# CAPTURED

## THE TORN SERIES BOOK TWO

## J.A. OWENBY

AUTHOR'S NOTE

Dear reader,

Thank you for continuing to read Lacey's story. I appreciate and value you.

Lacey's story happens every day. In 2014, twenty people were victims of intimate-partner violence *every minute*. Approximately 4,774,000 **women in the U.S. experience physical** violence every year. It's a nightmare of an epidemic.

If you think people in abusive relationships are weak and should "just leave," please know that approximately 75 percent of the women killed by their batterers are murdered when they attempt to leave the relationship, or after they've already left it. No one wants to be abused, and it's not a weakness. It's fear.

I was one of the lucky ones. I got out and hid for three terrifying years, and today my life looks wonderfully different. I reached out for help, and I was determined to change my life.

There is hope and help—just take the first step and never look back. Please contact the National Domestic Violence Hotline at 1-800-799-7233 (1-800-787-3224 TTY), or online at www.thehotline.org.

In hope,

J.A. Owenby

SIGN UP FOR J.A. OWENBY'S NEWSLETTER and receive bonus scenes, updates, and participate in giveaways.

Enjoy giveaways, the inside scoop about J.A. Owenby, and never miss a new release again! Sign up today at https://www.author-jaowenby.com/newsletter

1

My blood-curdling scream ripped through the night and jolted me from my sleep.

"—Lacey! Lacey! It's me, Emma."

"Wh-what?" I asked, peering into the darkness. As my eyes adjusted, I could see Emma standing in the doorway.

"It's okay, you're safe," she said as she turned on the light and approached me.

Tossing my covers off, I sat up in bed, wrapping my arms around myself in an effort to still the violent tremors that traveled through my body. Sweat trickled down my spine as a wave of nausea washed over me. I hopped out of bed and made it to my tiny bathroom in time for my stomach to empty its contents from the night before.

"Oh gosh, are you okay?" Emma asked.

"Yeah." I flushed the toilet and splashed my face with cold water. "Dammit!" I said, slapping my hand down on the bathroom sink. "Please tell me that did not just happen."

"I think it did happen."

Emma joined me in the bathroom, her house shoes flopping with each step she took. She lowered the toilet seat and sat down. Concern spread across her face.

I tucked a piece of long, blond hair behind my ear and sat on the side of the white bathtub.

"I'm so sorry. I—"

"—Don't apologize. I'm just worried about you."

My chest filled with a deep breath, and I tried to focus on the way the tile felt under my bare feet, the warmth of the night air on my skin, the hardness of the tub, anything to bring me back from that horrible place.

"The dream—I was trapped at Mama's." My voice barely hovered above a whisper. "But this time, she locked me underneath the house. There was only dirt and spiders. . ."

"Jiminy Christmas," Emma replied softly.

"Sorry I scared you. I didn't even know it was me screaming until I woke up and you were in my bedroom."

"Well, I know you're leaving tomorrow for Oregon, but I think you should reconsider your career choice."

"What do you mean?"

"Personally, I think you missed your calling. Those scream queens in the movies have nothing on you," she said.

A smile eased across my face. "You would know, you love those stupid movies," I said and stood up.

My body had calmed down some and I wasn't shaking uncontrollably anymore. Exhausted, I made my way back to my bed. I glanced at the clock; it blared 3:00 A.M.

"Ugh," I said and plunked down on my bed. "I'm tired but wide awake now."

"Yup, me too, so scoot your skinny butt over. We're having a slumber party."

I laughed and made room next to me for Emma.

A heavy sigh escaped me as I realized this was my last morning not sharing a room with someone. Emma and I had decorated it together, and I'd grown fond of it. I'd picked out a black-and-pink bedspread, which provided some much-needed contrast to my all-white furniture and the white apartment walls. I would leave my furniture with Emma, though; it wouldn't fit in my dorm room.

"I'm excited and scared at the same time about leaving tomorrow," I said. "What if I have nightmares like this while I'm there?" A long thread hanging off my bedsheet gained my attention and I pulled at it.

"Well, this is the only major one you've had lately. I think you're worried about the move—it's a lot to handle, but you've come so far in the last six months."

"Yeah, you're probably right. The nightmare just really scared me is all."

"Try not to think about it anymore. You have so many good things to look forward to. This time tomorrow, you'll be in Eugene! And I'm so excited to hear what your new college is like."

Turning, I looked at Emma. I knew she didn't want me to leave. She would be my only reason to stay, but it wasn't enough—we both knew it. The last few months had been torture.

We hung out and laughed about all the silly things we'd done while living together. We talked about what we would miss, and we made plans to visit each other a few times a year. I wanted her to visit me on campus and see what life was like outside of Arkansas, and I agreed to visit her the moment my schedule allowed me to.

As the first rays of sunshine spilled through my bedroom curtains, we made coffee, moved out onto the deck, and watched my last sunrise in Hot Springs, Arkansas.

I CHECKED my watch and glanced around the crowded Western Sizzlin'. It was Sunday, and everyone and their mother went to this place to eat after church. This afternoon was no exception. I scanned the entryway and the crowded front section of the restaurant for Emma's parents while she parked the car, which was loaded up with my luggage. I bit my lip as tears threatened my eyes at the thought of saying goodbye to them.

As if losing Walker weren't enough, I also hadn't spoken to Mama since the horrible night I moved out. If it hadn't been for Emma and her family, I wouldn't have had the strength to follow through with it.

Jim and Linda had supported me through an awful time in my life, and I loved them like they were my real parents.

When I finally shared everything with them—Mama's abuse, the imaginary demon possession, Walker leaving me, and the weeks I'd spent locked in Mama's house—I thought I'd lose them. I figured I'd come home one afternoon and find all my belongings on the apartment patio. But it never happened. They loved me and supported me while I healed enough to take a step out on my own.

Emma walked through the front door of the restaurant. "There they are," she said and waved at her parents.

I followed her through the crowded restaurant, scanning faces as I walked. Even though I hadn't seen Walker in months, I still looked for him. When you loved someone that deeply, they didn't just disappear overnight. Moving to Oregon would hopefully help me let go and move on.

"Hi!" I said as I hugged Jim and Linda.

"Are you ready?" Linda asked and grinned from ear to ear. "You know we're going to miss you, but this is an excellent step for you." Her manicured red nails flashed as she clapped her hands together. She'd recently colored her hair a soft brown which now matched her eyes.

"I am, and apparently, it's only eighty degrees there right now, too. Can you imagine the end of August in the eighties? Good riddance to the hundred-and-two-degree, muggy weather. And how is it possible I use half a can of Aqua Net and the minute I step outside, all my hard work collapses?" I asked, giggling.

"It sounds like you'll have a few months to settle in before the rain comes," Jim said as he stroked his salt-and-pepper beard.

"I love the rain, so hopefully it won't bother me at all," I replied, scanning the menu.

We focused on choosing our food and resumed our conversation after the waitress took our order. I promised Jim and Linda I'd visit as soon as I could. Emma mentioned planning a trip to Oregon. We chatted while we ate, and the butterflies began to flutter in my stomach the closer we got to leaving for the airport.

The waitress cleared our plates and filled our cups with coffee.

"Here, we wanted to give you something," Jim said as he placed a package on top of the table.

"Aww, you didn't have to get me anything," I said. "You've already done so much. I don't know how I'll ever repay you."

"It's not about repaying anything," Linda said. "It's about family."

I frowned and stared at the large present. It was wrapped in bright-blue paper with a white bow.

"Go on, open it," Emma said as she motioned for me to hurry up.

"Okay," I said and tore the paper open. My mouth dropped as I stared at a brand-new phone and answering machine.

"It's for your dorm room. You can call us anytime to say hello or if you need anything. You're family now, which means you're stuck with us," Linda said, laughing. "I couldn't stand the thought of you thousands of miles away, not being able to call us anytime you wanted to. You've come so far in the last few months. We're so proud of you."

Jim nodded in agreement as Emma leaned over and hugged me.

"I'm not sure what to say," I whispered. "Thank you—this means the world to me." Standing, I hugged Jim and Linda, wiping away the tears that were running down my cheeks.

Part of me didn't ever want to let them go, but I knew it was time. I'd worked hard for this.

"No crying," Linda said as she dabbed her eyes.

"Are you talking to yourself or Lacey?" Jim said, chuckling.

"I'm gonna use the ladies' room before we leave," Emma said as she pushed her chair away from the table and stood up. "Be right back."

As I turned to ask Linda a question, something caught my eye. Emma was talking to someone. When I saw who it was, my hand jerked and I knocked over my coffee cup. I jumped back in my seat and grabbed napkins to mop up the mess.

I searched for Emma again, but she was gone.

So was Walker.

"Are you okay?" Linda asked.

"Yeah, guess I'm just a little nervous about the move," I said and attempted a smile.

Linda and Jim helped me clean up the spilled coffee, my eyes darting nervously around the restaurant. I didn't see him.

*Maybe I hadn't really seen him at all.* But I knew better, and I'd recognize him anywhere.

"We'd better get going—we still have an hour-long drive to the airport," Emma said as she returned to our table.

Her cheeks were flushed, which confirmed what I'd seen. Walker was here, and I was about to leave and fly two thousand miles away. I'd managed not to run into him for nine months, and the day I was scheduled to leave, there he was.

I nodded, gathered my belongings, and said goodbye to Jim and Linda one last time as we all exited the restaurant and located our cars. Regrouping my thoughts, I tried to focus on the journey in front of me. It was over with Walker, and I was moving on.

"It sucked saying goodbye to your parents," I said, sliding into the passenger seat of Emma's car. "I don't wanna ugly cry all the way to the airport, so it's your job to make me laugh."

"Are you kidding? I'm trying not to cry too. If I do, I'll have to pull over on the side of the road, and you'll miss your plane."

"Oh Lord, let's not. I'm scared, but that doesn't mean I wanna miss my flight."

"Haha, I know, right?" Emma asked. "I'm so proud of you, but this sucks monkey toes. Never in a million years would I have thought my best friend would move so far away. I know you're gonna do great, but I'm gonna miss you so bad. Promise me you'll call me a few times a month. In fact, call me and then I'll call you right back so you don't have to pay for it."

"Emma, I can't."

"You will if it means I won't get to talk to you otherwise! I'm serious—it's not about you, it's about me."

I covered my mouth and tried not to giggle, but it escaped anyway. She glanced at me and giggled as well.

"I'm serious, now. This isn't all about you," Emma said, which made me laugh harder.

"Oh my God, stop!" I said, gasping for air. "I'll call, I promise. Just don't wreck the car."

"Lacey Anne, I swear, no one else makes me giggle over such stupid stuff."

"Same here."

My pulse quickened while I looked out the window and tried to decide if I should say anything about Walker. The painful reminder of him and Brittany at Susan's funeral resurfaced.

"Walker—I saw you talking to him," I whispered.

"Crap! You did? Jeez, he just had to show up when you were almost out the door. I wanted to give him a good pop in the arm."

"What did he say?"

"Do I really need to tell you? I mean, you're leaving. What good will it do?"

"Please, I just need to know."

"He saw me going to the bathroom and said hi," she said. Her grip on the steering wheel had tightened; her knuckles were turning white. There was something she didn't want to tell me.

"What else?"

"Don't make me tell you," Emma pleaded.

"Emma, now," I said firmly.

"He asked about you," she muttered.

"What? I don't think I heard you right."

She sighed and flexed her fingers, allowing the blood flow to return.

"He asked about you. I told him it wasn't okay—he doesn't get to ask about you after what he did."

"Oh, no. You didn't." Exasperation filled my voice. "He had no idea what happened with . . . he never heard the truth."

"I know, and he doesn't just get to saunter up to me and act like nothing happened. He asked if you were there and I told him he'd better stay away from you or I'd crack him upside the head."

I was too upset to laugh, even though the thought of Emma actually hitting Walker was funny.

"Oh my God, you did not say that!" I said.

"Of course I did. Why wouldn't I? He needs it if he's still married to Brittany."

"What?"

"Nothing," Emma said.

"What do you know?" I asked, narrowing my gaze.

Emma tapped her fingernails on the steering wheel.

"Look. I'm leaving, and nothing will make me stay," I said. "Just tell me so I can move on."

"I ran into him about a month ago while I was at the grocery store. He and Brittany were having problems. He asked about you then, but I told him to leave you alone and let you move on."

"Holy shit," I muttered.

"You can't stay here for him. They're still together as far as I know. He's married, you're not, and you're moving away."

"I wish it were that simple," I said.

"Go meet a nice, good-lookin' Oregon boy and move on."

I bit my lip and stared out the window. Walker had asked about me twice in the last month, and I was leaving. Emma and I rode the rest of the way to the airport in silence.

2

E mma and I made it through the crowded Little Rock airport to my gate. I had ten more minutes before I needed to board.

"Well, I guess this is it," I said, turning to face Emma. I slipped off my backpack and put it on the floor next to me.

"Please don't be mad at me—I couldn't stand it. I'm so sorry, I just didn't want to tell you," she said.

"I'm not mad at you. I'm lucky to have a friend like you," I said and smiled. "You don't need to wait with me, though. It'll just make this harder." My attention drifted to my feet as I tried to process saying goodbye.

"I'm not leaving until your plane takes off, so don't even suggest it."

"Alright, fair enough. I'd watch your flight leave too."

"You're gonna do great," Emma said.

"Yeah, maybe a change of environment will help," I said, tucking a stray piece of hair behind my ear.

"I bet it won't be long before you meet some amazing guy in Oregon who'll sweep you off your feet." Hope filled her face as the words left her mouth.

"Well, you'll be the first to hear about it if I do. I don't know if I'm ready, though."

"I know, but you'll have different classes and be surrounded by new people. I'm sure it will help."

I glanced out the window as the boarding call for my flight sounded through the airport speakers.

"Okay, call me when you get settled," Emma said.

"I will," I whispered as I hugged her.

"It's not goodbye, it's an 'I'll see ya later,'" she said, assuring me.

"I like that better," I replied, pulled away, and picked up my bag.

I took a few steps and then turned back around to see Emma wiping tears from her cheeks. My breath caught as I took one last look at her, at the airport, and at Arkansas. I was about to leave everything familiar and start over without knowing a single soul. Fear gripped me at the thought.

I waved to her. "See ya later, Emma," I said. Then I walked away before I couldn't.

I stepped onto the plane, located my seat, flipped open the overhead compartment, and tossed my backpack in. I'd been assigned the window seat, so I settled in before anyone else filed into my row. My eyes lingered out the window and I waved to Emma, but she couldn't see me. She already seemed far away, and we hadn't even left the ground.

I leaned my head back and sighed. Hopefully, I wouldn't be seated next to Chatty Cathy or her brother. Talking with someone wasn't at the top of my list today. I just wanted to have a smooth flight and get ready to start my new life.

Folding my hands in my lap, I closed my eyes as someone sat next to me. I figured if I established boundaries before takeoff, no one would bother me.

The flight attendant's voice floated over the PA system as the engines roared to life. I turned toward the window and watched as we began to move. Emma was in the same place she'd been ten minutes ago. She'd struggled with my decision to leave, but she had put up a strong front and never discouraged me from moving. She was a true friend. I mentally blew a kiss to her as the window went out of sight and we accelerated down the runway.

The plane gathered momentum, and I let out a small gasp as I was pushed back into my seat. I dared to peek out the window again once we'd gained altitude. Little Rock drifted farther away as everything—and everyone—became little specks.

"Goodbye, Mama. Goodbye, Walker," I whispered.

I still hadn't acknowledged the person sitting next to me. So far, my boundaries were working. I pulled out my Walkman and placed the headphones over my ears, drifting off to sleep as I listened to Prince's "I Could Never Take the Place of Your Man."

MY EYES SHOT open as the plane lurched forward.

"Oh God, we're gonna crash," I muttered under my breath.

I clutched the arms of my seat and squeezed my eyes shut. Then I remembered the flight attendant had told us to grab the little mask thingy in case of an emergency. But where was it? *Why hadn't I paid attention?*

With a lot of effort, I forced my eyes open and peered around. I bit my lip. No one else had oxygen masks on. I willed my heart to slow down as I realized I'd just freaked out in front of everyone.

"First time flying?" the guy next to me asked.

"No, I'm a frequent flyer," I replied with more sarcasm than I meant.

He leaned his head back against his seat and smiled.

"It's only turbulence. It makes the plane bounce around and it can be scary sometimes, but it wasn't too bad," he said. He ran his hand through his blond hair. It was about an inch shy of his shoulders; longer than most guys wore theirs back home.

"You must not be from here," he added. His brown eyes danced with mischievousness.

"Where's here, since we're on a plane and not exactly anywhere?"

"I meant Oregon. We're only thirty minutes away from Portland."

"No, I'm not from Oregon."

He smiled again, and my heart stuttered. Maybe moving on from Walker would be easier than I'd realized.

"My name's Xander," he said, gesturing to himself.

"Hi," I said.

"And you are?"

"Lacey," I said and extended my hand.

He chuckled as he shook it.

"And what do you find so funny? I seem to have an uncanny ability to entertain you," I said as a smile tugged at the corner of my mouth.

"It's your accent."

My eyebrow rose as I waited for him to continue.

"You're clearly from the South. I'd heard Southern women were beautiful, and I guess they weren't kidding."

A familiar flush crept up my neck and cheeks, and I swore mentally. I turned away and stared out the window.

"What brings you to Oregon?"

"College. I'm beginning my sophomore year at the University of Oregon."

"What a coincidence. I'm headed there myself. It's my senior year."

"Really? What's your major?" I asked. My curiosity was piqued.

"Criminal justice," he responded with a smirk.

"I've always found criminal justice and psychology fascinating."

"Yeah? The U of O has a great program—it's one of the reasons I chose it. And for the parties, of course." His smile softened.

"I don't care about those. I'm here to get an education, not a table-dancing degree," I said, wrinkling my nose.

"We'll see."

"Oh God," I muttered, grabbing the armrests again as the plane bounced.

"It's just turbulence," he said as he placed his hand on my arm.

I pulled it away, horrified he'd touched me. I didn't know him from Adam.

"Sorry. Look, there's Mount Hood." He pointed out the window.

I gasped as the mountain came into view. The snow-covered peak stood out boldly against the bright-blue sky.

"Holy shit," I mumbled.

"You like that word, don't you?"

"What?" I asked, not taking my eyes away from the window.

"Shit."

"Not as much as I like holy shit," I said, no longer paying attention to him as we flew over the mountain. "My God, this is beautiful," I whispered.

I wanted to suspend time and stay in this moment forever as we flew over the mountain and I saw the magnificent beauty of Oregon. I felt so tiny compared to everything down there, and for a moment, all the pain slipped away. Everything I'd lost—Mama, Walker, and the friends I'd left behind—seemed minimal compared to the scene below me.

The breathtaking scene below captured my attention, and I took it all in: the snow-capped mountain, the sunlight bouncing off the peak, the green trees dotting the ground. I had no idea any colors other than brown even existed in the summer. Suddenly, home *felt* two thousand miles away from Emma and everything familiar.

I leaned back and continued to watch as Portland came into focus. Within minutes, we landed, and everyone started to stand up. Xander slipped out and allowed me to step out in front of him. I exited onto the Jetway and into the airport.

"Welcome to your new home," Xander said. "Maybe I'll see you around campus sometime."

"Yeah, maybe," I said, giving him a small wave goodbye.

I stood still for a moment and watched everyone around me. Xander had caught up with a group of guys, and they all headed toward the baggage claim. I slipped my backpack on and decided I should follow. It seemed like the most logical step since I had to get my luggage too.

It was another forty minutes before I had my bags and rental car, and there was still a two-hour drive to Eugene. After loading up the car and pulled onto the interstate. I fiddled with the radio, found a good station, turned on the air conditioner, and got comfortable. I would reach Eugene by six. It felt weird being two hours behind

Arkansas, but I was grateful I would reach the university before nightfall.

I'm not sure if I was blessed or cursed, but for whatever reason, my roommate never made it and I had the dorm room to myself. Part of me was relieved in case I had more nightmares, but I'd also hoped to make a new friend.

I took advantage of the unexpected space and used the four days before classes started to decorate. I transformed the dull, white room to my taste: black and pink. Somehow, I'd managed to not rip my eight-foot Bon Jovi poster during the move, and he now hung on the back of my dorm-room door. My telephone service had been turned on, and I had a nice new phone and answering machine. Even though no one had called me yet, I checked it often.

SCHOOL STARTED after Labor Day in Oregon, which I found odd. Not only was I in a new city and state, but I was quickly finding out things were done very differently here.

I wrapped my towel around myself and padded down the hallway in my slippers to the showers. The bathroom was crowded with girls walking around naked. I left my towel on until I was in a shower stall with the curtain closed. My Southern shyness about my body would remain intact. Unlike some of the others, I would not be one of those girls who walked around naked and flaunted their assets.

One of my first lessons for the new school year was to shower fast, or you'll be left standing under cold water. I rinsed all the soap off, grabbed my towel, and hurried back to my room. Thirty minutes later, I was dressed in my favorite jeans and soft, green T-shirt, my makeup was applied, my backpack was slung over my shoulder, and I was ready to go. My pulse quickened as I pulled my dorm-room door closed behind me.

I stepped outside into the cool morning air and pulled my jacket around me. I'd been cold since I got here; the days were at least fifteen degrees cooler than they were in Arkansas. All the other students wore shorts and T-shirts, but I stuck with jeans.

I took my time and strolled across campus, absorbing all the colors. The thick green grass crunched under my shoes as I noticed the abundance of maple, birch, and pine trees. Large planters brimming with every color pansy possible hung from the lampposts, creating bright splashes of color against the green.

My building loomed in front of me and I stopped in my tracks. The single red-brick structure was bigger than half the campus combined back home. I ascended the stairs and fell in step with the other students as we filed through the front doors. Searching the hallways, I located my classroom.

"Holeeee shit," I muttered, entering my history class. The auditorium comfortably held at least a hundred students. I mentally kicked myself for not arriving sooner, but how could I have known the class would be so big?

Anxiety flooded me while I stood at the top of the stairs and scanned the room for available seats. I didn't want to sit up front or in the back. My comfort zone was in the middle.

I located an open seat and made my way down the stairs.

"Is the seat taken?" I asked and pointed six seats into the row. Six people groaned at me and stood up. I apologized as I scooted past them, trying not to step on their toes as I made my way to the seat I thought would be perfect.

The professor entered the room as I settled in.

"Welcome to Oregon History! I'm Professor Scott, and I'm here to make your life hell." He laughed. "I'm kidding, but don't think you can sleep in my class and pass. Show some respect and interest and I might give you a C," he said, smiling from ear to ear.

The class groaned as he turned his back to us and began writing on the board. I glanced around at the other students and realized I might blend in after all.

"My teaching assistant is giving the person at the end of each row a stack of papers," he continued. "Please take one and pass it down. This is the class syllabus. I don't care if you work ahead or behind, but by the end of the term, I want all your work turned in. Don't be late. I hate late. And if you think you're smarter than everyone else, you can write a thirty-page paper on the history of Oregon. If your paper passes with a C or better, you can skip the final. If you don't get at least a C on it, you'll still have to take the final. It's up to you. I couldn't care less if you actually come to this class or not, but you do have to pass this class to graduate."

He wiped his hand on his jeans, leaving a trail of chalk across his backside.

I muffled my giggle as he turned toward the class and put the chalk down.

"Wow, thirty pages," I whispered to the guy sitting next to me.

"Mhmm, he's a ballbuster," he said under his breath. "I don't care what he said—I've heard he loves to fail the papers so you have to take the final anyway. No thanks. I'll show up and take the test. Besides, he is *so* not hard to look at."

He handed me the stack of papers that was making its way across the row. I took one, passed the stack down, and began scanning the class syllabus.

"Is this your first year at the U of O?" I asked quietly as I peered at him. His jet-black hair was slicked forward with his bangs flipped up in the front, accentuating his flawless complexion.

He turned toward me and stared. His dark-brown eyes scanned my face as his eyebrows rose.

"No, I'm a sophomore this year. But you're definitely new here," he said, laughing softly.

"How do you know I'm not from Oregon?"

"Seriously? You did not just ask me that question, girl. You do realize your accent is as Southern as it gets, right?"

"It is?" I asked, frowning.

"Definitely," he replied.

"I'm Lacey," I said and extended my hand.

"George," he said. "And the first thing you need to learn is no one shakes hands here, so put it away." He nodded at my extended hand.

"Oh, thanks," I said as I put my hand in my lap. I dipped my head and focused on my shoes as the dreaded flush crept up my neck and cheeks.

Professor Scott began lecturing, and I grabbed my notebook and pen and took notes. History was by no means my best subject; hopefully I would find a few study partners who actually liked it.

Class wrapped up, and I stuffed my textbook and notebook into my backpack.

"So, Hillbilly, where exactly *did* you come from?"

I glanced up at George. He was already standing, waiting for me to get up and file out of the row.

"That's rude. Do you talk to everyone like that?"

"Yup," he said and motioned for me to hurry up.

I stood up, and a smile pulled at the corners of my mouth. At five foot six, I cleared George by a good inch.

"Yeah, I'm short, Hillbilly, so smile away, but move your ass. I've got another class across campus," he said as a grin flashed across his face.

I hurried down the aisle and joined George as we walked up the stairs.

"Do you just say anything that comes to mind?" I asked. I hated to admit it, but I was a little intrigued by how bold he was. People weren't this outspoken back in Arkansas.

"Sometimes. But you'll find most people are like that around here."

"Are you from here? Eugene, I mean?" I asked as we pushed open the door and walked outside. The fresh air tickled my nose.

"Born and raised. And you never answered my question. Where in the South are you from?"

"Arkansas."

"Oh, wow," he said as he looked me over.

"What?"

"Nothing," he said.

"Hey, I need help," I said, pulling out my class schedule and pointing at my next class on the list. "I need to find this room."

"Well, aren't you lucky. It's my next class too. Follow me, but you gotta keep up," he said and sped up. "You're gonna get your exercise here, Hillbilly. Our next class is on the other side of campus."

"Oh!" I said as I tried to keep up, barely managing to hang a few steps behind. "What's your major?"

"Interior design. What's yours?"

"Communications."

"You're gonna have to ditch your accent if you want to work in that field," he said, laughing.

"Okay, you're hired."

George stopped in his tracks and I bumped into him, almost knocking us both over.

"Hired? What do I look like?" he asked as he put his hand on his hip and glared at me.

"Well, if you're gonna call me Hillbilly and make fun of my accent, the least you can do is help me get rid of it. So, you're hired as my tutor," I said, waiting for him to agree with my logic.

"I'm not sure anyone can help you," he said as he began walking again. "But you're fun to listen to, so I'll check my schedule."

I wasn't sure if I wanted to laugh or roll my eyes as I jogged after him.

George was right, our sociology class was clear across campus. I would have to hustle from history on these days or I'd be late. No more gawking at the architecture and how green everything was.

We grabbed seats near the middle of the room and George introduced me to two other students he knew, Adalyn and Megan. They welcomed me to Oregon and asked about Arkansas, but unlike George, they didn't make fun of my accent. They were also in the same dorm as me, so we decided to meet up later in the evening. We chatted until the professor walked in and class started. Even though I'd already met a few people, my heart ached for Emma and Joss.

George pulled me aside after class and opened his planner. "I have time around nine tonight. I can come to your dorm then," he said.

I checked my schedule and realized all my classes were in the first half of the day, which left the afternoons free for studying. It also meant my evenings would be wide open.

"Perfect," I said and gave him my room number.

"Gotta run, Hillbilly. I'll see you tonight," he said, and then he took off in the other direction.

4

I waved at the dorm mom, Mrs. Walters, as I walked into the building. I'd heard a few older girls mention they were closer to her than their own moms. My Southern manners reared up as I realized I hadn't introduced myself yet.

I approached the front desk in the dorm lobby and waited for her to hang up the phone.

"Hi, hon, what can I do for you?" Mrs. Walters asked, her blue eyes dancing.

"Oh, I—I was just going to introduce myself," I said and cleared my throat. "I'm Lacey and I just moved here from Arkansas."

"Wow, you came all this way to be an Oregon Duck, huh?" Mrs. Walters asked, grinning.

"Yes, ma'am," I said, smiling.

"Well, get settled in and let me know if you need anything, and I mean anything. Stay with your friends if you're out at night, and make sure you have your ID on you at all times."

"Yes, ma'am," I said.

"Oh, and one more thing," she said and reached behind the desk. She produced a card and handed it to me. "If you're out at night alone, call this number, and someone will pick you up and bring you to your dorm room. Don't ever walk around alone late at night."

"Really? That's pretty cool."

"We take campus security very seriously here."

"Thank you. I need to go study, but it was nice meeting you."

"Same to you," Mrs. Walters said with a slight wave.

I reached my room and opened the door. Tossing my books onto the other bed, I crossed the small room to check my answering machine. A red number two blinked at me. My finger pushed the play button.

"Lacey, it's Emma. I haven't talked to you in a week and I can't deal with it anymore, so call me as soon as you can. I'll be home tonight."

I pushed the erase button and listened to the second message.

"Is it her?" a faraway voice asked, and then the message ended. My mouth dropped open.

"No," I whispered, playing the message again. I recognized the voice, and a shiver shot through me as I listened one more time. It couldn't be. I rubbed my face and reminded myself to breathe. There was no mistaking her voice in the background. Mama had managed to track me down, which meant either Patsy or Krissy had found my phone number.

"Shit," I yelled and slapped my hand on the desk. I'd naively thought she wouldn't be able to track me down, but no matter how far away I was, she found me. I didn't know what it meant or if she would call again, but I didn't want anything to do with her.

Fear rose to the surface as I crawled into my bed and huddled in the corner. I pulled my blankets around me and tried to stop trembling, but my mind had taken a dark turn. All I could think about were the days I'd spent drugged and locked in Mama's room. I'd lost Walker and everything else that had been important to me.

I bit my lip hard enough it almost bled. At least the pain gave me something else to think about. My head throbbed as I stared at the phone and then remembered Emma had also called me.

I crawled across my bed, grabbed the phone, dialed her number, and prayed she would answer.

"Hello?"

"Hey, Emma, it's Lacey."

"Lacey! Oh, my gosh, how are you? What's Oregon like? Have you met anyone there yet? What's your dorm like? I miss you!"

I smiled as I waited for her to settle down. As I heard the excitement in her voice, my fear dwindled into the background.

"I'm okay. I'm homesick right now, but I think it's because everything is so new."

"Is it really different?"

"You have no idea. But I've met a few people, and I started classes today."

"Was it weird not starting in August?"

"Yeah, but school goes later in the year to make up for it. It isn't hot here, either, which is nice. I have to wear a jacket most of the time."

"Tell me who you've met," Emma said. I could picture her face filled with excitement.

"Well, I met a guy named George today. I have him in history and sociology. He's interesting . . . And a couple of girls, Megan and Adalyn, who are in the same sociology class. I'm gonna meet up with them later tonight—they're in the same dorm as me. They seem really nice. Nicer than George, anyway."

"Is he mean?"

"No, I don't think so, but he calls me Hillbilly and makes fun of my accent."

"What? I never noticed you had an accent," Emma said.

"Me neither, but I guess I do, and I need to ditch it if I'm majoring in communications."

"Well, I hope he stops calling you Hillbilly."

"Yeah, we'll see. What about you? How are your classes? How are your parents doing?" I asked.

"We're good. My new roommate, Lisa, moved in this past weekend. It's so strange not having you here." She sighed.

"I know. I got lucky and have a room to myself, but what's a real trip is all the girls run around naked here. The showers are down the hall, so they streak everywhere they go. I am so not used to it."

"That would be different, for sure," Emma said, laughing.

I grew quiet and debated whether or not to tell her about the voicemail.

". . . Lacey Anne, I know you, and something's up. So, spill."

"You can tell over the phone?"

"Yup. Now what's up?"

"Mama called me," I whispered.

"What? Are you serious? Are you sure it was her?"

"Yeah. I'm not sure who actually called, but I could clearly hear Mama asking if it was my voice on the answering machine. She was in the background, and then they hung up."

"That was all they said?" Emma asked in disbelief. "Shoot! I wish I were there. I know it must've ruffled your feathers. After everything she did to you, to hear her voice again . . ."

"Yeah, to say the least. Hopefully, she doesn't call back."

"Do you promise you'll tell me if she does? I know you, and you won't wanna tell me for some dumb reason, like you don't want to worry me or something. Promise me."

I paused for a moment and debated if I would really tell her if Mama called me again. I wasn't sure; I didn't know if I'd want to worry her or not. But if I didn't promise her, she'd never let me get off the phone.

"Okay, I promise," I said.

"Alright then. If it becomes a problem, we'll figure something out. You don't have to go through this alone, never again. You understand?"

"Yeah," I said and smiled. "Gotta go, though. I wanna keep my phone bill low enough to call whenever I want to."

"Don't you worry. I'll call you in a few days, okay?"

"Sounds good. Thanks, Emma."

"Nothing to thank me for. We're family, real family. I love ya."

"Love you too," I said.

I held the phone until I heard the click of Emma hanging up. A calmness settled over me and replaced the receiver in the cradle.

5

On the days it wasn't raining, the sunsets in the Pacific Northwest were different than I'd ever seen. The sky would burst into bright pinks, oranges, and reds, but it seemed like they were only there for a second. The moment you blinked, they were gone and the sky was dark.

I felt like a little kid exploring. Everything fascinated me, from the green grass in September to the crystal-clear sky and crisp air.

Not only had my first day of classes gone better than I'd expected, but I also hadn't thought about Walker all day—until Mama had called. A chill shot through me as I thought about the message. All the memories rushed back, and I swallowed the lump in my throat as I realized I'd met him almost a year ago.

My shoulders slumped as I stood up, walked to the window, and looked out at campus. *I moved here to start over.* Mama wasn't here, and I was safe no matter how scared I felt. I pushed the memories away and glanced at the clock. There was only an hour to study before George stopped by, and I needed the distraction.

I turned my desk lamp on, got comfortable on my bed, and opened my history book. The next thing I knew, I was peeling my eyes open as someone knocked on my door.

The clock said 9:04 P.M., and I hurried to open the door. George pushed past me and into my room.

"Come in," I said, slightly sarcastically, as I tried to smooth my hair down with my hands.

"Ooooooh, honey," he said with a hint of disapproval in his voice.

"What?"

"Someone's getting adjusted to the time difference. Grab a brush, and you should also get rid of those raccoon eyes before we get started, Hillbilly," he said as he nodded toward my mirror.

"George, please stop calling me Hillbilly," I groaned, running the brush through my thick hair.

"I will when you lose the accent. You *are* gonna melt hearts, though," he said as he scanned me up and down.

"Why do you say that?"

"Well, even though you sound like a Hillbilly, you're gorgeous. Those green eyes will get you into any club, not to mention your ass. Turn around and let me see."

"Are you serious?"

"Yes! Now chop chop," he said as he clapped his hands together.

I spun around on one foot as quickly as I could and giggled. There was no way I was going to display my butt for him. He could continue to check out Professor Scott's ass.

"Oh, dear," George said and rested his head in his hands.

I grinned as my attempt to irritate him worked. That's what he got for asking.

"Should we get started?" I asked.

"We should. Why don't you tell me about where you're from?"

I frowned, not sure how it would help me lose my Southern accent. But he'd find out anyway if we became friends.

"I was born in Little Rock and raised in Hot Springs. I went to community college for a year, and now, here I am."

"That's the most boring story I've ever heard, which means there is *way* more to it," he said. He sat on the bed opposite of mine and leaned against the wall.

"Well, as a proper Southern girl, I don't divulge my secrets to strangers." There was no way in hell I would tell him about Mama. He'd never talk to me again.

"Who is he?"

"What?" My eyebrows knitted together while I walked to my desk, grabbed a hair tie, and pulled my hair back. I'd just met George a few hours ago and wasn't ready to talk about any of this.

"Okay, you don't have to tell me. *Yet*," George said.

I turned to face him. "What about you? I know you're from Oregon, but do you have family here?"

"Yup, my parents, two sisters, and my brother are right here in Eugene."

"If your family is here, why do you live in the dorms?"

"First of all, I have a full scholarship. Second, my house is way too crowded. And you'd be surprised by how many sophomores still live on campus. Rent is really expensive unless you want to live in a house with twelve people. And hell, it's not much different than a dorm anyway. I don't have a car, either, so campus is where I'm at."

"Makes sense. I wouldn't know where else to live anyway. Have you ever left Oregon?"

"I've only been up and down the West Coast from California to Washington, but nowhere else, yet. I plan on moving to New York after graduation, though. I'd love to meet a gorgeous hunk from the East Coast," he said, grinning.

"Oooh, sounds fun. Tell me more about New York," I said and sat on my bed.

"I have a cousin who lives there, so I have a place to stay. It's all of seven hundred square feet, but I figure if I've lived in a dorm room for a while it can't be much different, right?"

"I wouldn't think so," I replied.

George rolled his eyes. "We have a lot of work to do if you want to get rid of your accent."

"Well, shit," I muttered.

"Oh my God, I've never heard anyone draw out the word *shit*," he said, laughing. "Say it fast so there's no drawl in it. *Shit*, not *sheeyit*."

"Shit!" I said it as fast as I could.

"It's okay, Lacey. We'll work on it. Just try to talk faster, and don't spread your words out. Try to clip them for a little while—maybe it will work."

"What if I can't lose my accent? Hell, I didn't even know I had one," I said and bit my lip.

"Well, you can always make money as a nude model for the art department," George said, snickering.

A knock on my door stopped me before I could make a rude response.

It was Adalyn and Megan. "Hi! Come on in," I said, holding the door open for them.

"Hi!" they said as they joined us in my room.

Adalyn towered over Megan by at least a foot. They were both gorgeous, but they were opposites in appearance. Megan's platinum-blond hair flowed down her back and accentuated her big brown eyes. Adalyn's straight, brown hair hung in a carefree bob, and her athletic frame gave the impression she could eat anything she wanted to and never gain an ounce.

"Hey, George," Adalyn said as she plopped down next to him on the bed. "Sorry we're late. Megan and I were talking to Ms. Walters. She's the best dorm mom ever."

"I just met her this afternoon. She seems really nice," I said.

"Yeah, she's the go-to person here, for sure," Adalyn said. George and Megan nodded in agreement.

"So, did you hear who's having a house party tonight?" Megan asked George.

"A party? It's Monday night. Who parties on a Monday?" I asked.

All three of them stared at me.

"Who *doesn't* party on a Monday is more like it," Adalyn answered and smiled. "It's okay, Megan was from a small town too. We'll get you all settled in by the end of the week."

"I don't drink, so I'm not sure a party sounds like a lot of fun," I said.

"Are you sure?" George asked. "Xander Koffman has a house now, and he's throwing the first party tonight."

"Xander? I met a guy named Xander on the airplane."

"Blond, brown eyes, and so damned hot he makes you squirm?" Megan asked.

I laughed at Megan's description, but it was accurate. "Ya know, I didn't get his last name, but he had blond hair almost down to his shoulders, and he said he was a senior."

"That's him," George and Adalyn replied at the same time.

"You forgot to mention his ass, girl," George said as he elbowed Adalyn and fanned himself.

I giggled. "So, he's a big deal?"

"He's the star quarterback for the Ducks," Megan replied. "The only reason we can crash this party is because my cousin plays football with him—he gave me the address. It only takes about thirty minutes before they're too drunk to notice we're not upperclassmen anyway," she said, grinning.

I chewed on my bottom lip and pondered whether or not I was interested. The last party I'd gone to had ended with Walker breaking my heart. I intended to move on, but I wasn't sure if a party was the way to do it. I laughed softly to myself. Why did I assume I'd even meet someone?

"You guys are great, but I can't go tonight."

"Well, have it your way," Megan said as she stood up to leave. "We'll be sure to let you know all the juicy details you missed!" She motioned for the others to follow.

"Bye," they said as they closed the door behind them. And just like that, I was left standing in my dorm room alone, with no friends.

"Shit, shit, shit," I said over and over, as fast as I could.

December had arrived, and I was a little surprised I'd managed to attend the U of O for three months and not go to a party. It wasn't that it hadn't crossed my mind, but I'd moved two thousand miles away to start over, and parties weren't at the top of my list. I'd grown closer to George and the girls, but I still had a hole inside me and it wouldn't go away.

I'd had two more phone calls, but no one said anything; they just hung up. My night terrors escalated after the calls. I often woke myself up screaming and puked in my trash can more often than I wanted to think about. No one knew except Emma, and it was different than if she were here.

I considered asking George if he would stay with me, but I was worried if I had a nightmare, I'd never hear the end of it. Or, even worse, he would demand to know what had me so upset. How do you tell someone you're so scared of your own mother that she still haunts you from practically across the country?

GEORGE RARELY KNOCKED; this time was no different as he closed the door behind him and crawled into bed with me.

"Hi, George. You're in my bed," I said, not moving from my position on my stomach.

"Yup, and it's as uncomfortable as mine. You know, I keep telling you to lock your door," he said.

"Yeah," I muttered.

"That's it? You're not gonna tell me that back home you didn't have to lock your door because you lived in the country, and yada yada yada?"

I attempted a half-hearted smile as he rolled over onto his side.

"Such sad eyes, Hillbilly," he said. "What's wrong?"

I put my face in my pillow so I didn't have to look at him. George had a peculiar way of seeing past my facade.

"Nothing. I'm just a little homesick, is all," I said and faced him again.

"You know what you need, Hillbilly? You need a night out. We need to get you liquored up and go dancing!" George said as he smacked me on the ass.

I glared at him as I tried to hide my smile.

"You do realize I have a name?" I asked and propped myself up on my elbow.

"I know you do, Lacey Beaumont. And with your sweet Southern accent of yours, the boys are gonna fall all over you. And right after, they're gonna melt into puddles once they see your green eyes. Girl, you'll have them wrapped around your little finger."

"You're so dramatic. How in the world would you know?" I asked.

"Because it's exactly what would happen to me if I were straight," George said, snickering.

"It's a damn shame you aren't. I'd probably fall in love with you if you were."

"Honey, please. If I were straight, you'd run the other way. Someone broke your heart, and you can't tell me any different. I see how sad you are."

"Don't," I whispered.

"Stop," he said and raised his hand to halt me from saying anything else. "I don't need the details or to live in the despair with you. It's my job to help you move past it."

"Job? Have you taken me on as your pet project?" I asked, my eyes widening.

"You know it."

Maybe I'd finally raise the white flag and go out with my friends; maybe it would help. Maybe I'd even have a drink. I was sick and tired of being scared and lonely. I sat up in my bed, grabbed his face, and kissed him on his full mouth.

"What the hell?" he sputtered as I giggled and jumped off the bed.

"I'm gonna go shower, so I'll meet you back here in an hour."

"Good—you need to do something with your hair, girl, it's out of control. We actually brush our hair here in Oregon. Not sure what they taught you down South, but get it together, Hillbilly!"

I stuck out my tongue at him as I backed out of my dorm room.

AN HOUR LATER, George met me back in my room.

"Wow! Don't you clean up well after plucking the straw out of your hair and putting shoes on!"

"Yeah?"

"Come here," he said and motioned for me to move closer.

Approaching him, I waited for his final touches to my light-blue shirt and Guess jeans.

I gasped as he placed his hands underneath my breasts and lifted them up.

"Calm down, girl, you know these do absolutely nothing for me. I'm just adjusting your cleavage. The goal for tonight is to get you laid."

"George, I don't want to be with anyone," I said.

"That's what you say, but even I can see you need to get some. You've gotta move on, and the best way to do it is to find a new one, but this time, keep him as your toy. If you don't want to get hurt, don't fall in love."

"I wish it were simple," I said and sighed.

"It is, trust me. Let's go break some hearts," he said as he took my hand and led me out of my room to meet Adalyn and Megan.

George knocked on the girls' door, and Adalyn flung it open and ushered us in. I guess that's how it worked if you locked your door.

"Oh my God! I can't believe you're finally going out with us tonight," Megan said. She squealed and hugged me.

"I need to get out for a while and do something other than attend classes and study," I said, returning her hug.

"Well, it should be entertaining, for sure. There's never a dull moment at these parties," Adalyn said as she applied the last touches of her lip gloss.

"Where exactly is this party, anyway?" I asked.

"It's at the Pi Kappa Phi house," George said with a hint of amusement in his voice.

"It's almost ten, so we should go," Megan said.

7

I followed the group out of the dorm and across campus. We could hear the party from a block away, and as we rounded the corner, my mouth dropped open. The house looked like it was bursting at the seams—students were spilling out onto the porch and front lawn.

We made our way up the steps and into the house. The bass was thumping so hard it shook the floor. Everyone was dancing and jumping to the beat.

We pushed our way through shoulder-to-shoulder people, and I grabbed George's arm.

"Don't lose me!" I shouted over the music.

"Then don't let go," he said, laughing as he squeezed my hand.

The overwhelming smell of alcohol, sweat, and puke hung in the air, and I tried not to make a sour face. Why in the world would anyone want to be here?

I scanned the living room and spotted Megan and Adalyn; they'd already found their places next to some rather gorgeous guys. George steered me through all the people and straight to the alcohol.

"Here," George said, handing me a red cup filled halfway with a fizzy, dark-colored drink. "This will help you loosen up a bit and have some fun. You might even like it—it doesn't taste a damn thing like alcohol."

"What is it?" I asked as I sniffed it.

"Coconut rum and Dr Pepper!" he shouted and guzzled his down.

I took a deep breath and did the same.

"Wow, it's actually good," I said, grinning.

George refilled our cups and motioned for me to drink up. He joined me, and then he proved his friendship to me. He handed me a cup of water.

"What's this for?"

"If you don't wanna be puking your guts up, then drink a ton of water. It will reduce your chances of having a hangover."

"Aww. Thanks, George," I said and giggled again. "You know I love you, right?" My eyebrows rose in surprise as soon as the words left my mouth. I wasn't in the habit of telling my male friends I loved them.

George threw his head back and laughed. "Well, it seems like the alcohol has hit your system. I love you a little bit too, Hillbilly," he said and winked.

I squeezed through the people as George led me to the living room, where Megan and Adalyn were snuggling up to some of the guys and gyrating more than dancing. Although I'd had a few drinks, I still felt out of place. I wasn't sure the party scene was for me, and I'd started to regret coming when George pulled me into the group of sweaty bodies and started dancing.

"Come on, Hillbilly. Have some fun!"

I glanced around. No one was paying any attention to us, so I joined in with the best moves I had, which weren't many. I laughed as George danced around me and bumped me with his skinny butt. I grabbed his arm and hung on as the large group began to jump. As we jumped in unison and the alcohol calmed my nerves, I wondered—for a split second—if I might be able to actually fit in here.

The music slowed, and George and I made our way to the kitchen for another drink. But I didn't slam this one; I took my time and sipped on it.

"I've gotta take a leak, so I'll meet you back here in a few minutes," George said.

My gaze followed him as he walked away to find the bathroom. Just then, a hand grabbed my ass. I spun around to find a guy wobbling and reaching toward the wall for support.

"Wanna find a room?" he asked, slurring his words.

"No! And if you ever lay a hand on me again, you'll walk away unable to have children," I said, glaring at him.

"Bitch," he muttered and moved on to the next victim.

Some fresh air sounded good, and I pushed my way through the crowd and out the front door. Stepping onto the porch, I took a deep breath, and noticed the porch swing wasn't taken at the moment. My love for porch swings went back to childhood; they reminded me of home. I ignored the couples making out along the railing nearby and sat down.

I leaned back into the swing and tilted my head back as it swayed. The stars twinkled against the darkness of the sky. It was beautiful.

"Well, if it isn't Lacey from the South."

I snapped to attention, turning to see who had said my name. It was Xander, from the plane.

"Can I join you?" he asked.

"Sure," I said as he settled in next to me. "'Lacey from the South,' huh?" I asked, my eyebrow arching.

"I never caught your last name," he said. His brown eyes danced with the same mischievousness they'd had when I met him.

Megan and Adalyn's words ran through my mind as I held his gaze. I was sitting next to one of the most popular guys in the entire college. My heart fluttered while I took a sip of my drink, hoping it would calm my nerves.

"Beaumont," I said.

"Lacey Beaumont from the South," he said and smiled. "You know I'm just teasing, right?"

"No, not really. I mean, I'm never sure if people are teasing or making fun of me. Regardless, I don't care for either. I can't help where I grew up."

"Well, I'm smitten by your accent and how beautiful you are. You put most girls to shame—you have no clue."

My cheeks flamed with his words, which made him chuckle again.

"Is that why you laugh at me? Because you're smitten?" I tilted my head and waited for his response.

"Something like that." His smile widened as he ran his hand through his hair. "Where are you from? Arkansas? I would've asked you on the plane, but as I recall, you were in the middle of thinking we were about to crash."

I covered my face with my empty hand and shook my head. He laughed softly again. I took another sip of my drink and peered up at him over the rim of my cup.

"Yeah, well, maybe I won't be so scared next time. And yes, I'm from Arkansas—it was my first time on a plane. If you need to crack any jokes, go ahead and get it over with." I sighed and leaned back into the swing again.

I glanced around the porch, but there were only a few other couples outside with us. Secretly, I was glad we weren't alone, even if the other people were busy sucking face and didn't have a clue we were there.

"My mom grew up in Little Rock, so I've visited her side of the family a few times," Xander said. "She would take us to Hot Springs, and her best friend lived in Hope."

"Oh my God!" I squealed. "I grew up in Hot Springs." I tried to contain the excitement in my voice, but I could feel the rum warming my veins. I'd finally met someone who had at least visited where I'd grown up. "It's so nice to talk to someone who . . ." My voice trailed off.

"What's the matter?" Xander asked.

"Nothing, I'm sorry. I'm being silly."

"No you're not."

"I—I'm so homesick," I whispered. "Oregon is beautiful, but it's so different. Sometimes I feel like I shouldn't really be here."

"Why are you here?"

I stared into my cup and then took another sip.

"School," I said, glancing up at him.

Xander held my gaze. As hard as I tried to hide it, I got the feeling he knew there was something else.

"There you are," George said loudly as he walked out onto the porch. Startled, I turned to see him standing beside us with his hand on his hip. "I've been searching everywhere for you. I was worried sick someone had picked you up and taken you upstairs. Megan and Adalyn hadn't seen you anywhere, either. You can't do that to me *ever again*." He wagged his finger at me.

"Upstairs? What do you mean?" I asked.

George shook his head, and a smile slowly crossed Xander's face. George's jaw dropped as he realized who I'd been talking to before he burst through the door and onto the porch.

"Oh—uh, hello, Xander. I'm George, Lacey's best friend."

It was my turn to laugh as George ogled him. I peeked at Xander, but it didn't seem to bother him at all.

"Hey, George. It's nice to meet you," Xander said with a little wave.

"What's upstairs?" I asked again, glancing from one guy to the other.

"Nothing, but I don't ever want to find you up there," George said as he narrowed his eyes at Xander. I'd never seen George give anyone a dirty look before.

"Don't get bent out of shape, bud, we're just talking," Xander said. "I do think it's cool you watch out for her, though—you're a good friend."

The tension eased from George's shoulders. "Fine. Lacey, I'll be dancing with the girls, so come find me when you're done *talking*." He turned and walked back into the house.

"Sorry," I said.

"He's just watching out for you. I like him already," Xander replied. He paused for a moment. "How about dinner sometime?"

"Huh?" I asked.

"Dinner. I'd like to take you to dinner."

"Me?" I asked as I pointed to myself.

"Yes, you," Xander said.

"Uh, wow, um, okay," I replied.

"Well, are you sure?" he asked with a hint of surprise in his voice.

"Yes! I'm sorry, you completely caught me off guard," I said. "You surprised me, I wasn't trying to blow you off."

His expression softened. "I won't take you to McDonald's. I'd like to take you to a nice restaurant."

"Oh—I don't own anything other than jeans."

"There's no dress code, so don't worry about it. But I won't take you out for a five-dollar date. You deserve better," he said.

I tilted my head and waited for him to elaborate, but he didn't. I don't know what he saw in me that was special enough to qualify for a nice restaurant, but maybe it was time I let go of Walker and found out.

"Okay, sounds really nice."

"I know we have finals next week, so how does next Friday night work?"

"Yeah, perfect."

"What's your dorm-room number? I'll stop by at seven and pick you up."

A shy smile eased across my face. I was about to go on my first date since Walker, and it was with the star quarterback.

"My room number is 212 and I'm in Barnhart Hall. I'll be ready," I said and stood up. "I need to find George and my other friends."

"I'll come back inside with you," Xander said.

We made our way back into the house and over to the living room. We were greeted by a large group of guys chanting in unison. I scanned the room for Megan and Adalyn and quickly spotted them dancing on a table. The guys yelled and cheered as they moved. My eyes widened. I had no idea they could dance like that.

"I told you table-top dancing was a degree here," Xander said, laughing.

I shook my head and watched my friends.

8

Another gray, rainy morning woke me. I hadn't seen a clear evening since the frat party last weekend. Most of the time, the rain was light enough you could get away with just wearing a coat and toughing it out. But when the rain was heavy and the wind joined in, no coat—or umbrella, for that matter—could survive its wrath.

After finishing my last final, I literally ran across campus to my dorm, relief washing over me. I waved at Mrs. Walters as I wiped my shoes on the entryway rugs. The lobby was almost empty. Only a few students were left, scattered on couches and at tables with their noses in books.

Christmas break had officially started, and I had three-and-a-half weeks of no classes. I'd hoped to fly back home, but it just wasn't going to happen; money was too tight. Thank God the U of O didn't close over break. I knew I wasn't the only person staying, so although the dorm would be almost empty, I felt better knowing I wasn't alone.

A pang of sadness crept through me, and I brushed it off as I rushed up the stairs and thought about my date with Xander.

I unlocked my door—I'd started locking it more often after Mama's message—and checked my answering machine. No numbers blinked at me. As much as I loved having a phone in my room, my heart pounded against my chest every time I saw a message waiting for me. I wasn't positive Mama had called again, but only a few people had my number.

My eyes rolled at myself. She was thousands of miles away; she couldn't hurt me anymore.

I glanced at the time and turned on my radio. Bon Jovi's "I'll Be There for You" filled my small room as I got ready for my date. It had been over a year since I'd been on one, but I pushed the memory of Walker out of my mind.

After one final look in the mirror, and applying my lip gloss, there was a knock at my door. I frowned. Xander was early, but I'd rather he be early than late.

I pulled my door wide open and gasped.

"Well, don't stand there with a stupid look on your face. Pack your things—it's time to come home. I've had enough of your nonsense," Mama said.

"What are you doing here?" I grabbed the door and tried to control the tremble that coursed through my body as I realized she was standing in front of me—in Oregon.

"I told you, it's time to come home. You've had several months to see the error of your ways. I can forgive you, but you have to give up this evil life you've created for yourself. This isn't God's plan for you."

"Really? And what would his plan actually be then? Holding me hostage?"

Mama's fist tightened, and her face turned a light shade of red.

"You need to listen to your mother," Patsy said as she walked toward us. Her heels echoed through the empty hall.

"No!" I said. I tried to close the door as fast as I could, but it wasn't fast enough. Mama had wedged her foot in, and now she was leaning her full weight against the door. I struggled, but my boots didn't have any traction, and I slid backward.

"Stop! Get out!" I screamed and hoped someone, anyone, would hear me. This could not be happening again. "Go home. I don't ever want to see you again," I yelled, straining to close the door.

Mama began praying under her breath as she and Patsy won the struggle against my door and let themselves into my dorm room.

"I told you a while back, Lacey, I love you and I won't give up until your soul is saved from burning in hell. Eternity is a very long time."

Tears streamed down my face. "I'm not sick, Mama. You need to leave."

"You don't get it, do you? I can see college hasn't made you any smarter," she said, smirking. "Patsy and I are staying at a hotel here in Eugene. We aren't leaving without you."

I choked back a sob and then screamed as loudly as I could, but all I could see in my mind were the empty hallways.

I didn't see Mama's hand come up until the palm of her hand stung my cheek.

"Shut up, Lacey! I'm sick and tired of your games. You always have to be the center of attention. We came all the way out here to help you, and you're going to thank us by screaming? My God, you've gotten worse since you moved. Are you going to parties and sleeping around? You know how those demons love it when you're a little slut."

"Stop it! Get out!" I yelled.

Mama reached out and grabbed my arm. I tried to jerk away from her, my heart pounding, but she only tightened her grip.

"You can either be quiet and leave with us in a peaceful manner, or I'll drug you again and haul your ass right outta here," Mama said quietly.

A chill shot down my spine at the calmness of her words.

"Let go of my arm," I said loudly.

Mama tightened her hold and pulled me closer to her.

"Patsy, get her purse and a change of clothes. No one will even know she isn't here since it's Christmas break. Lacey, you'll spend Christmas with your family."

I tried to tug my arm away as tears continued to stream down my face.

"No," I whispered. "I won't go."

"And the crazy thing is you think you have a choice in the matter."

Although I struggled against her, but Mama had more strength and weight on her side. I sat on the floor and tried to make it more diffi-cult as Mama dragged me out of my room and down the hallway. Patsy followed with my purse and clothes.

I glanced around the hallway, but no one was there. Where was Xander? What time was it? I squeezed my eyes closed and prayed for him to show.

Mama pushed the button for the elevator and jerked me to a standing position. "If you try to run or scream, you'll regret it for the rest of your life," she hissed.

The ping of the elevator made my breath catch. The doors whooshed open, she pulled me in, and the doors slid back into place. My heart pounded as we descended. We walked out of the elevator, and I scanned the now-empty lobby. Mrs. Walters wasn't even at the front desk.

I racked my brain for a way to escape, but once Mama had made up her mind, it was nearly impossible to beat her. I'd learned the hard way.

Patsy pushed open the front door of the building, and we stepped outside and into the drizzle. Some students were walking across the distant edge of the parking lot, but they were too far away to help me. Mama pulled me toward a blue Buick and unlocked it. I took a deep breath and screamed at the top of my lungs.

"Lacey!" a voice thundered across the parking lot.

"Xander, help! Please!" I yelled as he ran toward me.

"Hey, what the hell is going on here? Let her go," he said and grabbed Mama's arm. Mama released me, and I pulled away from her and stepped toward Xander.

"Get me out of here," I hiccupped. "Please, just get me out of here."

"You need to leave before I call the police," Xander said to Mama. "I don't know what's going on, but if I see you again, or I see you near Lacey, I'll call the cops."

Mama glared at him as she turned and got into her car.

"Not very smart on your part, Lacey," Patsy muttered and got into the passenger's side of the Buick. Xander wrapped his arms around me as they pulled out of the parking lot.

"Are you okay? Who the hell were they?" Xander asked. Worry spread across his face as he waited for me to answer.

"Get me back upstairs, please," I said, ignoring his question.

I willed my body to calm down, but it wasn't working, and I trembled against him.

"Okay, I'll take you up there," Xander said as he tightened his arm around me and guided me up the sidewalk and into the dorm.

I opened my door and glanced around. If it hadn't been for Xander, I wouldn't be standing in my room at all.

I covered my face as sobs ripped through me. Not only was I not safe anymore, but she was also no longer two thousand miles away. Mama was in Eugene.

Xander pulled me into him and held me while I cried.

"What can I do? I don't know how to help," he whispered.

"You can't," I said between hiccups. "I've tried, and nothing's worked. I ran, Xander. I lost everything and moved across the country, and it didn't work."

No way could I look at him right now. I hadn't sobbed like this since Mama locked me in her bedroom. My ugly cry looked awful, and I couldn't stand for him to see it. I pushed away from him and walked out of my room, down the hallway, and into the bathroom. It amazed me how fast the dorm had cleared out for the break. Xander, Mama, and Patsy were the only people I'd seen in a few hours.

Ten minutes later, I returned to my room and found him sitting on the floor.

"I'm sorry, Xander. I just don't think I'm up to going out tonight."

He studied my face as he stood up, straightened his broad shoulders, and clenched his jaw.

"I don't know what happened, but you're not staying here," he said, rubbing his neck. "You're obviously terrified of those women, and I don't want to leave you here alone. Are any of your friends here during the break?"

"Yeah. George is going to stay with me later tonight. He's at his parents' house right now."

"When's he coming by?"

"In a few hours," I replied.

"What if you and George came over to my house tonight instead? I have some guest rooms, and maybe being in a different place with your friends will help you feel better. You can figure some things out—whatever those things might be."

"I couldn't impose, and . . ."

"What?"

I held his gaze. His typical mischievousness had vanished; he was serious about helping.

"You can't save me. No one can," I said and bit my lip.

As my words sank deep into my soul, I walked to my desk and brushed my hair. I couldn't stand for him to see me like this.

"She took my purse and some of my clothes," I muttered, shaking my head. I squeezed my eyes closed, unable to process what had just happened. Sitting down, I stared at my reflection in the mirror. My green eyes were red and swollen. Xander stood behind me, his brow furrowed and his arms crossed in front of him.

"Shit," he said and ran his hands through his hair. "Listen, I'll take care of it and get your purse and clothes back. Please, don't worry about it. It's under control."

"How? I don't even know where she is . . . somewhere in Eugene," I said and turned toward him.

"I have connections—let me take care of it. I'll need you to tell me who they were and what the hell they wanted, but we should get you situated first. Then you can tell me what I need to know."

"That would be amazing if you could get my stuff back and I wouldn't have to see her." A small amount of relief washed over me at the thought of it.

"For now, call George at his folks' house. At least this way I'll know you're safe tonight."

"I'll call him and see what he wants to do," I said, picking up the phone.

9

The air was thick with tension when George entered my room. He took one look at my red, swollen eyes and walked over to me, grabbing my hand. He didn't even bother calling me Hillbilly.

We silently followed Xander out of the building and into the parking lot. "My truck's over here," he said, leading us to a new, black Chevy pickup.

George and I glanced at each other as he unlocked the doors. We handed him our backpacks, and he placed them in the back of the extended cab.

"Hop in, you guys. There's room for everyone in the front," he said as he climbed into the driver's seat.

I slid in next to him, and George took the window seat next to me.

"This is a beautiful truck—is it yours?" I asked softly, worried I was being nosy.

"Yeah, my grandma passed away this summer and left me her house, and . . . well, I've got money for a while if I'm careful," he replied.

"Oh, I'm so sorry. What about your parents?"

"My parents are in Europe. I don't see them often, but they call every now and then. For the last four years I've lived with Grandma, so I could afford to go here. I miss her a lot, but she was in so much pain. She fought cancer for several years."

I sucked in my breath and stared out the passenger window, willing the tears to stay away as I thought about Susan. George squeezed my hand.

"Yeah, I know how hard it is," I replied, frowning as the sadness of those memories washed through me. George placed his other hand on top of mine.

Xander turned on the radio, and we rode the rest of the way without talking. We followed a road I wasn't familiar with and headed out of Eugene toward Springfield. It felt like we'd been driving for an hour, but only twenty minutes had passed when we pulled onto a gravel road and drove a few more minutes before parking in front of a two-story, beige bungalow. Black trim surrounded the windows and planters were strategically placed at the corners of the porch.

"This is home," he said and turned off the truck. George and I slid out the passenger side while Xander grabbed our backpacks from behind the seat.

I glanced at George and silently thanked him for being there with me. Since I didn't know anything about Xander, I was a little nervous. We walked up the front steps and followed him into the house.

"Wow," George said as we stepped into the foyer, which had beautiful wood floors. I tugged on his arm and motioned for him to check out the wainscoting in the dining room. My eyes wandered into the living room next, where I noted the crown molding, and the beautiful stonework around the fireplace.

"Yeah, she's a beaut," Xander said as we followed him down the hallway and into the kitchen. He placed our backpacks on the table, opened the fridge, and pulled out a few beers.

"No thanks," I said, scrunching up my nose at the thought of the taste.

"Not a fan of beer, I see?" Xander asked, smiling for the first time all evening.

"I am. Thanks," George said as he accepted one.

"Well, I've got something else for you then," he said and opened a kitchen cabinet.

"Really, I'm okay," I said.

"No, no, you're not anywhere close to being okay, so no arguing," he said and pulled down a bottle of rum.

"Lacey, you like rum. It'll help you relax some," George encouraged.

I nodded as Xander proceeded to make a drink with half rum and half Pepsi.

"This should help," he said and smiled.

I took a sip and winced.

"Wow! A little strong," I said, wiping my mouth with the back of my hand. "Thank you," I added. "None of this was necessary."

Xander waved me off and picked up our backpacks again.

"Come on, I'll show you the guest rooms," he said.

George elbowed me as we followed him up the stairs.

"My God, his ass," he whispered and fanned himself. I covered my mouth and stifled a giggle.

"George, you can have this room," Xander said as he opened the door to a small, but beautifully furnished, bedroom.

"Lacey, I'm going to give you the bedroom in between George's and mine," he said as he opened another door and placed my backpack inside it. I noted the queen-size bed and dark hardwood furniture. A bright-colored area rug spanned the room. I wondered why anyone would want to cover such beautiful wood floors.

"The guest bathroom is across the hall and there's one downstairs as well, so you guys make yourselves comfortable."

"Wow, I don't have to run down the hallway in a towel tonight. I'm kind of excited," I replied.

"Well, we certainly do *not* want to see that," George piped up.

"Speak for yourself there, buddy," Xander said, laughing.

The familiar flush crept up my neck and cheeks, and I took another drink and hoped they wouldn't notice.

"Why don't we go downstairs and get something to eat," Xander said.

"Or maybe another drink," I replied and smiled. "Pretty sure I started feeling better about two sips ago." A giggle escaped me as they looked at me.

The guys laughed, and we made our way downstairs and settled into the living room. Xander grabbed the rum and Pepsi, sandwiches, and chips.

The rain pounded against the windows, and I settled into the love seat as Xander built a fire. George took a handful of chips and situated himself into the couch with his beer, which left the seat next to me available. Xander didn't pass up the opportunity.

"How're you doing?" he asked.

"I'm okay, thank you," I said and raised my glass.

"Lacey doesn't really drink, so we might want to ply her with water as well," George said. "My Hillbilly is a lightweight."

"Hillbilly?" Xander barked out a laugh.

"Seriously, George? Like I wasn't having a shitty day already," I said and glared at him. It was one thing for him to tease me, but not in front of Xander.

"It's okay, Lacey, I won't tell anyone, and I certainly won't call you that," Xander said as he chuckled.

The fire crackled, and I took another sip of my drink.

"My mother," I said and stared into the flames.

George and Xander looked at me and waited for me to say something else.

"The women in the parking lot," I continued. "One was my mother, and the other one was her girlfriend. I moved here to go to the U of O —I was honest with you about that. But I also wanted to start over and leave the past behind. Stupidly, I thought it would work, but here she is . . ."

"Wow, that is so messed up. I'm sorry you had to deal with that shit," George said.

"Yeah. No one should have to go through that," Xander said.

"Welcome to my life," I said and sighed. "Let's change the subject."

Neither one of them pressed me for any additional information, and it was all I was going to share anyway. George cleared his throat and broke the silence.

"Do you miss football?" George asked Xander.

"Yeah, sorta crazy it was my last year," he said and ran his hand through his hair. "I love the NFL, though. Steve Largent is kicking ass again this season for the Seahawks. That'll keep me focused on football for a while. I'm off to the real world next June though, no more classes or teachers. That'll be when it really hits me. It'll be a bit weird, but I'm excited about getting a job and starting my career."

"Mmmm, a job," I said and held up my empty glass. "Maybe I should get one of those too? I saved enough money to last me a year while I got adjusted to a new, well, everything, but . . . yup."

"How ya feelin' there, Lacey?" Xander asked. He didn't bother trying to hide the amused expression on his face.

"Better, like, much better. Can I have some more, please?"

"Sure," Xander said and reached for my glass.

"Thank you and your amazing smile," I said and peered up at him.

Xander grinned as he walked out of the living room and into the kitchen.

"Water—she needs some water too if you don't want her puking on your gorgeous floors," George called after him.

"George, you're right," I whispered loudly. "He's totally hot! And nice. Like, what the hell, right? Just pick us up and let us stay at his house for the night? And what a house!" I squealed.

"Lacey," George said as he slid into the seat next to me. "Shhh, girl, you're all sorts of wasted already." He laughed.

"Oh God, my neck doesn't hurt anymore either. It's a miracle. I should drink more often. It melts the stress away," I said as my head rolled to the side and I smiled at George. "I love you, George. I really do."

"Yeah, I love you too, Hillbilly, and that's why I'm here. I don't know what happened to you tonight, but I'm really glad Xander had you call me. I'm here," he said as he took my hand.

"I wish straight guys were as sweet as you. They might get laid more often," I said.

"Yeah? I'll keep that in mind," Xander said as he entered the living room with another rum and Pepsi and a big glass of water.

"Shit," I said as my cheeks flushed bright red. I reached for the rum and Pepsi as Xander placed the water on the table for me.

"Don't worry, George, her drink is mostly soda this time. I didn't realize she wasn't a drinker."

"Thanks. Yeah, last weekend was the first time I ever saw her drink, and it wasn't much."

I leaned my head back and listened to George and Xander talk. The fire crackled, the rain pattered against the window, and the rum flowed through me. It was enough to completely forget everything bad that had happened in the last year. All the hell, the struggle to appear happy, and the constant hole in my heart—it all slipped away.

"Lacey!"

George nudged my shoulder, and my eyelids fluttered open.

"George? Where am I?" I asked and gripped his arm.

"You're okay, I'm here. We're at Xander's, in his guest room. You fell asleep, so he carried you up here. You had a nightmare. Are you okay? You said you were trapped, and it was hard to make out the rest, but I could've sworn you said you were going to die."

"Holy shit, I didn't," I whispered and covered my face with the blanket. Then I pulled the cover back down and peeked at the clock. It was two in the morning.

"Hey, what's going on?" George asked, nudging me.

I rubbed the sleep from my eyes and peered at him in the darkness. George had proven to be a good friend, and hopefully one I could trust with my past. And if Mama was staying in Eugene, I would need my friends.

"My mom's sick, and I don't mean physically sick." I sighed as the memories flooded back.

"You mean mentally ill?"

"Yeah. I tried to get her help last year, but she didn't want it," I said. "Things ended badly, and when I say badly, I mean she drugged me and kept me locked up for almost two weeks. I wasn't allowed to go outside or to work, school, or anywhere else. My boyfriend at the time was in the military, and I was supposed to take his mom and brother to visit him. When I didn't show, his ex-fiancée and his best friend drove them instead. Then, for some stupid reason, Walker thought I'd cheated on him, and he broke up with me. We were engaged. I dunno. I'm probably not making a lot of sense." I sighed.

"Walker?"

"What?" I asked, snapping to attention.

"You called out to him during your nightmare."

"Ugh, I cannot believe this crap," I said and rubbed my face. "Yes, his name was Walker."

"Okay, so now that you're actually awake, can I ask you a million questions? I'm confused about a few things."

"Sure," I said and propped myself up on my elbow. I wanted to see his reactions as I told him how screwed up I was.

"Okay, so your mom drugged you, but why? I mean that's fucked up times ten, and now I get why it freaked you out when she showed up at your room today. And wait, I thought she still lived in Arkansas. And she has a girlfriend?"

"George, it's two o'clock in the morning. I can only handle one question at a time."

"Okay. So why did she drug you?"

"She didn't want me to date Walker, or anyone for that matter."

"How old were you when this happened?"

"It was a year ago. I was eighteen."

"Whoa. How in the hell do you even wrap your mind around that? Your *mom* did that to you?"

"Like I said, she's not well. She . . . she's convinced I'm possessed by demons."

"Dear mother of God!"

"Seriously? I tell you I thought I was possessed, and you respond with that?"

"Shit, I'm sorry, but this isn't your ordinary family drama. And you said *she* thought you were possessed, not you."

"I believed it too. I didn't know any different until I met Walker and his family. His aunt was the first person to tell me she was mentally ill."

"So, you fell in love with Walker and he told you you're not possessed by demons and your mom is off her rocker?"

"Something like that," I said.

"Then she found out and drugged you to keep you from dating him?"

"In a nutshell."

"What in the hell happened next?"

"My best friend, Emma, and her dad helped me move out of Mama's house and then we got an apartment. I tried to move on, but I started having nightmares, and every time I went somewhere I didn't know if I would run into Walker, his wife, or Mama."

"Wife?" George squealed and bolted upright in the bed.

"Oh, yeah, after he broke up with me because he thought I cheated on him, he and his ex-fiancée got back together. They got married right before—" my voice hitched at the thought of Susan. "Before his mom passed away from cancer."

"I'm going to borrow your words. Holy shit!"

"I'd applied to college out here, and when I was accepted, I moved. I'd hoped I could get my shit together and start over. So, there it is— my dirty little secret. Promise me you won't tell anyone. Not Adalyn or Megan, not your mom, your brother, or even his cat," I said and glared at him. "These are my secrets to tell, no one else's."

George shook his head. "I wouldn't do that to you. Even though I tease you, you're my best friend, and that's so messed up. I'd be freaked out too."

"I don't know what I'm going to do," I said and squeezed my eyes closed. Maybe when I opened them, I'd wake up from this horrible dream. If only.

"You still love him," George said.

There was a light knock on the door. We glanced at each other, and George held his finger up to his mouth, motioning for me not to answer his question.

"Love who?" Xander asked and poked his head through the door.

"Hey, did we wake you up? I'm so sorry. I couldn't sleep, so we were talking," I said.

"No, I've been up," Xander said. "I'm gonna get some sleep, so I'll see you guys later in the morning. There's plenty of food in the kitchen, so help yourselves when you get up."

We waved goodnight as he closed the door behind him. His footsteps echoed down the hallway.

"Well, that was bad timing," George whispered.

"Yeah, it was. He just asked me out, and then he walks into that conversation. Do you think he heard anything else?" I asked, biting my lip.

"I have no idea—I'm still trying to piece all this together. It does make more sense now, though. There were days you seemed so sad it was almost like you were hollow. I know you've gotta be homesick on top of everything else, too. I'll do whatever I can to help you get through this. And maybe you should give me Emma's phone number . . . ya know, just in case," George said, giving me a worried look.

"I hope you'll never need to call her, but it's probably a good idea," I said, reaching for my backpack and writing her number down for him. "Please don't share it." I handed it to him.

"You have my word," he said as he slipped it into his pocket.

"I'm tired again," I said and lowered my head onto the pillow.

"Me too. I'll have more questions tomorrow, but for now, I'll hold your hand so maybe you won't have more nightmares."

"Thanks, George," I said and squeezed his hand as I drifted off to sleep.

## 11

The gray morning light filtered through the curtains, and the rain had slowed to a light drizzle. I slipped out of bed and crept down the stairs and into the kitchen. After a minute of searching the cabinets, I found Xander's coffee and made a pot for everyone. I grabbed a large glass of water and downed it as well. Thank God I wasn't hungover, but I didn't have time to feel tired or achy, either.

I glanced at the stove clock: 8:12 A.M. It was two hours later back home. I found Xander's phone and dialed Emma's number.

"Hello?" she said.

"Emma, it's Lacey. Can you call me back at this number?" I asked and then gave her Xander's phone number.

"Okay, I'll call you right back," Emma said and hung up.

I grabbed the phone before it fully rang.

"Hey, thanks for calling," I said quietly.

"Where are you? Are you okay?" Emma asked.

"Don't worry, I'm fine. It's sorta weird, but I had a date last night."

"And you spent the night already?" she asked. Her voice held a note of disapproval.

"Not like that, Emma. I was all ready to go out with him, but then Mama showed up at my dorm room."

"What?" Emma screeched. "Your Mama as in Crazy Mama? What in the world, Lacey?"

"I know. Needless to say, it wasn't going well, and then Xander showed up to take me out. If he hadn't come right then, I'm not sure what would've happened. Anyway, Xander invited George and me over, and we stayed in his guest rooms. He was super sweet."

"Pack your stuff. If she's in Eugene, you need to come home. I'll kick Lisa out, and you can have your old room back."

There was nothing funny about the situation, but I laughed.

"You can't kick Lisa out, and I'm not coming home, either. I'm surrounded by people all the time here. I'll be okay."

"I don't like the sound of this *at all*."

"Me neither, but I can't run forever," I said and sighed. "Let's talk about something else. What's going on with you?"

Emma filled me in on her nursing classes and family, and we agreed to talk in a few days. I hung up the phone and grabbed a few one-dollar bills from the pocket of my jeans. Folding them in half, I placed them next to the stove and put the salt-and-pepper shakers on top of them. Even though Emma had called me right back, I wanted to make sure to pay the phone bill.

I poured a cup of coffee and curled up in Xander's wingback chair next to the window.

"Did you sleep better?" George asked as he joined me in the living room.

"Yeah. Thank you for keeping me company last night. There's coffee if you want some." I nodded toward the kitchen.

"Thanks, I think I'm gonna need it. It was a long night," he said as he patted his rumpled hair and made his way into the kitchen. He rejoined me in the living room with a cup of steaming coffee.

"I'm not going to call you Hillbilly anymore. You've been through enough without me making things worse. Besides, you're not a hill-billy. I don't think I've ever seen you without shoes," he said and smiled over his cup before he took a sip.

"Thanks," I said, shaking my head and grinning.

"There's more to your story, isn't there?"

"You heard the highlights, but there was a lot of stuff in the middle, too."

"I'm sorry you had to go through that. And I won't lie—after you told me all that stuff last night, I'm really worried."

"So is Emma. I called her this morning, and she wants me to come back to Arkansas since Mama is out here now. But I can't. I like Eugene, and I can't keep running, right?"

"Mmm, I would. I wouldn't want to be in the same city with her, or even the same state."

"Is it crazy that some days I miss her?"

"No, not really. I mean, she is your mom, and it's not supposed to be like this."

I nodded and sipped at my coffee.

"Do you have a picture?"

"Of who? Mama?"

"Walker. I want to see the guy who shattered your heart."

"I do, in my dorm room. It's in a box with Susan's obituary and some pictures. I'll show you sometime."

"Morning," Xander said as he leaned on the door frame between the living room and kitchen.

"Hi," I said and smiled. George shot me a look and wiggled his eyebrows.

"Damn, he looks good, even in the morning," George muttered under his breath.

I stifled a giggle as Xander sat on the love seat and propped his feet up on the coffee table.

"Thank you again for letting us stay here last night," I said.

"You bet," Xander replied as he ran his hand through his hair.

"I'll need to go back to the dorm today—would you be able to give me a ride back?"

"Will you be okay by yourself?" Xander asked as concern spread across his face.

"George will stay with me. I'll be alright." I wasn't about to tell him

George was leaving tomorrow to go to Mexico for the rest of Christmas break. I didn't want him to think I was a charity case.

"Give me a call if you need to come over again."

"Thank you, it means a lot to me."

"And me," George chimed in. "If she's with you, I'll know she's safe," George said and shot me a look out of the corner of his eye.

Xander glanced at George and then back at me.

"Wait a minute, I have to ask. Are you in danger?"

I glared at George for giving up too much information. We'd had a long night, but he had to be more careful.

"I don't know. I'm not gonna lie to you—I really don't know." I sighed, leaning my head back against the chair and staring out the window.

If I were honest with myself, I'd admit that anytime Mama was around, I was at risk of being in danger. But who wanted to admit something like that about their parent?

"It's okay, I won't push you. But if you need a safe place to stay, or if you're ever in trouble, I'm here. I want to help," he said.

I stared at him for a moment and searched my tired brain for something to say. I'd talked with Xander a total of four times now, and he was offering me a place to stay.

"Thank you, but I'm sure it'll be okay."

"Promise me you'll call me if you need to."

I paused for a moment and nodded.

"Why don't you take a shower and then I'll take you guys back to the dorm in a little while?" Xander stood up.

"Okay," I agreed and took the last sip of my coffee.

George hopped off the couch and left Xander and me alone in the living room as he headed upstairs.

"So, I'm serious. About calling me, I mean," he said.

I stood up and crossed my arms in front of me self-consciously. Xander walked around the coffee table and closed the gap between us.

"You're welcome here anytime," he said as he reached out and tucked a stray piece of hair behind my ear.

"Thank you," I whispered. "I really appreciate it."

Xander held my gaze and then leaned forward and gently brushed his lips against mine. He pulled back and ran his thumb across my lips and cheek.

"You're so beautiful," he whispered as he dipped his head and kissed me again. My lips parted as I welcomed the warmth of his mouth.

He wrapped his arm around my waist and pulled me closer. I ran my hands up his arms and lingered on his muscular biceps. Heat spread through me. A deep yearning I'd locked away since I was with Walker resurfaced as Xander kissed me.

I sighed as he pulled away.

"How about a redo of our date?" he asked and smiled softly.

"I'd like that."

"Tonight then? I'll pick you up at seven?"

"Sounds perfect," I replied, grinning.

Xander leaned down and kissed me on the forehead. Then his hands slipped away from my waist and he walked away into the kitchen. A moment later, I heard him on the phone and decided it was a good time for a shower. I made my way upstairs and glanced at the clock on the nightstand next to the bed. It was already noon, which meant I only had seven more hours until Xander picked me up. My stomach fluttered with excitement as I grabbed my clean clothes and walked across the hall and into the bathroom. I'd forgotten what it felt like to have privacy.

I poked my head around the shower curtain as I heard the bathroom door open and close. I'd been thinking about Xander and I hadn't locked the door behind me. I should've known better; George never knocked, and he had no issue with talking to me no matter where I was.

"What the hell, George?" I asked, adjusting the curtain. I didn't care if my body did anything for him or not; I didn't want him to see me.

"Well, I figured we could talk here and not get interrupted. I have questions."

"For God's sake, let me take *one* shower in peace. You know what the dorms are like."

"If you're worried I want to see your lady parts, you need to chill out. You know they won't do a damned thing for me," he said.

"Out!" I demanded and pointed toward the door. "Your questions can wait."

He stood up and huffed as he walked out of the bathroom.

I rinsed the conditioner from my hair and laughed, wishing Emma could meet George. They'd get along really well—they were both always full of questions.

12

Xander loaded our stuff in the truck, and we all slid into the front seat. I wrapped my arms around myself as Xander blasted the heater. I'd been so distracted with Mama earlier I'd left my coat in my dorm room.

"I don't get it," I said. "It's warmer here in the winter than it is back in Arkansas, but I'm still freezing all the time."

"It's the rain," Xander said.

"Once you get wet and the wind whips through you, it's over— you're cold until summer," George said as he pulled his coat tighter around him.

"My coat's in the backseat if you can reach it," Xander said.

I turned and strained to get it, finally managing to pull it toward me. I smiled, snuggling into his coat and warming up.

"Thanks," I said and beamed at him.

George elbowed me in the ribs and raised his eyebrow at me. He probably had tons of questions about Xander now, too.

"George, are you hanging out with Lacey tonight?" Xander asked.

"Hell yeah. I'm not leaving her until I have to," George said.

"Well, I'm going to take her out, so she might not be back until late."

"Ah, the missed date from last night," George replied. "Well, you two go have fun. I'll hang out at my parent's house for a while since Megan and Adalyn are in Portland for winter break."

"Yeah, the dorms will be pretty empty," I said, biting my lip and remembering Mama and Patsy cornering me in my room.

"I'm leaving for Mexico tomorrow, too," George added. "I won't see you for the rest of the break."

"That is totally unacceptable," I said and stuck my lip out. "What am I gonna do without you, especially now?" I leaned my head back and closed my eyes at the thought of everyone being gone except me.

"Wait. You're going to be gone the rest of the break? Lacey, you didn't tell me," Xander said with a hint of surprise in his voice.

"Didn't think I had to," I retorted.

"That's not what I meant. If there's no one with you and the dorms are nearly empty, then I'm worried."

"I'm alright," I muttered, frowning at George. I didn't want Xander to think of me as a train wreck he had to take care of. I'd figure something out.

We pulled into the parking lot in front of my dorm. I'd never seen so many available spaces before, and Xander parked his truck close to the front door.

He grabbed our backpacks, locked the truck doors, and reached for my hand.

"I'll walk you up," he said and squeezed my hand.

I nodded as George and I followed him up the sidewalk and into the dorm, which felt abandoned. Would anyone be here over the break? As I walked down the hallway and into the elevator, my stomach churned with uneasiness. If the dorms were this quiet, was Xander right? Was I safe here? Would Mama show up again, or would she leave me alone now that I'd told her I didn't want to see her? If she did show up again, how would I protect myself?

"You okay?" Xander asked softly as the elevator pinged, announcing we were on my floor. I nodded as the doors whooshed open. The sound of our footsteps echoed through the hall.

We stopped at my door. I dug into the pocket of my jeans for my key, but then I noticed the door wasn't quite shut all the way. Hesitating for a moment, I pushed it open and gasped as we walked in.

"Where the hell is your stuff?" George asked from behind me.

"Holy shit," I said, scanning my room. Everything was gone. My desk was empty; my bedspread, poster, and alarm clock were all missing. The white walls and mattress were completely bare. I opened my closet door and found it empty.

"What the hell? Where's my stuff?" I asked, my eyes widening with shock.

"Lacey, this has your name on it," Xander said as he picked up a folded piece of paper from the desk and handed it to me.

My hands shook as I unfolded it.

*Lacey, I have your belongings. If you want them back, you'll have to come get them. Patsy and I are waiting for you. It's time to get yourself together once and for all and stop being led around by the demons you're allowing to run your life. We're at the Holiday Inn, room 118.*

A tear streamed down my cheek as I handed the note to George.

"Are you kidding me?" George exclaimed. "She took your stuff to make you come visit her? You can't go over there."

"What's going on?" Xander asked.

I nodded at George, and he handed the note to him.

Xander took it and read it.

"That's bullshit. She can't do that," Xander said and frowned.

"Well, she just did," George said. "I just don't get it. Lacey, maybe Xander can help. You need to fill him in on everything that's going on."

I sighed as I pulled away from Xander and crawled onto my bare mattress. Xander sat at the foot of it, and George settled in on the opposite bed. I told Xander what I'd shared with George, except I kept Walker out of it as much as possible and didn't even mention his name. My gaze traveled to him, searching for his reaction, but I couldn't read his face.

"That's fucked up," he said as his jaw tensed.

"Those were my words too," George said.

"George, can you stay with Lacey for a while? I need to make some calls. I'll be outside in front of the dorm. Keep your door locked," Xander said, turning his gaze to me.

I stood up and locked the door behind him.

"He's pissed," George said.

"He's definitely something, but I can't tell what. I don't think he's gonna come back. You can't blame him—it's a hell of a lot of drama to dump on someone who just asked me out."

"He'll be back," George assured me.

I stretched out on my bed and stared at the ceiling as a tear rolled down my cheek.

"Dammit, I have nothing, not even a toothbrush," I said. A combination of anger and fear swirled in the pit of my stomach.

"Scoot over," George said and patted my side. "I know you're scared, but Xander said you have a place to stay."

"No, that was before he realized how crazy my life is. I guarantee the offer is no longer on the table. My God, what am I going to do?" I asked, unable to hide the tremble in my voice.

"Hey, we'll figure this out. It's going to be okay," George whispered.

A knock on my door startled me as I wiped my tears away.

"Lacey, it's Xander. It's okay to open the door."

I crossed the room and let him in.

"Okay, I called a friend, and you should have your stuff back in a few days since she told us where she's staying in her note. In the meantime, you're staying with me. George, you're welcome to come over until you have to leave. I think Lacey feels better with you around." He paused. "So? Let's go."

George and I stared at each other, speechless.

"How?" I asked, scooting off my bed and stood up. "How are you getting my stuff back?" I frowned as I tried to imagine how that was even possible. There was no way Mama was going to give it back.

"I have some connections. Don't worry about it. You'll have it soon," he said and reached for my hand. "Like I said before, I know people."

I nodded and took his hand.

"Do you have your key, Lacey?" George asked.

"Yeah. I'll lock the door, even though there isn't anything left to steal," I muttered.

We followed Xander to his truck, and within thirty minutes, we pulled up to his house. We filed in and made ourselves comfortable in the living room. Xander brought George a beer and a drink for me that I suspected had more rum in it than Pepsi.

"Thank you," I said as he sat next to me on the love seat.

"You're safe now," Xander said as he wrapped his arm around my shoulders and pulled me to him. I flushed as he kissed my forehead.

## 13

Xander and George did their best to take my mind off Mama. We spent the afternoon shopping for a toothbrush, pajamas, underwear, jeans, and shirts to get me through a few days. I promised Xander I'd pay him back, but he insisted it was an early Christmas present. It wasn't in my nature to accept gifts from someone I barely knew, but I had little choice unless I wanted to stink and walk around with bad breath.

We dropped George off at his house at eleven that night. It had been a super long day, and I was sad I had to say goodbye to him for the rest of Christmas break. I walked him to his front door and hugged him.

"Try not to worry. I think you're in good hands, and safe, with Xander. That's the most important thing, right?" he asked.

"Yeah, but I wish you weren't going to Mexico. I mean, I know you'll have an amazing time, but we can't even talk on the phone while you're gone. What if I need you?"

"We'll catch up the minute I'm back, and I feel better knowing Xander's around."

"Yeah, I agree," I said and kissed his cheek. "Merry Christmas. I'm gonna miss you."

"I'll be back before you know it, and I'll expect all the juicy details about you and Xander," he said and smiled.

"Okay, I promise," I replied, chewing my lip as he stepped into his house and closed the door. I sighed as I made my way down the sidewalk to the truck.

"You okay?" Xander asked as I put on my seat belt.

"Yeah, just a little sad. I'd hoped to be in Arkansas with Emma and her family, and now that all this has happened and George, Adalyn, and Megan are all gone . . ."

"I get it. This is my first Christmas without my grandma," he said softly as we pulled out of George's driveway.

The truck's windshield wipers whooshed as we pulled onto the highway. The rain had grown heavy, and so had my mood. It had been one thing hanging out with George and Xander this afternoon, but now it was silent, and I was left with my thoughts.

I stifled a yawn as we pulled into his driveway. Xander parked the truck and walked around to the passenger door. He held his jacket over my head as we ran to the front porch and tried to stay dry.

"I've never heard it thunder here," I said as we walked into his house.

"You won't very often. We don't have storms like you do back home," he said and closed the door. "How are you doing with all this?" he asked as he hung his coat in the hall closet.

"Honestly? I don't know, and I have no idea what I would've done if you hadn't helped me. Thank you," I said as I glanced up at him.

"You're welcome," he said as he tucked a strand of wet hair behind my ear. "You can stay as long as you want."

"Yeah?" I asked.

"Yes," he said and smiled.

The rain pounded against the window as Xander wrapped his arms around me.

"I won't let anything bad happen to you," he whispered.

I nestled my head against his chest, realizing he was trying to help, but no one could keep me safe. I'd moved away and started over, and Mama had still found me. My eyes closed and I bit my lip, allowing his warmth to calm me. At least, at this moment, I was okay.

"Let's get you to bed," he said.

I followed him up the stairs and into the guest room.

"I'll be here if you need anything," Xander said, giving me a gentle kiss on the lips. "Get some rest."

I watched him as he smiled and closed the bedroom door behind him. I rubbed my arms and then rifled through a shopping bag for my new pajamas. My shoulders slumped while I stared at them, the last twenty-four hours sinking in.

I bit my lip as I realized Xander had been true to his word so far, and I *had* actually been safe with him. Mama had left when he showed up. Walker had stood up to Krissy, but never Mama. No one had ever stood up to Mama and gotten away with it. But maybe this time would be different.

I changed my clothes and slipped under the covers. It was almost midnight, and I was exhausted. I would figure things out tomorrow.

"LACEY! LACEY, WAKE UP!"

My eyes fluttered open as I recognized Xander's voice next to me. His hand was on my shoulder.

"What are you doing in here?"

"You started screaming. Are you okay? My God, you scared the shit out of me," Xander said and ran his hand through his hair.

"I'm so sorry," I whispered as I sat up. I wrapped my arms around myself and tried to still the violent trembles that traveled through my body.

"It's okay," he said, his face filled with concern. "Hey, it's okay." He sat next to me on the bed. "Come here."

I scooted closer to him and laid my head on his shoulder while he rubbed my back. After a few minutes, I stopped shaking and laid down again.

"I'll stay with you tonight so you can sleep," he said as he laid down next to me. "I don't know everything that happened to you, but I won't let it happen again," he whispered.

Xander pulled me close to him, calming me. I squeezed my eyes closed and swallowed my embarrassment. The nightmares were almost as bad as Mama herself, and they followed me everywhere I went. I focused on the rise and fall of Xander's chest until I drifted back to sleep.

"MORNING," I said, placing the last pancake on the plate.

"Wow, this looks amazing," Xander said as he walked into the kitchen and reached for the coffee pot.

"I wanted to cook you breakfast after everything I've put you through," I said.

"You're not putting me through anything. I asked you to stay here. I don't regret it."

"Well," I said as my cheeks reddened, "then the least I can do is try and keep you well fed." I smiled at him.

"It smells fantastic," he said as he pulled a chair out and sat down at the kitchen table. "I was thinking, now that you're here, what do you think about going with me to pick out a Christmas tree? We should decorate," he said as a grin spread across his face.

"Really?" I couldn't hide my excitement. One of the things I'd been missing the most was trekking into the woods and chopping a tree down with Mama. I didn't have a lot of good memories with her, but that was one of them.

"Yeah," he replied. "Let's do that after we eat and shower."

"Okay," I said and took a bite of my pancake.

"Grandma loved Christmas," he murmured.

"I'm so sorry. I lost someone last year around the holidays too, and it's so hard." I paused, realizing what I'd said. I didn't want to get into detail about Susan and Walker. My focus returned to cutting my pancake, and I avoided Xander's questioning gaze.

I scooted my chair back and refilled my coffee cup.

"Would you like some more coffee?"

He took a second to swallow his mouthful of pancake. "I'm good, thanks."

I started to replace the coffee pot, but I accidentally hit it against the counter. It shattered into pieces, and the remainder of the coffee splashed all over me. Startled, I dropped my full coffee cup, adding to the hot liquid and broken glass now all over the kitchen floor.

"Don't move," Xander exclaimed as he jumped up and grabbed a towel. "Stay still," he said as he dabbed the towel against my face, arms, and wet clothes.

"I'm—I'm so sorry," I whispered. "I'll buy you a new one. I didn't mean to."

"Are you okay?" he asked, ignoring my apology as he searched my face and body for cuts. "Stay still, I don't want you to cut your bare feet."

I didn't move as he examined me.

"I'm sorry," I said again.

"I don't give a shit about the coffee pot. I just don't want you to get hurt. Hang on," he said as he swept me off my feet and into his arms. The glass crunched under his shoes as he carried me from the living room and gently placed me on the couch.

"You're not mad at me?"

"Why in the world would I be mad?" He stood up and ran his hand through his hair. "I know there's history with your mom, and I don't know what else you've gone through, but I'm not going to yell at you over a coffee pot. Now stay here, and I'll clean everything up. You don't have any shoes on, and I don't want you in the kitchen. In fact, why don't you go on upstairs and shower. Just don't go into the kitchen again without shoes, okay?"

I nodded and watched him walk away.

"Shit," I said and rubbed my face. How stupid could I be? I'd never broken a coffee pot in my life. What was wrong with me?

I swore under my breath as I made my way upstairs and picked out an outfit for the day. Maybe a hot shower would do me some good. If

I kept breaking stuff, Xander would boot me out for sure, and I'd be left staying in my dorm room alone, with Mama only a few miles away.

"Merry fuckin' Christmas," I said, stepping into the hot shower and closed my eyes.

14

The week passed by quickly, and I'd managed not to break anything else. Xander and I had spent all our time together. We'd shopped and decorated for Christmas, watched movies, and gone out to dinner a few times. He'd been a perfect gentleman and had only kissed me, but the more time we spent together, the more I found myself wanting to take it further.

I stared at the bedroom ceiling as a ray of sunshine broke through the curtains. It was almost always sunny on Christmas in the South, but here, it had been more than a week since the sun had revealed itself. It was a nice touch.

I sat up and slipped into my house shoes. It was 9 A.M., which meant it was 11 A.M. back home. I couldn't wait to call Emma today. My heart ached at the thought of not being with her and her family for the holiday, but I was also grateful not to be alone.

I tiptoed across the hallway to the bathroom and shut the door behind me. If I stayed much longer I'd get spoiled not having to share a bathroom with a million other girls.

I quietly made my way downstairs and into the kitchen, still wearing my pajamas.

"Merry Christmas," Xander said from the kitchen table.

"I thought you were still asleep! I literally tiptoed across the hall so I wouldn't wake you." A giggle escaped me.

"Funny. I've been down here since seven. I poured you some coffee already," he said and nodded toward the cup on the kitchen table.

My cheeks flamed at the thought of the incident last week, but Xander hadn't brought it up again. We'd replaced the coffee pot the same day.

"Thank you, and Merry Christmas to you too," I said and smiled at him.

"Why don't we go into the living room," he said. His brown eyes danced with mischievousness.

I took his hand, followed him into the living room, and gasped. A pile of presents filled the space underneath the tree.

"What's all this?"

"Well, there's a gift for you, and then a few items you've been missing. I just thought it would be fun to wrap it all," he said and grinned.

"I bought you something too, but there are way more than two presents here," I said, confused.

"Here, start with this one and you'll understand," he said as he handed me a package.

I gently tore the wrapping open and pulled out a pair of jeans Mama had taken from my dorm room.

"Holy shit! Are you serious?" I squealed.

"Yes, it's all here."

I jumped up from my chair, hurled myself at him, and hugged him with everything I had inside me.

He kissed the top of my head and handed me another present. I tore the paper open and laughed as I pulled out my favorite green T-shirt. The next package was my purse. I opened each one until my belongings covered the floor around me. Xander had gotten all my stuff back from Mama.

"Thank you. Oh my God, you have no idea what this means to me. I have all my things back, and I didn't have to see her." I bit my lip and willed my tears back. At least this time they were tears of happiness.

"Okay, wait," I said, locating his present. "I know it's not much, but

I wanted to get you something," I said and shyly handed him the gift.

"You didn't have to get me anything. I'm just happy you're here."

"Open it!" I squealed and clapped my hands like a little kid.

Xander laughed and carefully unwrapped it.

"Wow, this is awesome!" He held up the Seattle Seahawks jersey to get a better look at it.

"Yeah? You like it?" I asked. "It's Steve Largent's number."

Xander stood up and drew me in for a hug. "It's amazing. Thank you."

He tilted my chin up toward him and brought his mouth to mine, but it wasn't a soft kiss, and my body responded instantly. I wrapped my hands around the back of his neck and stood on my tiptoes as he wrapped his arms around my waist and pulled me into him. Then he gently backed away, allowing us to catch our breath.

"Wow, yeah, I actually do have a gift for you." He laughed as he kissed the tip of my nose.

"I think the kiss counted," I said.

Xander stepped away and picked up a small box. He handed it to me.

"You didn't have—"

"—Shhh," he interrupted. "Just open it."

I carefully unwrapped the paper and stared at a small, white box. I lifted the top off and gasped. It was a thin, beautiful gold necklace with a delicate butterfly pendant.

"This is expensive!" I exclaimed. "You shouldn't have . . . I can't accept this. You've already done so much for me."

"Stop. Please, I want you to have it. While I was picking up groceries last week I walked past a jewelry store. This necklace was on display at the front window, and all I could think of was you. How amazingly beautiful, fragile, and strong you are all at the same time."

I stood still, staring at the delicate piece of jewelry. I glanced up at him. "It's beautiful. Thank you."

"Turn around so I can put it on you."

I handed him the necklace and turned my back to him. He slipped the chain around my neck and gently moved my hair out of the way.

His breath grazed my neck as he fastened the clasp. Goosebumps covered my skin as he ran his finger lightly down the back of my neck.

"You're so beautiful," he whispered in my ear. His soft kiss brushed my neck, and I stepped backward and pushed my body into him. His hand slipped under my pajama top and rested against my stomach. I sighed as I felt his arousal and nestled against him. It had been so long, and I was on the brink of losing myself to him.

Xander slid the buttons of my top open with his free hand and gently pushed it off my shoulders. My nipples hardened against the air.

"I just want to look at you," he whispered. He moved his hand down and slipped it under the waist of my pajama bottoms, stopping at the top of my panties.

"So beautiful," he said and kissed my neck. I rubbed my ass against him, and he grabbed my hip with his free hand.

"No, be still. I want to take this moment and see you for the first time. I'll never see you like this again, so give me this."

I nodded, relaxing my back into his chest and grabbing his leg to keep my balance.

His hand moved to my ass cheek, and he ran his palm across my skin. Then he hooked his thumb into the waistband and slid my pajama bottoms down, leaving me in just my pink thong.

"Turn around," he said.

I stepped out of the pants and kicked them to the side, along with the Christmas paper remnants. I turned toward him and glanced up. His eyes were filled with need.

He reached out and touched me between my breasts, his finger tracing down my stomach to my thong.

"Take it off," he said, his voice rough.

I slipped my fingers underneath the fabric and slowly slid them down my legs to my ankles. Stepping out of them, I moved toward him.

"No, don't come any closer. I just want to look at you," he said again and motioned for me to turn around.

I stopped and did as he said. His eyes took in every part of me as I turned and then stood still in front of him.

"Sit down," he said and motioned to the chair next to the Christmas tree.

I sat down and leaned back.

"All of you. I want to see all of you. Open your legs."

I gasped, not only at his request but at how turned on I was by him taking complete control. I opened my legs and watched as his eyes traveled from my face, to my breasts, to my core.

"My God," he whispered. He removed his shirt, his eyes only leaving me for a split second. He fumbled with the button on his jeans, flicking it open and unzipping his fly. Then he stopped, took a few steps forward, and kneeled down in front of me.

He grabbed my hips and brought me to the edge of the chair. His breath caressed my skin as he held me a mere inch from his mouth. I grabbed the armrests and dug my nails into them, waiting for his mouth to make contact with my skin, but he glanced up at me with heavy-lidded eyes and smiled.

My breath came in short gasps. If he didn't make a move soon, I wasn't going to be able to take it anymore.

His hands moved from my hips to the inside of my thighs and his fingers dug into my flesh as he pushed my legs farther apart, giving him complete access. He flicked his tongue across my clit.

"Oh my God," I sighed.

His tongue danced across my clit again, and I whimpered. He slid his hands underneath my ass and lifted me off the chair, bringing his mouth down to me. His tongue massaged me as his thumb entered me slightly. My back arched off the chair as he sucked and licked me.

He wrapped my legs around his neck, and I moved with him as my hands ran through his hair. His pace quickened and I knew I couldn't hold on much longer, but it felt so good that I didn't want him to stop.

"Xander," I gasped. "Holy shit. I can't make it much longer."

He quickened his pace and slid his finger into me, pumping it in and out of my wet center.

My body bucked against him as I released. He pulled away and smiled.

He stood up and slipped off his jeans. My eyes widened as he stood in front of me. Muscles rippled through his entire body. He took himself in his hand and stroked himself as he watched me.

"Do you want me, Lacey?"

I couldn't answer, so I just nodded as I felt my body react to him taking care of himself in front of me.

He sighed and closed his eyes as he continued. I was shocked at my reaction; I wanted him more than ever.

"I want you inside me," I said, my voice a gruff whisper.

He stopped, and a playful smile tugged at the corner of his mouth. He bent down and reached into the pocket of his jeans, which were lying crumpled at his feet. He pulled out a condom.

"I hate these things, so you need to get on the Pill," he said as he opened the packet and rolled on the condom.

"Okay," I whispered as I watched.

He stood in front of my chair and stared at me. Then he reached his hand out to me, pulling me out of the seat. He wrapped his arm around me and brought me to him. His fingers wound through the hair at the nape of my neck and he tilted my head back. His kiss was light as he tightened his hold on my hair. He trailed kisses down my neck and cupped my breast with his other hand. I groaned as his fingers teased my nipple. His hardness throbbed against me. He was as ready as I was.

He released my hair and led me to the couch. I laid down as he situated himself between my legs. I moaned as he entered me.

"Ahhh, my God, Lacey," he said as he gently moved in and out of me. I shifted and began lifting my hips with him.

"Don't stop. You feel so good."

He slid his hand under my ass and lifted me into him. He quickened his pace, and I dug my fingers into his back.

"That's it, babe," he said.

I moved my hands down his muscular back and continued to bring my hips up to meet him.

"Mmm, so good," I whispered.

My heart pounded as our bodies rocked against each other. He slowed and pulled out of me.

"What's wrong?" I asked and frowned, disappointed he'd left me.

"Nothing," he said as he sat up at the end of the couch. "Come over here."

I stood up as he grabbed me and guided me toward him. Straddling him, I gasped as he slid inside me again.

"Oh yeah, that's what I want. I want to see your face," he said.

He lifted my hips and brought me down on him again and again. I whimpered as he gently cupped my breast and took me into his mouth. My fingers threaded through his hair and held his head in place as his tongue massaged my nipple.

He pulled away and leaned back into the couch.

"You ready, babe?"

"Yes," I panted.

Xander continued to bring me down on him as he slipped his hand between us and squeezed my clit.

"Ahhhh!"

"Feel good?" he asked as he continued.

"I can't, I can't wait anymore," I gasped.

"That's my girl," he said as he pumped me and massaged my clit.

I threw my head back as I lost control.

"You're so beautiful when you come. So beautiful."

My movement slowed as I gasped for air, but Xander wasn't finished yet. He continued to slide in and out of me with a slow and steady pace.

I'd come so hard I was almost dizzy, but him still being inside of me made me want more.

"How?" I asked as I tried to catch my breath.

"How what?" he asked and grinned.

"How can you make me come twice, harder than I ever have in my life, and I still want more?"

Xander laughed and lifted me off him. I jutted my lower lip into a pout as our bodies parted.

"Don't worry, babe. Just turn around and straddle me again so your back is against my chest."

I turned around and lowered myself down slowly as he entered me again. He situated me a bit, lifted his hips off the couch slightly, and then took my breasts in his hands as he kissed my neck and moved in and out of me.

"See? Feels good, doesn't it? You're so damn wet, too," he said as he slid one hand down my stomach and found my clit again.

I moaned as he massaged my sensitive skin and moved in and out of me. It wasn't long before I released again.

"That's it," he said as he grabbed my hips and held me in place. "Now, lean forward and rest your hands on the coffee table."

I did as he told me. His hand ran up my back as he quickened his pace.

"You feel so incredible," he panted.

The excitement mounted in my body again as he began pounding me.

"Oh, you like this, baby. Come with me. Come on me again, Lacey."

His fingers dug into my hips as he thrust into me again.

"There it is," he said as we both came together.

Exhausted, I got up and laid on the couch beside him. I peeked at him as he smiled at me.

"Well, that was a pleasant surprise," he said.

"What?" I said, still struggling to catch my breath.

"I think we're gonna have a lot of fun," he said as his eyes sparkled.

"I don't think it would break my heart at all," I said, laughing.

I reached for my shirt and thong, slipped them both on, and began cleaning the living room of the wrapping paper.

"Merry Christmas," I said.

"You too," Xander replied.

"I was wondering if I could call Emma? I'll pay you for the call."

"Yeah, of course. You can call her from my bedroom."

"Oh, I didn't realize you had another phone. Thanks. I'm gonna call her and then shower if it's okay."

"Of course, you don't have to ask."

I nodded and left him sitting on the couch.

1 5

His bedroom door opened quietly as I stepped into his room. This was the one place I hadn't been in the house yet. His king-size bed was unmade and his closet door was open. I peeked into it and noted his multiple pairs of shoes and built-in shelving. A faint hint of Eternity cologne lingered in the air, and I took a deep breath and smiled.

His dark wood furniture matched the brown curtains that were pulled to the side of the window. My gaze traveled around the room for the phone and spotted it on the nightstand. His watch and some loose change sat next to it. I picked up the phone, sat on his bed, and dialed Emma's number.

"Merry Christmas, Emma!" I said when she answered.

"You too! I wish you were here. It's not the same without you."

"I know. I miss you all so much."

"Where are you today?"

"I'm at Xander's house," I said and grinned.

"Oh? Spill," Emma said.

I filled her in on the past few weeks, including Xander saving me from Mama trying to kidnap me, getting my stuff back from her, and our morning together.

"So, you're dating?"

"Yeah," I said and bit my lip.

"Okay, you know I love you, but I gotta ask. Do you really like him, or do you *think* you like him?"

"That doesn't make any sense. What are you saying?"

"I've known you for a long time, and when you talked about Walker, your voice literally changed. It was obvious to everyone you loved him. I don't hear that when you speak about Xander. And with your mom showing up, I'm curious if you're with him because you're scared, not because you're in love with him. At least not as much as you were with Walker."

I rubbed my face and tried to control my reaction. How could she even suggest something like that? I didn't reply.

"Well, shoot. I can tell I made you mad because you got quiet, so I'm gonna say something else. His timing sucks. I'm sorry, but what kind of guy gets you into bed when you're so vulnerable?"

"That is *not* what happened." The tone of my voice was sharp, and if Emma wasn't sure she'd pissed me off, she was clear now.

"I'm sorry. I mean, I'm not there and I haven't met him, but it feels off."

"You're right. You don't know him. He's smart, gorgeous, and he gave me a safe place to stay. It's obvious he cares about me."

"Okay. I just want you to think about it, that's all."

I sighed and closed my eyes. This wasn't the conversation I'd expected.

"I want you to be happy, and if it's with Xander that's fantastic, but I'm not gonna lie and say I'm not concerned. I'm not sure I can ever forgive Walker for hurting you the way he did, but he never took advantage of you when you were going through hell and back."

"I don't care about Walker. He's not a part of my life anymore. If you were here, you'd understand."

"You're probably right, but I'm not there, and all I can go on is my gut."

"Yeah, okay. I have to go," I said.

"I don't want to hang up with you mad at me. I . . . I'm worried about you is all."

"I know your heart is in the right place, and I love you, but I need to go."

"Okay, love you too. Call me soon."

I rolled my eyes and replaced the phone in the cradle. I definitely wasn't going to call her back for a while. The last thing I wanted to hear was her chatter on about someone she hadn't even met. No matter what she thought, I wasn't so fragile I couldn't take care of myself. And she was wrong. I cared about him. A lot.

I crawled off Xander's bed, walked across the hall, and took a shower.

Xander and I snuggled together in front of the TV, watched movies, and kissed for the rest of the day. It looked like I wasn't going to be sleeping in the guest room anymore.

THE REST of the break flew by as Xander I spent every minute together. I'd forgotten how intense a new relationship could be, and the constant craving you could have for someone.

Xander and I opened a bottle of champagne and brought in the new year together. It was the first time I'd ever really gotten drunk, and I felt like shit the next day. I winced as I thought about George telling me to drink water. Between the alcohol and the sex that night, I'd forgotten all about it. Thank God I had one more day before we returned to school.

I climbed out of bed and gasped when I glanced at the clock. It was noon; I'd slept most of the day away. Xander's side of the bed was empty, so I slipped my feet into my house shoes and made my way to the bathroom.

Thirty minutes later, I was clean and my head throbbed a little less. I couldn't believe the break was almost over. Excited to get back, I realized I'd missed school. I hadn't talked with George, Adalyn, or

Megan the entire break and I couldn't wait to see how they were doing and tell them about Xander and me.

I bit my lip as I remembered Mama was also in Eugene. It had been easy to block her out while I was at Xander's, but I had to return to the dorm tomorrow. I wished my dorm-room door had a peephole in it so I would know who was knocking. Hopefully with everyone back from Christmas break she wouldn't try again, but Mama defied logic.

I opened the guest-room door and grabbed my backpack from the closet. The majority of my belongings were in the corner of the entry-way, but I still had a few things here as well. I walked over to the window and stared at all the naked trees. Even with the leaves gone, you couldn't see another house. I wasn't sure where the closest neighbor was, but the peace and quiet had been incredible.

"Are you packing?"

I turned to see Xander standing in the doorway of the bedroom.

"Yeah, I'm just getting my stuff ready for tomorrow."

Xander entered the bedroom and sat on the end of the bed, frowning.

"How are you doing with everything?"

I shrugged, not really wanting to talk about it.

"Are you worried about your mom?" he asked as he ran his hand through his hair.

"Of course I am, but I'm hoping with everyone back on campus she'll stay away."

Xander didn't respond.

"Are you?" I asked. "I mean, are you worried about me going back? I miss school and my friends, and I'm ready for classes to start, but . . ." My voice trailed off, and I bit my lip.

"I don't want you to move back to the dorm," he said softly.

My eyes widened with surprise as I searched his face.

"Staying with you was only a temporary situation. I can't just move in with you."

"Why not?"

I paused and waited for him to say something more. Or maybe I was trying to process what he'd asked me. "Are you asking me to move in?"

"Yes, it's exactly what I'm saying," he said and stood up. He walked over to me and wrapped his arms around my waist.

"Don't go," he whispered. "Move in with me and let's put your stuff away."

"Are you sure? It's a huge commitment."

"It's what I want, but how do you feel about it?" he asked as he held my gaze.

Was it too soon? Was I rushing into things? Or was this what I'd hoped for? My body tingled at the thought of waking up next to him every morning. We'd spent so much time together already, and it felt right. He felt right.

"Yes," I whispered. "Yes, I'll move in with you."

Xander smiled and brushed his lips across mine. "Good, then you're officially all mine."

"I think I like the sound of it," I replied, my lips only an inch away from his mouth.

Xander slipped his hand underneath my hair and pulled my head back. His kiss grew more intense as his thumb stroked the front of my neck.

He turned me away from him, and as I faced the window, he pulled my shirt over my head and removed my bra. I was once again grateful there weren't any neighbors nearby as he cupped my breasts. My body responded to him as he kissed my neck and slid his hand down the front of my jeans.

"These have to come off," he said, his voice heavy with need.

He slipped my jeans and panties down to my ankles, and I stepped out of them. Then he unbuttoned his pants and let them drop to the floor. I reached behind me and took him in my hand. He was ready, and with Xander, it never took me long to be ready either.

"Bend over."

Doing as he asked, I was amazed at my body's response as he took control. I sucked in a sharp breath as his fingers lightly brushed up and down my back. I grabbed the windowsill as he held my hips and slid into me.

"My God, Lacey," he said as he gently grabbed my hair and pulled my head back. His rhythm was slow and steady as he massaged my clit. "That's my baby. You're so wet."

He picked up the pace as I moved against him, taking him in deeper. He pumped in and out, the familiar feeling building up inside me.

"God, what are you doing to me?" I gasped as my fingers dug into the windowsill.

"Say you're mine. Tell me you belong to me," he demanded.

"I'm yours and only yours," I replied.

"Don't ever forget it," he said as he grabbed my breasts and squeezed. I couldn't hold back any longer as we released together.

My body relaxed and I stood still for a moment, catching my breath. He trailed soft kisses across my back as he pulled out of me and stepped backward.

He turned me toward him and kissed my forehead.

"How does it feel to officially belong to me?" he asked as a mischievous grin spread across his face.

"Amazing," I said as I stood on my tiptoes and kissed him.

"I'll clean out a few drawers and make some room in the closet for your clothes. Why don't we get you settled in?" he said as he pulled up his jeans and buttoned them.

"Sounds perfect," I said, locating my clothes and got dressed.

# 16

Mondays typically sucked, but today I was out of bed early and waiting for Xander downstairs. I couldn't wait to see my friends and arrive on campus with him. Mama didn't even worry me today.

Xander walked me to class and kissed me goodbye as he headed in the opposite direction. He'd made me promise I wouldn't go anywhere alone, and he insisted on walking me to every class even if it meant he would be late to his.

I spotted George as soon as I walked into the room and hugged him as hard as I could.

"Oh my God, I missed you!" I said.

"I missed you too! How was your vacation? You're all smiles today, I see," George said as his eyebrow rose. "You have something juicy to tell me. I can see it written all over your face."

"Yes, but I want to tell Adalyn and Megan at the same time," I said, sitting next to him. We'd all signed up for the same health class this semester; it was a required course anyway, so we figured we might as well all take it together. "Tell me how Mexico was while we wait."

"It was so nice, but I couldn't call anyone, and it sucked. I shouldn't complain, but I wanted to tell you about every detail."

"Hey," Megan said as she slid into her seat next to us.

"Hey!" I said and reached over to hug her.

"I heard some shit about you," Adalyn said as she walked into the classroom and sat down next to us.

"Me?" I asked as I hugged her.

"Well, go on," George motioned for Adalyn to hurry up and share.

"Xander Koffman, huh?" Adalyn asked as she grinned at me.

"What?" Megan said, glancing from me to Adalyn and then back to George.

"Lacey and Xander are living together."

"No fucking way," George said.

Megan's mouth hung open, and all eyes were on me. My cheeks burned bright red.

"How the hell did that happen? I mean, I'm only gone for three weeks and I miss all the good stuff," Megan said.

"Wait, how did you even know, Adalyn?" I asked.

"A group of girls were whining he wasn't available anymore," she said, laughing.

"Well, he is one of the most popular guys on campus," George chimed in.

"So? Dish," Megan said as she leaned toward me.

"Well," I stammered as they all stared and waited for details.

"He asked me to move in with him yesterday, and I said yes," I said and shrugged as though it weren't a big deal.

"Holy mother of God," Adalyn said. "Do you have any idea you just snagged the most unavailable guy in this university? I mean, he dated all the time and definitely had a reputation for one-night stands, but I've never heard of him committing to anyone before."

"You must be damn good in bed," Megan said and elbowed me.

"Damn straight," I said and laughed with them.

"I'm happy for you," George said. We locked eyes for a moment, and he winked at me. I knew George was happy for me, especially with all the Mama drama, and his support meant the world to me. Too bad Emma didn't feel the same way. Loneliness washed over me at the thought of her, but I pushed it out of my mind. She should have supported me.

"Welcome back, everyone," the professor said.

I turned toward the front of the classroom and tried to focus, but I couldn't wait to see Xander again after class.

George, Megan, Adalyn, and I filed out of the building an hour later and stood on the covered walkway. The rain had slowed to a drizzle, but it was still cold and damp. I scolded myself for choosing a skirt instead of jeans.

We chatted about the holiday and the presents we got. I pulled out the butterfly necklace from underneath my shirt to show everyone as an arm slipped around my stomach and a warm kiss landed on my cheek.

I smiled up at Xander as he joined us.

"Hey, everybody," he said.

Everyone stopped mid-speech and focused on him. I wasn't sure if Megan or George drooled more when Xander was around. It didn't even faze him anymore.

"So, I was thinking since everyone's back now, I should have a party at my house this Saturday."

"Hell yeah!" Adalyn said.

"What do you think, Lacey?" Xander asked and smiled at me. His brown eyes danced, and I found myself suddenly wanting to kiss him.

"I think it would be awesome," I said, grinning.

"Yeah, we can let everyone know you've moved in with me," he said and nuzzled my neck. "Alright, so why don't you guys come over tonight and we can plan it. Does that work for everyone? I can pick you all up around seven at Lacey's old dorm."

"Old dorm?" I asked.

"Yeah, I talked to the lady who runs the housing department and told her you wouldn't need the room anymore. She and my grandma knew each other for years, and she was a real sweetie and expedited a check for you. You got some money back," he said as he reached into his back pocket and pulled out a piece of paper.

"What? Oh my gosh, so amazing! Thank you!"

I caught a glimpse of George's face as I hugged Xander. A pang of frustration filled me, unsure what to make of his expression.

"Okay, we'll see everyone tonight then," Xander said as he tugged on my hand to leave.

I tucked the check into my purse and waved goodbye.

I followed Xander across campus and behind the maintenance building. He led me under an empty covered walkway and laughed as he pulled me to him.

"The amazing thing about us being together is I can have you anywhere and anytime I want."

"Xander!" I giggled. "Here? It's freezing cold, and anyone could walk around the corner and see us."

"That's the whole point," he said as he slid his hand up my skirt.

I gasped as he slipped his finger into my panties and massaged my clit.

"You're okay with it though, right?" he said as he cupped the back of my neck with his other hand.

I responded with a moan as he eased his finger inside me.

"That's my girl, you're already wet. You like it, don't you?"

I didn't reply, but I unbuttoned his jeans and took him in my hand.

He removed his finger and tugged the back of my hair, pulling me down. I realized what he wanted and lowered to my knees, glancing up at him as I took him in my mouth.

"Ahh," he said as his head went back. His hand tightened on my hair as I sucked him, his hips moving with my mouth.

"That's it, babe."

His pace quickened and then he abruptly stopped and pulled me into a standing position. He lifted my skirt and turned me around toward the wall. He pulled my panties aside and slid inside me, one hand massaging my clit and the other teasing my nipple. The cold air whipped around us, but I wasn't cold as he grabbed my hips and picked up the pace. I clutched at the wall as the familiar feeling swirled inside me.

"Oh God," I whimpered.

I finished before he did and enjoyed every last moment before he lost control.

His hand slid up the front of my neck as he placed a kiss on the back of my head.

"I love fucking you," he whispered as he wrapped his fingers around my throat and gently squeezed. "I love being inside you and knowing I'm the only one." His hand slipped down from my throat and into my top and bra. He squeezed my nipple and then flicked it.

"Ow!" I squealed.

He stepped back and pulled out of me while he laughed.

"That hurt," I said, crossing my hands over my chest. I didn't bother trying to hide the frustration and surprise in my voice.

"It didn't hurt me," he said as he adjusted himself and buttoned his jeans.

I stared at him as I lowered my skirt and made sure my top was in place.

"Let's go," he said and walked away, leaving me standing there alone.

Confused at his sudden change in mood, I followed him to the truck.

We rode the entire way home in silence as I puzzled over what had just happened.

## 17

Xander was fine the rest of the week, and neither of us brought up the incident of him hurting me. We had fun planning the big party, and he continued to walk me to all my classes. I hadn't seen Mama anywhere. I'd stopped freaking out every time I turned a corner now Xander was with me everywhere I went. He made sure I was never alone, and if he wasn't with me, George, Megan, and Adalyn were until he arrived.

The doorbell rang at 10 P.M. and I practically ran from his bedroom and down the stairs to answer it. George and the girls were coming to the party a little early, and I couldn't wait to see them.

"Hi!" I said as I opened the door.

George hugged me and gave me a quick peck on my cheek. I smiled, taking their coats and leading them into the kitchen to get something to drink.

"This house is beautiful, Lacey," Megan said as she looked around the kitchen and living room. I sipped on my rum and Pepsi as I showed them around.

"Here's the bathroom. There's another one upstairs, down the hall and on the left," I said.

"Other than the location of the alcohol, it's the most important thing to know at a party," Adalyn said and laughed.

"Where's Xander?" George asked.

I glanced at him as I noted the lack of excitement in his voice. I tilted my head, studying him and trying to figure out why. Maybe he was tired.

"Right here," Xander said as he walked into the kitchen.

"Hey," Megan and Adalyn said.

"Hi, ladies," he said and nodded at them. "Hey, buddy," Xander said as he patted George on the back. "Glad you guys could make it. I think Lacey misses you now that she doesn't live on campus any longer."

"Yeah, it's a little isolated out here," George commented with a hint of annoyance as he took a sip of his beer.

What was up with George? I was going to have to find a minute to pull him aside and ask.

The doorbell interrupted my thoughts as I excused myself to answer it.

Several of Xander's teammates from the Oregon Ducks filed through the front door, and within forty-five minutes the house was filled with music and laughter. Adalyn and Megan were dancing in the middle of the living room. Xander made his rounds between the living room, kitchen, and dining room and directed everyone to the alcohol.

George chatted on and on about Mexico as we drank. I danced with Xander a few times and then joined Megan and Adalyn. George didn't seem interested in dancing; he just leaned against the wall, watching everyone.

"Hey, the guys and I are gonna go play some cards," Xander said.

"Okay, take all their money," I said and laughed.

Xander pulled me in for a long kiss before he broke away. I watched as he and some of his friends walked through the swinging door of the den and disappeared.

I refilled my rum and Pepsi and made my way over to George.

"Alright. What's up? You love parties and I thought you liked Xander, but you're not excited about either tonight. Are you okay?"

He took a drink of his beer and leaned his head back against the wall.

"You know I love you, right?"

"Yes, and I love you too." I paused and waited for him to continue.

"I just thought it was strange the other day when Xander said he'd canceled your dorm room and gotten a check for you."

"What do you mean? He was just taking care of it for me. I'd been meaning to do it anyway."

"But that's the point. You should've *had* to do it. They never give checks to other people. You have to show your ID and sign for it."

"I don't understand what you mean."

"Okay," he said and took another sip. "Do you remember in August when you showed up on campus? You got your schedule and showed your driver's license, and then you got a school ID. You had to sign papers for your dorm room, too."

"Yeah, I remember."

"You have to go through even more to cancel your room. *You* have to do it—no one else can do it for you. Otherwise, people would be pulling pranks on students and it would cost them their rooms."

"What's your point?" I asked as my irritation rose.

"How did he do it without you, and why are you never alone anymore?" he asked as he frowned at me. "Like, *never* alone."

"George, you're the one person other than Xander who knows what happened with Mama. He's keeping me safe. I'm terrified of her showing up again and him not being there."

George sighed and leaned his head against the wall.

"Okay," he said.

"Okay what?"

"If that's what he's doing, then okay."

"What else would he be doing? You heard him—the lady at the housing department was friends with his grandma, and he called in a favor. I'm grateful he took care of it."

"I don't know what's bothering me. He just spends an unusual amount of time with you. I would almost think you weren't allowed to go anywhere without him."

"That's absurd. I can go anywhere I want without him, but as long as Mama's in Eugene, I prefer to be with Xander."

"I guess it makes sense when you explain it. I worry about you is all. I'm allowed to, you are my best friend."

"Everything is fine," I said and grinned.

"Wow. The sex must be really good, judging by the expression on your face."

"Mind-blowing," I said and giggled. "I've never had sex like this before."

"Well, in all fairness, you haven't been with anyone other than Walker, right?" George asked.

"Who?" I asked and laughed.

"Well, well. Someone is whipped," George said, smiling.

"Not yet, but maybe soon," I said and wiggled my eyebrows.

"In all seriousness, though, I'm always here for you."

My smile faded as I held his gaze. My stomach sank as I realized he was genuinely concerned.

"I know. Hey, I'm gonna go find Xander. I'll catch up with you in a few minutes, okay?"

George nodded as I smiled and made my way through the crowded living room and into the kitchen. I filled my glass with water and drained it. I realized George was being a good friend and watching out for me, but something in the back of my mind tugged at me. I refilled my cup with more rum than Pepsi and took a big swig. My head swam as the alcohol took effect.

I made it through the crowd of people and pushed open the swinging door where Xander and his friends were playing poker. Then, my feet stopped in my tracks as I tried to process what was in front of me.

"Xander?" I asked.

Xander snorted the white line off the table and leaned back in his chair. He wiped his nose and smiled.

"What the hell?" I asked, stepping backward.

"It's no big deal, Lacey. Don't be a nag," he said as he stood up and let the next guy snort a line.

My mouth dropped as I watched another guy do a line after him. I was drunk, but I knew what was happening. There was no way I could deny it. I shook my head as I stepped back through the swinging door, ran upstairs, and locked myself in the guest bedroom.

I put my cup down, crawled into bed, and tried to piece together what I'd seen, but my mind was too fuzzy and I couldn't process anything.

1 8

A thin ray of sunlight piercing through the heavy curtains woke me. I groaned as I attempted to rub the grit from my eyes, and realized I must have passed out. I sat up and searched the room. Where was Xander? The moment I thought of him, everything came rushing back. I couldn't stay. I couldn't stay with him if he was doing drugs.

The clock blared: 7:23 A.M. I stood up and crossed the room, unlocked the door, and poked my head into the hallway. Beer cans and red Solo cups lined the stairs. I peered to the right. Xander's door was cracked open. I inched my way down the hall so I wouldn't wake him.

"I'm not in there."

I jumped at the sound of Xander's voice and spun around to see him standing at the top of the stairs.

"We need to talk," he said.

I stood where I was and waited for him to say something.

"I'm sorry about last night. The party got out of hand, and I feel like shit about you walking in on that."

"On that?' You guys were doing lines of coke, for shit's sake." I crossed my arms and glared at him.

His jaw clenched as he held eye contact. Then he dropped his shoulders and stared down at the floor for a moment. "I'm so sorry."

"Drinking and having a party is one thing, but I'm not okay with drugs. I don't want to be with someone who uses coke, or anything else for that matter."

"I know, and I agree. It was a one-time thing, I promise. Please— don't leave me."

Xander's words stung as I stared at him. Worry danced across his handsome features as he waited for me to say something. My heart sank as I stood there trying to decide what to do.

"One time? As in it will never, ever happen again? Because if it does, I'm done. I'm outta here before you can even blink. It is *not* okay with me."

"Okay, okay," he said and walked toward me. He pulled me into him and wrapped his arms around me. "Don't leave me. I couldn't take it. I love you," he whispered.

I pulled away and searched his face for proof I'd heard him right. "You do?"

"Yeah, I do. I knew it before I asked you to move in."

"You did?" I couldn't hide the surprise in my voice. I bit my lip as I tried to think clearly.

My head throbbed from the drinking and everything that had just happened with Xander. Just minutes before, I'd been ready to leave. But it wasn't what I wanted. I didn't want any drugs around, but I wanted to stay.

"I love you too," I whispered.

"So, you'll give me another chance? You won't leave?" he asked with anticipation written across his face.

"I won't," I replied and linked my arms around his neck.

I put my head against his chest and listened to his heartbeat as he held me and swallowed my tears as I took a deep breath. It was going to be okay. I pulled away and smiled.

"This place smells like a brewery, and so do I," I said, scrunching up my nose.

"That's the nature of a party. Wait till you see downstairs. We have a big-ass mess to clean up."

"Yeah?" I asked as I felt the tension begin to dissolve from my neck and shoulders.

"Yeah," he said and squeezed my hand. I followed him as we descended the stairs.

"Holy shit!" I said, scanning the living room, dining room, and kitchen. Beer cans and red Solo cups littered the floor and tables, and there were people passed out everywhere. I jumped as someone started snoring.

I turned and giggled into Xander's shoulder, glancing up at him as I felt a chuckle rumble through his chest.

"Even when you're hungover, you're beautiful," he said as his finger trailed down my cheek and neck. He leaned down and kissed my forehead.

"Well, let's start in the kitchen and make some coffee," I suggested.

I grabbed a kitchen trash bag and began clearing the table and counters. Leaning over the sink, I opened the window a few inches. The cold, fresh air was a welcome renewal of my senses. I stood on my tiptoes, leaned toward the opening, and took a deep breath.

"Girl, are you huffing fresh air?"

I started at the voice behind me and dropped the bag of cans. I grabbed my head as it clattered to the floor.

"Morning, George. Did you pass out on a couch somewhere?"

"Nope, he stayed with me," a tall, athletic guy said as he entered the kitchen.

I peered at him for a moment, and it dawned on me he'd been in the den playing cards with Xander. I had no idea if he'd done any coke, but I wasn't sure I liked him.

I glanced at George as a smile spread across his face, and then I really understood. George had hooked up with him.

"Why don't you give me a minute, Andy?" George said. He nodded and pecked George on the lips before he left the kitchen.

My eyes widened as I pieced it all together.

"Oh my God!" I squealed as I ran across the kitchen and hugged him. "Who is he? Details, details," I said and pulled out a kitchen chair for him. We sat down, and I waited for him to wipe the silly grin off his face and fill me in.

"Yeah, I had no clue he was gay, but am I glad he is," he said, laughing.

I motioned for him to continue.

"I couldn't find you anywhere," he said. "I was about to look upstairs when Andy stepped in front of me and kissed me. He was obviously drunk, so I led him to the back of the living room so we could talk. And, well, we did, until five in the morning, and then Xander let us stay. The couch in the den folds out so we, well, you know," he said as a shy smile spread across his face.

"Oh my God! Is he nice? Do you think it will last, or was it a one-night thing?"

"I don't really think it'll go anywhere, but it's hard to tell. I guess if he calls me in a few days it wasn't a one-night thing."

"I'm so excited for you," I said, clapping my hands together.

"Don't get too excited until I figure out what this is, if it's anything at all."

"Uh-huh," I said, laughing.

"Hey, I couldn't find you anywhere last night after you went and checked on Xander. What happened to you?"

I frowned at the memory of walking in on Xander snorting coke.

"I—I got too drunk, then went upstairs and passed out in the guest room. I woke up about an hour ago."

"Wow, you *never* drink that much."

"Well, I guess I do now. Do you wanna help me clean up?"

"No, but I will," George said as we stood up and began gathering bottles together.

Four hours later, the house was cleaned up and the stragglers had left. I closed the door behind George and Andy and sank to the floor. The party had drained me of every drop of energy.

"You okay?" Xander said as he walked toward me.

"I'm exhausted," I said and stood up.
"Yeah?" he asked as he picked me up. "This better?"
"Much," I said, leaning my head on his shoulder.
"Let's go watch TV in bed for the rest of the day."
"Mmm, it's perfect," I said as he carried me upstairs.

19

The next week it started snowing, but they didn't cancel classes. I stood in the front yard and turned my face toward the gray sky. The plump snowflakes were falling fast, dusting my coat and hair.

"It's beautiful, isn't it?" Xander asked as he closed the front door and walked toward me.

"Yeah, I love snow," I said and grinned like a little kid.

"Your nose is already pink." He laughed and kissed my forehead. "Let's go before we're late. The traffic won't be pretty," he said and opened the truck door for me.

An hour later, we pulled into the campus parking lot. Xander walked me to my health class and I hurried in, ready for the warmth. Class had already started, so I sat in the seat closest to the door. I waved at George, Adalyn, and Megan, who were on the other side of the room. I was glad they'd made it okay.

My seat had a good view outside, and my eyes continually drifted from the professor to the snow. Even though Xander had a truck, I was getting nervous about the drive back home.

Class ended, and we all walked outside and checked the snow level on the sidewalks and grass.

"Hey, I heard another professor say they're canceling classes for the rest of the day," Megan squealed.

"Party in the dorm!" Adalyn said and laughed. "George, you can stay in our room so you don't have to trek back across campus."

"Won't Ms. Walters know?" I asked.

"You'd be surprised how much we get away with," Adalyn said, grinning.

"Sounds good to me," George said. "But we should go to my place first so I can get a change of clothes and the vodka I have stashed."

"What about you, Lacey?" Megan asked.

"I can't. I need to head home with Xander."

"Speaking of Xander," George said and pointed.

We all turned to see what George was talking about. Xander stood laughing in the middle of a group of girls. It wasn't so much the group of girls that bothered me as it was one girl in particular. She was hanging on his arm, giggling at every word he said.

"What the hell?" I bit my lip and tried to calm the butterflies that were suddenly doing backflips in my stomach. Although I tried not to jump to conclusions, I was *not* doing a very good job.

"Who is she?" I asked, unable to hide the irritation in my voice.

"She's the captain of the cheerleading squad, and she is a class-A bitch," Megan replied. "If she's interested in a guy, she doesn't care if he's committed or not—she goes after him with everything in her power."

"Pretty much sums it up," George agreed and sighed.

"Well, Xander could tell her to get the hell off him. I mean, seriously? I live with him, and he *just* told me he loved me . . . dammit," I muttered, realizing what I'd said.

George raised his eyebrow as the girls turned toward me with their mouths hanging open.

"Oh my God! How in the hell could you not tell us something like that, Lacey?" Adalyn asked.

"It's just so new. I was planning on hanging out with you all more today, but with the snow and Princess Bitch hanging all over my boyfriend . . . well, it just didn't come up."

"If he told you he loves you, you've got nothing to worry about," Adalyn said. "I'm sure Xander will take care of Brittney."

"Are you kidding me? Another one?" I clenched my hand into a fist, unable to hide my anger and frustration. I'd already had one Brittany ruin my life, and come hell or high water, it wasn't going to happen again.

"What do you mean, another one?" Megan asked.

"Nothing, it's a long story. I'll tell it to you sometime, but Xander's finally unglued himself from her, so I need to go. You guys be safe walking back to the dorms. Have a drink for me!"

They said goodbye and started making their way in the direction of George's dorm. I watched them leave as George turned back toward me, his face filled with concern. He waved and then joined the girls again.

"Hey, beautiful," Xander said as he came over and kissed me.

I glared at him, turned on my heel, and headed toward the truck without him.

"Hey, wait up. What's that for?" he asked as he caught up with me.

"You tell me," I muttered. I refused to look at him but continued my trek through the snow.

"What?"

"How's your friend Brittney?"

"Uh, she's good actually, but why do you care?"

I stopped and turned toward him. "Are you shitting me? If I had some guy hanging on me like that you'd be all over him, but it's okay for the cheerleading captain to rub her boobs all over you and hang on your arm? I'm confused here, Xander. You just told me you loved me, so what the hell do you want?"

A few students heard me and slowed down to watch the show.

My heart stopped as anger clouded his face. I'd never seen him mad, and he went from zero to pissed within seconds. Fear ripped through me as I realized I'd crossed the line.

"Let's go," he said as he grabbed my arm and led me toward the parking lot.

"Let go, you're hurting me," I whispered loudly.

He didn't let go, and he didn't say a word to me as he led me to the truck. He unlocked it, picked me up, put me in the seat, and shut the door.

My hands shook as I reached for my seat belt. It took me three tries before it clicked into place.

Xander got in and started the truck. He didn't speak to me the entire ride home. My heart pounded so hard my head hurt by the time we got to the house. He hopped out and pulled me out of the truck, up the porch steps, and through the front door. Then he let go of me, walked straight into the kitchen, and poured a rum and Pepsi.

"Xander?" I asked, unable to hide the tremble in my voice as I entered the kitchen behind him.

"I love you, Lacey. I wasn't kidding, but I won't put up with you nagging me just because some girl is being friendly."

"Friendly? You call that friendly?" My voice shifted from scared to pissed. "Okay, so just so I'm clear on our relationship, it's okay for some guy to hang on me and maybe grab my ass a little? You're okay with that?"

Xander's glass flew across the kitchen and shattered against the cabinets. Soda slowly dripped down the doors and onto the tile floor.

He crossed the kitchen and backed me into the wall, pressing himself against me.

"I'll make this clear for you. If anyone else *ever* touches you, I'll fucking kill them. You're mine, and I can't even stand the thought of another guy with his hands on you."

His words pierced my heart. I'd never seen anyone other than Mama get so angry. I squeezed my eyes closed as he pressed into me. I gasped. He was excited and ready to go. I could feel his arousal through his jeans.

"Open your eyes and look at me," he said, his voice cold. "Girls like me, so deal with it. And take a minute to remember that I opened my home to you and saved you from your crazy, fucked-up mother. Take a moment to think about that if you wanna leave. No one has ever taken care of you like I have. No one loves you like I do," he said and lifted my chin up toward him. "No one."

A tear streamed down my cheek as I looked into his eyes. The same beautiful brown eyes I'd come to love so much had suddenly turned dark and cold. My heart sank. I didn't know this Xander.

He gently wiped the tear from my face and traced his thumb down my throat.

"You're so beautiful it makes me crazy," he whispered as he slid his hand around the back of my neck and gently grabbed my hair. "What you're doing to me?"

I bit my lip as I watched his eyes soften. As quickly as he'd gotten pissed, he returned to the Xander I knew.

"I love you, I do," he said.

"Xander?" I asked, my voice barely audible. "I'm sorry. I'm sorry I doubted you." I hiccupped as another tear streamed down my cheek. "You're right, you've done more for me than anyone else. You've kept me safe from Mama, and you were there when I needed someone the most. Please, don't be upset with me."

"It's okay, babe. It's okay." He leaned down and kissed me.

My arms wrapped around his neck as I stood on my tiptoes, returning his kiss. I couldn't bear for him to be mad at me, and he was right about Mama. Even Walker had never had the guts to stand up to her.

I sighed as his mouth parted and our kiss deepened. He lifted me up, and I wrapped my legs around him as he kissed my neck.

"I forgive you, babe. Now you can make it up to me," he whispered in my ear.

"I plan on it." My heart sped up again, but this time it wasn't because I was scared.

2 0

---

Xander was once again the sweet guy I fell in love with, and we didn't have any other incidents for the rest of the week. But I knew better than to accuse him of something stupid again, too. I'm not sure what I'd been thinking in the first place. He'd been nothing but good to me, and he hadn't deserved my reaction.

Xander walked me across campus to my building as the wind whipped against us. I shivered as I wrapped my coat tighter around me. We stopped before my building, and he kissed me goodbye and left for his class.

"Yo," Megan said and waved at me.

I waved back and met her on the steps.

"Hey! What're you doing out here?"

"I'm waiting for Adalyn," she replied. "How are you and Xander?"

"Good," I smiled shyly.

"What's it like living with him?"

"Awesome. It all just fell into place—even our schedules, since he brings me to school."

"Yeah, you're never alone anymore. What's up with that?"

I bit my lip. Megan and Adalyn didn't know about Mama, and I wasn't willing to share.

"Lacey!"

I turned as I recognized Xander's voice. He was running toward me.

"Xander? What's the matter?"

He stopped when he reached me and grabbed my arm. My concern deepened as he frowned.

"She's here. We have to go. *Now.*"

My stomach dropped as his words sunk in, my eyes widening as I glanced at Megan.

"Let's go, she's right around the corner," he said, glancing back over his shoulder.

Fear spread through me as Xander took my hand and tugged me forward. She couldn't be here again. What did she want? If Xander hadn't seen her, what would have happened? We took off running without telling Megan goodbye. I knew she'd have questions, and I didn't know what I'd say to her.

"Get in," Xander said as he opened the truck door.

"What happened? Where was she? Are you sure it was her?" I asked, struggling to catch my breath and buckling my seat belt.

"She was right around the corner. Thank God I had class in that building or she would've gotten to you again."

Chills shot down my spine as I remembered the last time she'd shown up. I turned to stare out the window as we exited the university parking lot.

"I don't know what I would've done." I turned to look at him while he was driving. "What would I do without you?"

"You don't have to worry. I told you I'd take care of you, and I meant it," he said and took my hand.

I leaned my head back against the seat and closed my eyes to control the tears that were threatening to spill over.

"What the hell am I going to tell Megan?"

"We'll figure it out before classes tomorrow, okay? Don't worry about it. I'll think of something."

I stared out the window until we pulled into the driveway and made it safely inside the house.

I hung up my coat as Xander pulled me in for a hug.

"It's okay. Let's have a drink and figure things out."

I flopped onto the love seat while Xander made our drinks and started a fire. This was my favorite room in the house. No matter what was going on, I felt safe here.

"Do Megan and Adalyn know about your mom?" Xander asked as he handed me my glass.

I took a long drink, paused as the rum traveled through me, and glanced at the half-full glass. There was no reason not to finish it. Then I sighed and placed it on the table.

"Stressed?"

"This shit sucks," I said as I rubbed my face. "What am I gonna do?"

"Well, you could always just tell Megan and Adalyn the truth. Maybe not everything, but that someone from your past is looking for you."

I nodded, not really sure they'd be satisfied with that little of an explanation.

"There's another option," he said.

I stared into the fire, waiting for him to continue.

"You can withdraw from school."

My body snapped to attention, and I stared at him. Was he serious?

"You're kidding me, right? I can't just quit school. What the hell kind of idea is that?" I stood up, grabbed my glass, and walked into the kitchen. I refilled the glass with two-thirds rum and a splash of Pepsi and the joined Xander in the living room again.

"Just think about it. It's only for a little while. We have to keep you safe."

My head swam from the rum and all the emotions that coursed through me. I hated Mama. Why? Why wouldn't she leave me alone?

"I don't wanna think about it right now, but I'll talk to Megan tomorrow," I said and finished my drink.

"Okay," Xander said as he rested his hand on my leg.

I stretched my legs across him and closed my eyes.

I woke in our bed, alone. Xander must have carried me up here. The clock read 1:13 A.M., and he wasn't in bed with me. Concerned, I sat up and peered around the room, but I didn't see him anywhere.

I was emotionally and physically exhausted and laid back down. My eyes fluttered closed, and I drifted back to sleep.

"Morning," Xander said as he handed me a cup of coffee.

"Thank you," I said. "It's amazing what a shower can do for you after drinking too much."

"Yeah, you were out pretty quick. I know this is hard on you."

I pulled the kitchen chair out and sat down. Classes didn't start until ten, so I had a few minutes to enjoy my coffee with Xander.

"I missed you last night. I woke up once and you weren't there."

"Yeah, I couldn't sleep, and I didn't want to keep you up. So I decided to watch a movie and figure out what to do."

"I'm not your responsibility, you know. And I can handle Megan. I'm also not dropping out of school. I don't care if Mama sits in my classes with me. She doesn't get to win this one."

"I love that about you—your determination."

"Yeah?" I asked and smiled at him. "Mama always said I was possessed and stubborn. I like determined better."

"Fuck your mom. Sorry, but she just wants to control you."

"I know," I whispered.

Xander crossed the kitchen and took my coffee from me.

"We have a few minutes before we have to leave," he said and grinned.

I reached for his jeans button and flicked it open.

"Is this what you want?" I smiled as I looked up at him.

"Always."

2 1

I stayed close to Xander the next day as we kept an eye out for Mama or Patsy. I'd crossed over to a new level of paranoia and thought every short, dark-haired woman might be Mama.

I heaved a sigh of relief when classes were over and I hadn't seen her anywhere. Thank God the weekend was here, too. I'd hoped to hang out with George, but he had other plans. So I decided to study and rest instead.

Nineteen and no social life. A glimmer of resentment about what my life had become rose inside me. I had no freedom thanks to Mama and Patsy. At least I had Xander, George, and the girls on occasion.

My thoughts drifted toward Emma. My heart ached thinking about her, but our last conversation had left me feeling frustrated, and I wasn't ready to call her yet. If she couldn't support my new relationship, I didn't want to talk to her.

I rubbed my neck and settled into our bed, reaching for my books and notes.

"Hey, how's the studying going?" Xander asked as he leaned in to kiss me.

"It's okay."

Xander grabbed his keys and wallet from the nightstand.

"You going somewhere?" I asked.

"Yeah, I'm getting together with the guys tonight. I need a night out."

"Oh," I said. I couldn't hide the disappointment in my voice as a dark blanket of loneliness settled over me.

"I've gotta have a break sometimes."

"Okay. I've brought a lot of baggage with me. I'm sorry. Go have fun with your friends," I said and attempted a sincere smile.

"Keep the doors locked and stay here where you're safe."

"I will, promise. I'll find a good chick flick on TV after I'm done studying. I know how much you love romantic movies," I said and laughed.

"Have at it. There's plenty of food and alcohol," he said as he kissed me.

"What time will you be back?" I asked.

Xander paused and stared at me. Surprise registered on his face at the question.

"Did I say something wrong?"

"I'll be home whenever I feel like it," he said and walked out, leaving me sitting in the bedroom alone.

I didn't understand. Why was it a bad question? Wasn't it something you communicated to each other when you were in a relationship? Otherwise, how the hell would I know if he was dead in a ditch or just out having fun with his friends?

I slammed my book shut, ran to the window, and watched his truck back down the driveway. My stomach sank as he disappeared from sight.

I PACED across the living room, pulled back the curtain, and stared out the window for the hundredth time. The clock read 3:58 A.M., and I hadn't heard a word from Xander. Fear traveled down my spine and I swallowed, willing my food to stay down. Even though he'd been frustrated when he left, I never imagined he would stay out so late and not even call me.

I curled up on the couch and closed my eyes, but all I saw were images of him on the side of the road covered in blood, his truck smashed to pieces. Then I racked my brain for anyone I knew who might know where he was, but I couldn't think of anyone. George didn't have a phone in his dorm room, and neither did the girls. I had no car and no way of getting anywhere.

My head pounded as I tried to think of some way to find out if he was okay. I didn't understand. The cops would call if there had been an accident, right? So, if Xander was okay, where the hell was he?

My mind turned over and over as I explored different scenarios, but all I knew was he wasn't home.

Hours passed, and I bolted upright as I heard the door open. I jumped off the couch and ran toward him.

## 22

"Are you okay?" I said breathlessly. "My God, I've been worried sick." Tears filled my eyes.

"I told you I was going out. What the hell is your problem?" He pushed past me into the house.

My jaw dropped as I watched him walk down the hall and into the kitchen. I followed him.

"You left at seven o'clock last night, and it's noon the next day. That's not *going out.* I've been waiting, and was really worried something had happened to you. You don't know how to use a telephone and call me?"

Xander filled his coffee cup and turned toward me.

"Holy shit, you're high again!" I said as I saw the look on his face.

"It's none of your fucking business, Lacey," he said as he set his cup down. "I'm gonna shower and go to bed. Don't wake me."

My head swam as he climbed the stairs without even a backward glance. I told him before if he ever got high again, it was over. My feet flew up the stairs after him.

"Xander, I told you before, I'm not doing this," I yelled and ran into the guest room.

I opened the closet, found my suitcase, threw it on the bed, and unzipped it. The sound of the zipper echoing through the quiet room. There wasn't much room, so I would only be able to take a few things with me. But I suddenly had an overwhelming urge to get out of there, fast. I hurried down the hallway and into his bedroom to get some of my clothes.

Xander stood in front of the dresser with his arms folded in front of him, his face void of any emotion.

"Move. I was very clear about the drugs. We're over. I want my clothes."

He sneered at my words.

"You think you're so much better than everyone, don't you?"

"What? Where's this coming from?" I asked, dumbfounded at his question.

"You think everyone is here just to take care of you. You don't care about anyone else, or how much it affects us to have to put up with your shit day in and day out."

My eyes widened, his words penetrating me like needles.

"You're high. You don't mean that."

"Oh yes I do. I don't ask for any rent, I pay for your food, I drive you everywhere, and I give you a safe place to stay. *I* was the one who saved you from your mother when she tried to kidnap you, and you're gonna act like a spoiled little bitch when I go out for a night and have some fun?"

I stepped backward and shook my head.

"That's not true. I—"

"—Shut up, Lacey. I give you everything. If you wanna leave, go ahead. Have a nice walk to the university, and good luck running from your mother. You won't make it twenty-four hours without me."

He smirked as he pulled off his shirt and tossed it on the floor.

"I'm gonna shower, and then you're coming to bed with me. You look like shit—you need some sleep."

He shut the bathroom door behind him, and I ran into the guest room. My brain scrambled and I gasped for air, attempting to process what he'd said. I had no car, no place to live, and no real money to speak of.

My shoulders sagged as I walked over to the bed and sat down. I had no one except Xander. Tears slipped down my cheeks as I realized he was right. He'd spent almost every minute with me, kept me safe, and paid my bills. No one else would've done that for me. And maybe he wasn't high; maybe he was just tired. Was I even sure what someone looked like when they were high?

Wiping my tears away, I realized I'd only panicked because I loved him. I'd overreacted out of fear, and I'd pissed him off. I didn't want to lose him. Maybe the next time he went out by himself we could figure something out so he didn't feel like I was smothering him.

My pulse quickened, and I picked up my suitcase and put it back in the closet. None of this felt right. I wanted to work things out with him, and hopefully he would want the same.

I went back down the hall and returned to our bedroom. Xander had just stepped out of the shower, and beads of water trickled down his muscular body. My breath caught at seeing him naked.

"Sorry. I'm sorry I said that shit to you. It was a long night, and I'm exhausted," Xander said.

"Yeah?" I asked, afraid to get my hopes up.

"Yeah, I'll call you next time. I'm not used to someone worrying about me. I've done what I wanted for years. Grandma always went to bed at eight and never even knew I left," he said and chuckled.

"Okay, I can work with that," I said and took a deep breath.

My eyes traveled across his chest and down his stomach. He was ready to go, and I was ready to make things better.

"Come here," he said as a smile tugged at the corner of his mouth.

I walked toward him slowly until I stood in front of him.

"Take your clothes off."

My stomach fluttered with the familiar excitement as I unbuttoned my shirt and slid it off my shoulders. I released the front closure of my bra and dropped it on the floor.

"Your jeans," he said, his voice husky.

I unbuttoned my jeans and slid them and my panties over my hips and to the floor, kicking them out of the way.

Xander picked me up, and I wrapped my legs around him as he

carried me to the bed. He tossed me backward as I landed on the large mattress. He knelt on the floor, spread my legs apart, and dipped his head between my thighs.

His mouth made contact with me and I moaned in response. My back arched off the bed as he flicked his tongue across my clit. I grabbed his hair and moved my hips against him.

"Oh my God," I whimpered.

He increased his intensity and, just as my world was about to shatter, he stopped.

"No! Where are you going?" I asked, reaching for him.

He stood up and stepped away from the bed. He took himself in his hand and stroked himself in front of me.

"Xander, I need you inside me," I said, unable to stop watching. "Please."

"Ahhh," he said as he closed his eyes and continued. "Shit," he said as his hand moved quicker.

"Xander? Don't finish, I'm right here. Come inside me," I pleaded.

He ignored me as he continued, his muscles tensing. My eyes widened as I watched him finish. Confused, I shook my head.

"Why did you do that? I don't understand." I couldn't hide the hurt in my voice.

"Sometimes you're just not worth the effort," he said as he walked into the bathroom and closed the door behind him.

What had just happened? Had he just punished me for being upset that he was out all night? Did he not want me anymore? What kind of guy jacked off when his girlfriend was ready and willing right in front of him?

I suddenly wanted to put my clothes back on, and I scrambled to get dressed before he came out of the bathroom. Even though he wanted to sleep, I didn't want to be next to him right now. I slipped out of the bedroom and closed the door softly behind me. Shame hovered over me like a dark cloud as I hurried back to the guest room, locked the door, crawled into bed, and cried myself to sleep.

## 23

My stomach growled, waking me. I peered around the guest room and glanced at the clock. It was close to dinnertime. Maybe cooking Xander a nice meal would help smooth things over. Or, maybe if I stopped being a pain in the ass, he would want me again.

My heart ached at his earlier words. I should get my hair cut and my nails done. Had I gained weight? Maybe I should weigh myself. I obviously wasn't taking care of myself well enough for him to want me. And if I wasn't always worth the effort, was it worth it with someone else? Is that where he'd been all night? Getting high and sleeping around?

Hopefully, a hot shower would help me clear my head and stop the heartbreaking thoughts that hammered my brain. Afterward, I applied a little makeup and put on his favorite jeans and top. I peered at my reflection in the mirror and dabbed on some lip gloss. My breath caught. Was that me? My eyes were dull, and I looked exhausted. No wonder he didn't want to sleep with me.

I reached for my concealer and dabbed it under my eyes. Even though I could cover the dark circles, no matter what I did, I couldn't cover the growing emptiness inside me. I thought coming to Oregon and starting over would help, but now I wasn't sure I'd made the right choice after all. Maybe I needed to call Emma.

I dried my hair and recalled my last conversation with Emma. Although I was still mad something tugged at me. I just didn't know what it was.

My shoulders straightened as I finished up in the bathroom and saw Xander's bedroom door was still closed. I quietly went downstairs and into the kitchen. I checked for all the ingredients, and then I made beef stroganoff and lemon meringue pie from scratch. Hopefully he would like it, and after some sleep would be in a better mood when he woke up.

I still couldn't shake the pain of what he'd done to me, though. How could someone you love not be worth the effort? Walker never . . . no, he was in the past, and as long as I didn't screw things up again, I had a good future with Xander. I hoped.

"Something smells amazing," Xander said as he approached me from behind and wrapped his arms around me.

"Hope you like it," I said, trying to gauge his mood.

He moved my hair back and gently kissed my neck. I tensed, unsure what to expect.

"Hey," he said as he turned me toward him.

I couldn't look at him. He tilted my chin up and gently kissed me.

"I know we had a rough start to our day, but I love you. We'll figure everything out, okay?"

I didn't respond. A tug of war stirred inside me and I was torn between wanting to fix things and leaving.

He leaned around me, turned the stove off, and pulled me into him.

He kissed me again, and even though my heart was broken, my body responded.

"I love you, babe," he whispered as he unbuttoned my jeans. "Let me make it up to you."

And he did.

AFTER THE SHITTY WEEKEND, I was excited to return to school on Monday. I missed George something awful. I'd seen him briefly in classes, but Xander had been in a hurry to leave campus ever since Mama had shown up again. I rarely got to spend time with him and the girls anymore.

Silence hung over me on the ride to school.

"You okay?" Xander asked as he reached over and squeezed my hand.

"Yeah," I said and smiled. "I'm just tired."

"I love you."

"I love you too."

I settled into my seat and closed my eyes for the rest of the drive.

Twenty minutes later, Xander kissed me and left me at my classroom door. I heaved a sigh as he left. My emotions were royally screwing with me. One minute I loved him, the next I wasn't sure what I wanted anymore.

Identifying an empty seat, I slipped into one directly behind George; I didn't see Megan and Adalyn. George turned around and scanned my face.

"Something's wrong, isn't it?"

I nodded. "I need to talk, but Xander will be here right after class. He always has an excuse to hurry and leave, and since he's my ride and we live together, I have to go. I can't ever talk to you anymore. I miss you." Tears pooled in my eyes.

"Hey, I'm here," he said and patted my hand.

"Can we cut class? I'll still need to be outside to meet him at the same time, but maybe we can find an empty classroom?"

"And no worries, I know the perfect place," he said and smiled. He gathered his books, and I followed him out of the classroom. I didn't really want to miss class, but I needed to talk to someone.

I followed George down the hallway and into a dark classroom. He turned on the lights and we settled into the empty seats.

"What's going on?"

"I don't know what to do," I whispered. "I'm doing something wrong with Xander, and I don't know what."

"Wait, hold on. What do you mean, you're doing something wrong? Are you cheating on him?" he asked as he leaned toward me, waiting for my answer.

"God no! That's not my thing, at all." I paused as I remembered that thanks to James, Walker's so-called best friend, I'd already been labeled a cheater once before. "You can't tell anyone."

"Oh, it's one of those secrets?"

"It's Xander. He went out with his friends the other night, which was fine, but he didn't come home until noon the next day. I never heard from him—he didn't even bother calling me. When he came back, I was happy he was okay, but I'd waited all night for him. I was terrified he'd been in a car accident."

"So not cool," George muttered. "I don't give a shit who he is, you don't deserve that. You've been through enough."

"It gets worse."

George stared at me, his gaze growing more intense.

"I think he was high when he came home. I'm not positive, but I think he was. I've never been around someone using drugs, but his behavior has been . . . *different* a few times. And"—I paused, trying to collect my thoughts—"at the party we had at the house in January, I caught him snorting coke," I blurted out.

"Fuck, are you serious?" George asked as he sat up straight.

"Very. I saw him snort the line myself. And there's something else, too. I don't know who else did any drugs, but several of the guys from the football team were playing cards with him."

George leaned back in his chair and shook his head. He sat speechless longer than I'd ever seen before.

"Say something, please. How to fix it? I don't want to lose him!"

"Well, first of all, drugs change people or bring out the darkness that's already inside them. I've always liked Xander, but the more he's around you . . . there's something that bothers me. I just haven't been able to put my finger on it. Maybe this is it?"

"Shit. I shouldn't have bothered you with all this. I'll get it figured out," I said. "He's been nothing but good to me, and he's the only person who's ever stood up to Mama. I know he loves me." I smiled and mentally kicked myself for telling George.

"Hey, if you want to stay then you know I'll support you, but keep your eyes open. Maybe he wasn't high, maybe he was, but you're the only one who knows what's going on behind closed doors."

I nodded. "Enough about me, how are you? Has Andy called?"

"No, I guess we just had a great night together," he said and shrugged.

"I'm sorry. You're an amazing guy, and friend. I know you'll find someone who will love you for you and make you happy."

"Thanks, and that goes for you, too." He reached over and hugged me.

"Thanks for not calling me Hillbilly anymore," I said and laughed.

"You're so much more."

Was I? I didn't feel like much of anything anymore.

"Have you seen your mom again?"

"Oh, geez! I have some explaining to do to Megan. Last Friday, Xander walked me to class and said goodbye. Megan and I were waiting for Adalyn to show when Xander came running back. I mean, running like he was on the football field again. He'd seen Mama on campus. We had to leave so fast I didn't even tell Megan goodbye. I don't even know what to say to her."

"It's okay. I took care of it. She did mention it, and how weird it was."

"What did you say?"

"That there was someone you didn't want to see, and it wasn't my story to tell. Believe it or not, even though she wanted to know more, she respected that and dropped it. At least for now. I know you and I are closer than you are to Adalyn and Megan, but you can trust them. They would be there for you."

"Really? Even with all the craziness I bring with me? I couldn't take the chance of Mama hurting them. What would she do if they stepped in?" My stomach knotted at the thought. "There's no way I can't risk it."

"I totally get it, but keep it in the back of your mind."

"Shit! Class is almost over," I said and grabbed my books.

George and I slipped out of the empty room and walked down the hallway to our door. Within seconds, it opened, and students filed out of the room. George and I fell in line and walked out the front door, where Xander was already waiting.

I glanced at George as we approached Xander.

"Hey, Xander!" George said. "I feel like I haven't seen you in a while. How's it going?"

"Good," he said as he reached for my hand. "We'll have to catch up soon. Maybe another party at the house?" he asked and smiled.

"I'm always up for a good party."

"You ready to go?" Xander asked me.

I nodded and took his hand.

"See you later, George," I said as Xander tugged my arm.

"How was your class?" Xander asked as we walked across campus.

My stomach flipped as I wondered if he knew George and I had skipped.

"Good," I muttered.

"What did you discuss?"

I frowned at his persistence.

"You know, health isn't my favorite class, and I'm a little embarrassed to admit I thought about you most of the time," I said and beamed up at him. My heart melted as he smiled back.

"Yeah? I'm okay with that," he said as we reached his truck.

He opened the door for me and then slid into the driver's seat.

"So, I thought we should go out tonight," he said. "On a date. I guess with everything that's happened with your mom, we've tried to keep you safe at the house. You probably need to go out and have some fun. What do you think?"

"Really?" I couldn't contain the excitement in my voice. For the last few months, I'd gone to school and Xander's, nowhere else.

Xander chuckled and reached for my hand.

I SPENT THE AFTERNOON STUDYING, and Xander did the same. He rarely cracked open a book, and yet he still held a 4.0 GPA. He was smart, and he absorbed information without trying. Unlike him, I struggled a little bit and worked my ass off for a B average.

Glancing at the clock, I realized it was time to get ready for our date. I hopped off the bed and opened the closet, gasping at the emerald-green, backless dress that was hanging in front of me. I reached for it and looked at the label. It was my size. Xander had bought it for me.

A wide smile eased across my face as I grabbed it and ran to our dresser. I found the blue lace bra and G-string I'd saved for a special occasion. He was trying to make things better, and I loved him for it. And I wanted to give him a night he'd never forget.

I went to the guest bedroom, hung the dress in the closet, and walked across the hall to the bathroom. For some reason, I never really used Xander's bathroom. I knew he liked his space, and honestly, I liked not sharing a bathroom.

The spray of the hot water seeped through me as I shaved my legs, and deep-conditioned my hair. After I toweled off, I moisturized my skin and dried and curled my hair. I put it in a loose bun, allowing a few soft, curled strands to frame my face. Next, I put on my butterfly necklace, applied my makeup, and finished everything off with a light dusting of Obsession perfume.

The door creaked as I opened it and peeked down the hall. Xander was nowhere in sight, so I made a mad dash into the guest bedroom.

The plastic cover crinkled as I removed it from the dress. The material caressed my skin while I slipped it over my head. It fell right above my knees, and the deep green brought out my eyes.

I smiled, and for the first time in a while, the smile actually reached my eyes. My stomach fluttered as I realized I was nervous. Xander and I hadn't gone on many dates. I'd never worn such a beautiful dress before, either. At that moment, I realized I didn't have shoes other than my Nike tennis shoes and calf-high boots.

*Shit.* What was I going to do? I didn't have any heels. My face fell as I realized our date wasn't going to happen after all.

My shoulders sagged as I left the room and descended the stairs, staring at my feet. I glanced up to see him waiting for me. My breath caught when I saw him. He looked incredible. His broad shoulders filled out his gray suit jacket, and his dark-green shirt matched my dress.

"My God, you're breathtaking," Xander said as he stood at the bottom of the stairs. His eyes traveled from my face down my body and back again. "I knew the green color would be beautiful on you," he said as he extended his hand and helped me the rest of the way down the stairs.

"Xander," I whispered. "Thank you. Thank you so much. It's beautiful, but . . ."

"Hold that thought," he said as he walked into the living room and returned with a pair of black heels. "I didn't forget."

"Oh my God. I love you," I said, laughing.

Xander kneeled down and held the shoes as I slipped my feet into them. I was suddenly three inches taller.

He smiled at me as his eyes did another slow pass of my body. Excitement traveled through me, and I could feel my body responding to him. His hand moved gently up the inside of my leg and met my G-string. He massaged me through the thin material and then stood up.

"After dinner, babe. Until then, I want you to squirm while you think about me inside you."

My entire body flushed with heat as he squeezed my ass and kissed me lightly. He grabbed a black wrap and covered my shoulders with it.

"You didn't have to buy all this for me," I said, blushing at his generosity.

"I wanted to do something special for you," he said as he offered me his arm and escorted me out of the house and into the truck.

"Where are we going?" I asked.

"It's a surprise," Xander replied and grinned.

Xander merged onto the highway, and we headed into Eugene. Half an hour later, we walked into the Excelsior Inn and were seated in a back corner that gave us some privacy. Xander pulled out my chair for me and seated himself across the table. He ordered us drinks as I glanced at the menu.

"It's really expensive here. I can't ask you to spend this kind of money," I whispered as I put the menu down.

"Pick up the menu and order whatever you want. I've wanted to bring you here for a long time."

"Really?" I asked shyly.

"Really."

I returned to the menu and selected a salad, but when the server came, Xander ordered us both steak and lobster.

"I can't believe you did that!" I whispered.

He laughed and took my hand.

"How are you doing about your mom?"

His question took me off guard, and I pulled my hand away.

"I'm sorry," he said. "I didn't mean to just spring the question on you, but I haven't asked lately."

"It's hard," I said as I took a sip of water and wished it were a rum and Pepsi. "We have a complicated past."

"So, you haven't told me everything?"

"You know the important parts. I don't want to relive it over and over, ya know?" I put my glass back down on the table.

"Okay. I just wanted to see how you were doing."

"Thanks," I said. I hoped he would let it go.

We spent the rest of the meal talking about his upcoming graduation and where he wanted to apply for jobs. I also wanted to work over the summer, meet more people, and get my own car. Xander had been amazing about driving me everywhere, but I couldn't sit at home and wait for him all day, either. I didn't care if Mama was around or not. I would just buy some pepper spray and keep it on my keychain.

## 25

Two hours later, Xander paid the check and escorted me back to the truck.

The rain had started, and it pattered against the windshield as we drove home. I scooted along the truck's bench seat to be closer to him. His free hand slipped underneath my dress and caressed my thigh. I reached over, unbuttoned and unzipped his slacks, and took him in my hand. He adjusted himself in his seat as I rubbed him. I realized we were being risky while driving, but the idea excited me.

He moaned as I moved my hand up and down the length of him. The harder he got, the more I was ready for him to pull over.

"Oh yeah, babe. That feels good. We're almost home," he said and smiled. I grinned as I unbuckled my seatbelt and took him into my mouth.

"Fuck!"

He pulled into the driveway and parked the truck. He grabbed the back of my head, slid in and out of my mouth, and then lifted my head and brought his mouth to mine.

His hands ran up my legs and then lifted my dress over my head. I shivered against the cold as he paused for a moment and then lifted me onto his lap. I smiled as I straddled him.

"Shit, babe. I haven't seen you wear this blue bra-and-panty set before. I'm gonna come just looking at you."

The familiar flush ran up my neck and my face.

His hand ran down my stomach and slipped under my G-string, moving it out of the way.

"So fucking ready for me," he whispered.

He grabbed my hips and entered me. I leaned into him and propped my hands against the back of the seat as he rocked me, our rhythm in sync and steady.

Xander unhooked my bra and slid it off. My nipples hardened against the cold. He took my breast into his mouth. My fingers wound through his hair, pulling him closer.

"You feel so good. Don't stop."

I whimpered when he lifted me off him. For a moment, I panicked that we were about to have a replay of that awful night, but he slipped my G-string off and threw it onto the floorboard.

"What are you doing?" I giggled as he opened the truck door and got out. "It's pouring rain out there and it's cold."

He pulled on my leg as he brought me to the edge of the seat.

"I want you in the rain," he said. "You can use my jacket."

He removed his suit jacket and covered my shoulders as he picked me up and placed me on the hood of the truck. The rain had slowed to a soft sprinkle, and I laid back on the hood as it chilled my skin. The only thing I was still wearing were my black high heels, but the expression on his face told me that was all he wanted. I parted my legs and welcomed him.

He traced kisses down my stomach and nipped at the inside of my thighs. I moaned as his tongue caressed my clit and he slid his finger inside me. My back arched off the truck as I wrapped my legs around his neck. I couldn't hold back and released within a few short minutes, but I knew my Xander, and it wasn't over yet.

He smiled and lifted me off the truck, turned me around, and bent me over the hood.

"Oh yeah. Nothing like my girl in heels in the rain," he said as he entered me slowly.

I threw my head back and moaned as he maintained a slow rhythm. One of his hands held my hip for leverage as the other slipped between my legs and massaged my clit. I moved against him, wanting him to pick up the pace, but he refused.

"Slow and steady until you're begging me to fuck you harder."

I moaned as he kept true to his word and I begged for more.

"Please, baby. Harder. I need you."

He took hold of my hair, pulled my head back, and ran his other hand over my breast and up my neck. His fingers tightened slightly around my throat.

"Tell me again, babe."

"I need you."

His fingers tightened more as he picked up the pace.

"Say it. Say you want me to fuck you harder."

"Harder," I whispered.

"Not until you say it."

"Oh God, Xander. Please, baby, please fuck me as hard as you can."

His hand tightened even more as he pounded into me.

"That's it. Now I'll give you what you want," he panted.

I gasped for air, but I grew more excited as I felt him inside me. Black dots danced across my vision as I released with him.

Xander chuckled as he planted light kisses down my bare back. My fingernails dug into the palm of my hand as I tried to catch my breath.

"You're sexy as hell against my truck with those heels on," he whispered as he pulled out of me.

I turned to face him and smiled.

"That was crazy. I've never done anything like that before. What if someone had shown up?" I asked, my eyes widening at the thought.

"Then they would have gotten one hell of a show," he said and laughed.

He grabbed his jacket off the truck and tossed it around me as we hurried into the house.

"Why don't you go shower and I'll get your clothes out of the truck," he said.

"Okay," I said and hurried up the stairs to get under the hot spray of the shower.

2 6

It was almost midnight when we crawled into bed.

Xander wrapped his arms around me as I snuggled back into his chest. A smile eased across my face as my thoughts returned to our adventure on the truck. I loved exploring new things with him almost as much as I loved him.

"Lacey, can I tell you something?" he whispered in my ear.

I began to turn to face him, but he stopped me.

"No, stay where you're at while I tell you. I've never told anyone this before."

I stayed still and waited for him to continue.

"I wasn't honest with you. I don't ever talk to my parents, and I've lived with my grandma since I was fifteen. My parents sent me away."

"What? Why?" My heart ached at the thought of his parents not wanting him. I understood too well, and maybe it was even worse than what I'd gone through.

"I had a brother, Steven. He was a few years older than me, but he'd always been sick. He wasn't a strong kid, and he wasn't in sports or anything. Most of the kids made fun of him . . . and then there was the accident."

My brow furrowed. I was grateful I wasn't facing him, and the darkness masked my expression.

"Our house caught on fire and even though we all got out, Steven suffered horrible burns all over his body. Afterward, everything we did was for him. We left Minnesota, where I'd spent my entire life, and moved to Texas so he could be treated by the best burn doctors in the country.

"My parents stopped spending time with me, they missed my sports events in school, and even if they had planned to go, something with Steven always came up. Although he did get better, he was never really normal again, not mentally or physically. One day we asked Mom and Dad if we could go down to the swimming hole, and even though I was younger than him, they made me promise I'd take care of him. A big part of me was so sick and tired of everything about Steven. I hated him.

"Anyway, we went down to the swimming hole, and the current was stronger than normal. I didn't realize it until we were already in the water. Steven lost his balance and slipped off a rock. I reached him quickly, but then something inside me snapped. Here was a kid who was in constant mental and physical pain. He had no friends, and no life to speak of. And in that split second, I let go of him, held his head down, and watched him struggle to make it to the surface. I crawled out of the swimming hole, sat on the rock, dried off, and watched his limp body float to the top of the water."

My eyes widened as his words soaked in. My God, what was he saying?

"How old were you?" My voice cracked.

"I was eleven."

"Baby, you couldn't have really understood what was happening. I'm sure you were just in shock. You never meant to hurt him."

"I didn't, I mean, I was angry and wanted to scare him, but it went too far. But afterward, I wasn't really sad. It just was what it was. I thought I would have some guilt, but I didn't."

His arm tightened around me as he kissed my neck.

"I've never told anyone about it before, and the reason I chose you is that I love you. I love you so much that the mere thought of you lying to me or leaving me makes me crazy. I know you skipped your health class today and spent time with George."

My breath caught in my throat and a chill shot down my spine.

"So, I'm going to make this very clear. You're mine, and I tell you what you can and can't do. Don't you ever lie to me again. Ever."

He paused as he ran his finger down the side of my face and settled on my left breast.

"And if you ever leave me, I'll hunt you down and you'll join my brother. Do you understand?"

My mind scrambled for the right words. My boyfriend had just admitted to murdering his own brother and having no feelings about it. Would he really do the same to me?

"Just do what I ask and everything will be great, just like tonight— good food and good sex. Okay?"

I nodded as my heart pounded, realizing he could feel my fear as he squeezed my breast.

"Get some sleep, and remember, I love you." He kissed my cheek, laid his head on the pillow, and didn't let me go for the rest of the night.

I didn't sleep at all.

FAINT LIGHT PEEKED through the curtain as I glanced at the clock that now blared 6:22 A.M. I hadn't slept all night, and Xander hadn't let go of me until now. I tried to sleep, but his words haunted me. My feet landed quietly on the floor as I slipped out of bed and tiptoed out of the bedroom. I gasped for air as I stood on the other side of the door.

Even though I was exhausted, my mind was going a hundred miles an hour. I crept downstairs and made coffee, staring blankly at it as the coffee dripped into the pot.

What was I going to do? Had he been serious about his brother? How did he know I'd been with George? Was he following me? Would he really hurt me?

I pulled up a chair at the kitchen table and sipped my coffee, wincing as it burned my tongue. My eyes squeezed closed and I rewound last night's conversation once again. No matter how many times it played through my mind, I came to the same conclusion. Xander had been the only one to protect me from Mama. Yes, he was moody, but the times he'd gotten really angry, I'd pushed him.

Confusion clouded my mind as I sifted through his words. I could understand him not wanting me to lie to him, and I wouldn't again. I'd just explain to him I needed to see my friends more often, and I sometimes felt alone and isolated out here. He didn't have a problem with George anyway; it was that I'd lied. I wouldn't be happy if Xander had lied to me, either. Apparently it was a hot button for him, but I could fix it.

As for Steven, Xander had admitted it went too far, and he didn't mean to hurt him. I bit my lip and imagined what it would be like to hate your brother. My heart stuttered at the thought of eleven-year-old Xander feeling so scared and confused he thought he'd killed him. The pain of losing Steven and his parents must have overwhelmed him. He must not remember it correctly. How could he? He was so young when it happened.

*Why would he go to such a great extent to protect me from Mama, move me in with him, tell me he loves me, and then hurt me?* It didn't add up.

Relief flowed through me as things fell into place. It was his first time sharing a confusing and scary moment with someone, and he was mad I hadn't told him about George. We all say things we don't mean. I had certainly said things I didn't mean in the heat of the moment.

I took a deep breath and rubbed my aching neck.

"Good morning," I said, setting coffee and a plate of eggs and bacon on the kitchen table for Xander.

"Wow, this looks great," he said and kissed my cheek. "You generally don't cook breakfast on days we have class."

"I know, but I wanted to talk to you for a minute before we left," I smiled as I sat down at the kitchen table with him. My hands squeezed together under the table in an attempt to hide my frazzled nerves.

"What about?" he asked between bites of bacon.

"Well, I've been thinking about what you said last night," I said and glanced at him, trying to gauge his reaction. "My heart hurts for you. You were only eleven, and I know you didn't really mean to hurt Steven. I know you'd never hurt me, either. In fact, you've done the opposite. You've protected me. So, I just wanted to say I know it might feel like you hurt him on purpose, but you were a scared and confused kid. I'm so sorry your parents sent you away, Xander. I love you. I won't leave you like your parents did. And I won't lie to you again. I'm so sorry. I miss my friends, and . . . it won't happen again."

Xander put his fork down and leaned back into his chair. His eyes traveled over my face, and I returned his gaze.

"Thank you. I don't know what I'd do if I lost you."

"You don't have to think about it," I said, standing up from my chair and walked over to him.

Xander reached for me, pulled me into his lap, and wrapped his arms around me. Relief washed over me as my fear and the misunderstanding dissipated.

"I love you," I whispered. "We'll figure everything out, but I don't want you to worry."

Xander nodded and then brushed his lips against mine.

# 27

Spring wasn't much different than winter in Eugene. The temperature was only a few degrees warmer, and the rain kept coming. I was sure Noah had built his ark here.

The doorbell startled me out of my studies. My brows knitted together, and I closed my book, and hopped down the stairs. I had no clue who it was. Unless we were having a party, we rarely had anyone over. Xander always went out, but he at least called or came home at a reasonable hour these days. I'd learned to enjoy the time when he was gone.

I opened the door to two men standing on the porch. Both could've passed for thirty-five or so, but one was short and stocky while the other easily cleared six foot two. I didn't recognize them.

"Hi, can I help you?" I asked.

The taller one shifted a bit. His broad shoulders were almost as intimidating as his height.

"Yeah, we're looking for Xander. Is he home?" he asked as his eyes roamed over my body.

I bit my lip and debated what to tell them. If they knew he'd gone to the grocery store, would they want to come in and wait? I didn't want them to know I was alone, either. My stomach clenched as I tried to decide what to say.

"Sorry, he's in the shower," I said. "Can I let him know who stopped by?"

The taller guy shifted again and the glimmer of metal caught my eye. Who were they? And why in the hell was he carrying a gun?

"If you would be so kind as to let him know Agnus said hello."

"Agnus?" I asked. "Your name is Agnus?" I tried to stifle my giggle. Who in their right mind would name their son Agnus?

Agnus took two steps toward me and sneered.

"And who are you?" he asked. The smell of alcohol tickled my nose as he spoke.

"I'm his girlfriend," I said, grabbing the door tighter and attempting to hide the tremble in my legs.

"Mmhmm. Well, you tell your boyfriend he needs to take care of his business or we'll be back, and next time, I'm going to invite myself in."

He chuckled as he backed away. The two men turned around and walked back toward their black Mustang. I shut the door and locked the deadbolt as soon as they were off the porch. Then I leaned against the wall and slid down to the floor. What was wrong? Who were they and what did they want?

I made my way to the kitchen and grabbed the almost-empty rum bottle. Xander would be home soon with more, so I filled my glass and downed it straight. My eyes teared up as it burned my throat.

"I'm home!" Xander yelled. The door shut behind him.

"Lock the door," I said as I ran out of the kitchen and turned the deadbolt.

"What the hell?" he asked while he made his way to the kitchen. I followed behind him and grabbed the new rum bottle. I poured another shot and drank it.

"Shit!" I said and put the glass down.

Xander stared at me as surprise flashed across his face.

"Did you see your mom?" he asked as he unpacked the rest of the grocery bag.

"No," I said and helped him put the items in the cabinet. "No, two men showed up here for you. They told me to tell you 'Agnus said hello.'"

"Fuck!" Xander said as the jar of mayonnaise slipped from his hand and shattered on the kitchen floor.

"What else?" Xander asked, frozen in place.

I glanced at the broken glass and spattered mayonnaise, and then looked at Xander. His eyes widened as he stared at me.

"Say something, dammit!"

"Oh—no, they didn't say anything else," I muttered, grabbing the mop and bucket from the storage closet. "Who are they? One of them had a gun, Xander. And not a rifle, ya know the kind you go hunting with and bring back dinner? A real fucking gun!"

My voice gained an octave as I continued. "Why were they here and what did they want? I know one thing they wanted, and that was me, so please tell me what's going on."

Xander walked toward me, the glass crunching beneath his shoes as he approached.

"Don't ever open the door for them again," he whispered. "Don't open the door, don't ask me any fucking questions, and clean this shit up."

Tears threatened my eyes as he walked out of the kitchen and up the stairs.

I sighed as I looked at the mess and began cleaning it up.

Xander didn't reappear until evening. Since we had missed classes, I studied downstairs in the living room and left him alone.

"Your dinner is on the stove," I said as he came into the living room.

"Thanks, but I'm going out."

"You are?" I asked. I couldn't hide my surprise after earlier today.

"Yeah, and I'll be out late, so don't wait up. And don't open the door for anyone, either," he mumbled.

I stared at him as he walked down the hall and out the front door and glanced at the clock: 7:18 P.M. My stomach flipped as I felt a nudge that I wouldn't see him until tomorrow. I hated it when he went out all night.

An overwhelming urge to call George came over me, but he didn't have a phone. I nestled into the love seat and turned on the TV, but nothing was really on. My mind replayed the scene with the two men at the door. I knew it wasn't good news the moment I saw them, but why wouldn't Xander tell me who they were? Was he in some kind of trouble? And if he was, did that mean I was as well?

"What a fucked day," I muttered, making a large rum and Pepsi and drank until I passed out on the couch.

2 8

---

"Wake up, dammit! Where the fuck is my food?"

I swallowed and tried to clear the sleep from my eyes.

"Xander?" I asked as I sat up on the couch.

"You didn't cook?"

"No, I thought you'd be out all night."

"What the fuck? Don't think. Just do what the hell you're supposed to do."

I sat up on the couch and glared at him. My stomach lurched. He was high again, and there was no way either of us could deny it this time. He looked like shit.

"Sit down and I'll make you something to eat. I'm sorry," I said, hurrying out of the living room and into the kitchen. I'd hoped he wouldn't follow me, but I wasn't so lucky.

"Well, what did you do all night?" he asked.

I stiffened at the tone of his voice. Fear and anger warred inside me. What did he think I'd done all night? I drank myself into oblivion while I sat stuck in the house with no friends and no boyfriend.

I tried to dodge the question. "I'm sorry, I'm making you some-

143

thing right now. In fact, it will taste better because it hasn't sat in the refrigerator all night." I grabbed a pan and some eggs.

"I asked you a question. What you did all night?"

A beat of silence hung in the air and then I cracked the eggs into the hot pan and tossed the eggshells into the garbage.

"I had a drink and then fell asleep. How about you? The cocaine treating you well?" I asked, unable to hide the irritation in my voice. He'd been out all night with his friends while I sat at home, and he still expected me to cook. What the hell?

The hot pan and eggs flew by my head as they crashed into the kitchen wall. Pain shot through me as he slammed me into the wall beside it.

"I'm sorry, I'm sorry," I said, unable to control the tremble in my voice.

"What did I tell you about asking questions? It's none of your fucking business what I do," he said as he leaned into me.

"Okay. You're right, baby. I—I just get worried when you're like this. You're scaring me."

Xander paused for a moment and leaned back a bit, allowing for a small amount of space between us. I tentatively placed my hand on his chest, but he grabbed my hand, twisted it, and squeezed.

"You're hurting me," I gasped as the pain shot through my hand and wrist. "Please, stop. I'll make it up to you, I promise."

Xander sneered as he tossed my hand away from him and walked out of the kitchen and into the living room.

I pulled out the kitchen chair and slipped into it before I collapsed. I glanced at the wall and grabbed the kitchen towel to clean up the eggs before he came back. My legs shook so badly I couldn't stand up, so I slid from the chair and crawled over to the mess on all fours. Maybe if I gave him a few minutes to come down from the coke, he would calm down. What was I going to do? I bit my lip as pain shot up my arm.

My chest shuddered with a deep breath, and then I finished cooking for him. I brought a plate of eggs, bacon, and toast to him.

"Here you go," I said, placing it down on the coffee table.

He glanced at me as he reached for a piece of bacon. "Your feelings hurt that I got pissed?"

My eyes widened. "I feel bad, and I hate it when you're upset with me. It's been a shitty day," I replied.

"Well, leave if you don't like it. If you think me taking care of you and paying your bills is mistreating you, by all means, walk right out the fucking door."

"I didn't say that."

"What are you gonna do? Run back to Mama? You want George to help you?" Xander asked and laughed. "The sooner you realize you have no one else who gives a shit about you, the better off you'll be."

I winced at his words. He didn't mean it, not really; it was the cocaine talking. He was mean when he used.

I stood still, unsure of what he would do next. He leaned back in the love seat and chewed another piece of bacon as he stared at me.

"Can I get you anything else?" I asked softly.

"No. I don't even wanna fucking look at you. Get out of my sight and go to bed. It's five in the morning, and you look like shit when you don't get enough sleep."

I turned and walked out of the kitchen, releasing the breath I didn't realize I was holding in. Tears streamed down my cheeks while I quietly went up the stairs. I paused at the guest room and debated if I wanted to sleep in there, but I wasn't sure of what he would do if I wasn't in his bed. Fear won, and I went to his bedroom, closed the door behind me, and crawled into bed.

"Scoot over," Xander said as he slid underneath the blankets.

I did what he asked, and then I stayed still and waited to see which Xander was next to me. He was like Jekyll and Hyde on the nights he went out and used. I hated it, and I hated him as much as I loved him. I bit my lip as his arm slid around my waist and he pulled me into his chest.

"I'm sorry. I love you, babe," he said as he nuzzled my ear.

"I love you too," I whispered, realizing he was back to normal. I let out a soft sigh as he slipped his hand into my panties and teased me.

Xander did things to me that night I'd never dreamed of. I didn't know if it was the aftereffect of the drugs or if he was genuinely sorry, but in those moments every bit of fear and anger melted away. I knew that no matter what, this was who I'd become—Xander's.

I knew I couldn't leave; I knew no one else wanted me. I just needed to accept it and join him instead.

2 9

It felt like it had been weeks since I'd seen George and the girls, but really it had only been a few days. The sun warmed our backs as we stood outside and welcomed the spring air. The cherry trees were in full bloom, along with the dogwoods. I'd never seen anything so beautiful. Oregon continued to surprise me with the turn of every season.

"You're awfully quiet," Megan said and nudged me.

I winced as pain shot up through my arm.

"What's the matter?" George asked.

"What?"

"You acted like Megan hurt you. What's up?"

"Oh, nothing," I said. "I was helping Xander put the groceries away and I dropped a jar of mayonnaise and it burst on the floor. Then I slid in it and busted my ass. I caught myself funny, and now my arm is sore."

"I could totally see you doing something like that," Adalyn said and laughed at my clumsiness.

"Yeah, well, it wasn't pretty," I replied as my thoughts returned to the other night. My cheeks flushed with the memory.

George peered at me, his eyebrows narrowed and slightly raised in the middle. I wondered if he could see through my lie. There was no way I could tell any of them what had really happened. They wouldn't understand Xander's recreational coke use, and I didn't want them involved. When he was high he was scary, and I couldn't take the chance of him coming after them. Besides, I was learning to handle his moods, and we would be fine.

"What're you guys doing tonight?" I asked, redirecting the subject.

"Partying!" Megan and Adalyn answered at the same time.

"Oh? Are you going too, George?"

"Yeah! Why don't you come, Lacey? You haven't been out with us in a really long time."

"I know, I just stay so busy with Xander and studying. My scholarship depends on my grades," I said and shrugged.

"Well, let us know if you change your mind," Megan said.

"Sure," I replied.

"We have to go, so we'll see you soon," she continued.

I watched them walk toward the dorms as I waited for Xander. My heart sank. I wanted to go with them, but there was no way Xander would let me. Maybe we could do something else instead. I smiled as an idea crept into my mind.

"Where the hell is this coming from?" Xander asked and laughed. "You're serious?"

"Yeah! I mean, why not?"

"Well, you've always thrown a fucking fit when I come home high, and now you're telling me you want to go to my friend's house with me this weekend and try it?"

"Well, I miss you when you're gone all night," I said and jutted my lip out. "Please?"

Xander pulled me into him and searched my face. "You're not gonna act like a spoiled bitch in front of my friends, are you?"

His words stung, and I tried to pull away from him.

"No, no," he said and laughed again. "I'm just teasing you—

don't be so sensitive. I just wanted to make sure you can handle what goes on at these parties. They're not like the ones you're used to."

"What do you mean? You guys play cards, snort coke, and what else?" I tilted my head and waited for his response. I ignored the uneasy feeling that began gnawing at me.

"Well, it gets a little crazy sometimes," he said. A smile tugged at the corner of his mouth. "But I tell you what. I'll bring you this once, and if it goes well then I'll bring you *some* of the time."

"Really?" I asked and beamed up at him. "Thank you," I said. Then I stood up on my tiptoes and kissed him.

FRIDAY NIGHT FINALLY ARRIVED, and Xander held the truck door open for me. The rain had returned, and the wind whipped through the trees. Butterflies danced in my stomach. I hadn't been to a party since we'd had ours in January, and I missed being around people outside of the classroom.

He started the truck and we pulled down the driveway. I hummed to the radio and stared out the window. Ten minutes later, we parked along the street and walked up a short driveway. I pulled my jacket around me and shivered as Xander rang the doorbell and we waited for someone to answer.

"Hey, guys! Come on in." It was Andy.

I gasped, glancing at Xander and back to Andy. "You come *here*? To Andy's house?"

"All the time," Xander said as he placed his hand on the small of my back and nudged me into the house.

"Xander, you know where to hang up your jackets. We're waiting for you to start, so come on back," Andy said as he hurried down the hallway.

"I had no idea," I said and laughed, thinking about George and Andy that night.

Xander smiled as he took my hand and guided me down the hall.

"You still wanting to try some coke?" he asked as he peered down at me.

"Yup, if you're doing some tonight then I'm going to join you. I want to try it," I assured him. I glanced around Andy's house as we walked side by side, holding hands.

"Okay, then no drinking. I don't want you to end up in the emergency room the first time you get high," he said.

"Really? That could happen?" I asked and frowned.

Xander stopped in his tracks and turned me to face him. "You do know what coke is, right?"

"Yeah, of course I do. I just hadn't thought about not drinking, and you know how much I like my Pepsi and rum," I giggled. My nerves were starting to get the better of me.

"Whatever happens tonight, stay close, okay?"

"Okay." I had no intention of leaving his side.

"Hey!" everyone yelled as Xander and I entered the living room. I glanced around and bit my lip as I located the poker table and six guys sitting around it. I heard a giggle and looked over to the group of girls sitting on the couches. A silver tray was on the coffee table with lines of white powder on it. One of the girls waved at Xander as she wiped her nose.

*Holy shit, it's Cheerleader Brittney.*

Xander tugged on my hand as he took a seat at the table and pulled me into his lap. All the guys introduced themselves, and I nodded as I tried to remember their names.

"Let's play, mother fuckers!" Xander howled.

Andy dealt the cards, and I settled into the chair between Xander's legs. I could see his hand that way without him showing his cards. He shifted in the seat, pulled out his wallet, and tossed several hundred-dollar bills on the table. My eyes widened.

"Awww shit, dude! You didn't tell her we play with real money?" The guy by the name of Bill asked. "You're in deep now." He laughed and smacked Xander on the back.

"Nah, she's good with it. Aren't you, babe?"

I nodded. There was no way I was going to act like a spoiled bitch, as he called it, but I wondered what else I didn't know about.

"Whatever you say, man. The expression on her face says otherwise."

"Well, watch this shit," Xander said as he tossed his cards on the table. The guys groaned as they put theirs on the table. Xander stood up and gathered all the money.

"You always start out strong," John said as he shook his head. "Let's see if you're going to leave with your dick in your hand, though." He laughed.

"You wish," Xander replied as Andy dealt another hand.

I watched as he won three more hands, laughing as the other guys gave him a hard time about taking their money. It was great.

"You ready, babe?" Xander whispered in my ear. I nodded and stood up to let him out of the chair. He walked over to the group of girls. I'd been so engaged in watching Xander play poker I'd almost forgotten they were there.

Xander came back, placed the tray on the table.

"Your house, you first," Xander said to Andy.

Andy took a rolled-up hundred-dollar bill, snorted a line, and then passed it to Bill. One by one, the guys each snorted a line. When it was his turn, Xander grabbed a bill, rolled it, and snorted his own line. There was only one line left now, and he pushed the tray in front of me.

"Here, babe," Xander said as he held out the bill to me. I took it, smiled, held it over the coke and snorted the line. My nose instantly started dripping into the back of my throat; it burned and tasted bitter. I felt the effects almost instantly.

I handed the hundred-dollar bill back to Xander and searched his face. Then I leaned back in the chair and took a deep breath.

"Fuck," I said.

"You alright?" Xander asked.

I stood up so he could sit in the chair again. Then I sank into his lap and looked at everyone around the table.

"Wow," I said and bit my lip. I turned toward Xander and giggled. "Take all their money," I said and winked at him.

"Sounds like your girlfriend is feeling pretty good," Andy said.

"Good enough to take your money," I said, laughing.

One of the girls laughed too, and I turned to look at them just in time to see Brittney licking her lips and checking out my boyfriend. Xander chuckled as he patted my leg.

"Calm down, babe, we're at a party," he whispered in my ear.

I took his hand and slid it up my shirt. He squeezed my breast as I stared at her.

"Easy, girl," he said and grinned. "I think I might like you high."

I leaned back against his chest. "You win more hands, and I'll give you anything you want," I whispered in his ear.

"Alright, boys, let's play some fucking cards!" he yelled.

I giggled as the cards were dealt. I peered over at Brittney and the group of girls again, but they weren't paying us any attention.

Xander lost the first hand.

"Too bad for you," I said.

"Oh, it's not over yet. We're just getting started."

One hour and three hands later, Xander had lost all the money he'd won, and more. I bit my lip and kept my mouth closed. My excitement was dwindling, and Xander's temper was warming up.

Andy took the tray and loaded it up with coke again. We all snorted another line and within minutes I was feeling better again and so was Xander. After several more hours, rounds of cards, and lines of coke, I'd completely lost track of the time. Xander had won part of his money back, and his mood had improved a little.

"Alright, I've gotta take a break," Xander said as he lifted me off his lap. "I'll be back in a minute," he said. I watched him as he left the living room and went down the hall.

"Having a good time?" Andy asked me.

"Yes, thank you for having me," I said. Guess my Southern manners still showed through, even when I was high. I stifled a giggle.

"How's George?"

I tilted my head and tried to read his expression, but I couldn't. Did he care about George, or was he just making conversation? Andy moved to the vacant seat next to me while a few of the other guys got up and grabbed beers.

"Do you like him?" I asked, my eyes widening at the thought of them together.

"Yeah. I mean, who wouldn't."

"Then why didn't you call him?" I asked and propped my elbows up on the table.

"I don't know," he said. "Guess I just figured we were at a party, and that's all there was to it."

"He likes you, so you should call him," I said and smiled.

"Okay. I know you two are close, so I trust you. You have classes with him, right?"

"Yup! Can I tell him we talked?" I asked. I couldn't hide the excitement in my voice.

"Sure. I'll find him next week, but yeah, let him know I'm looking for him," Andy said as a shy smile crept across his face.

I leaned back in my chair as Xander's hand snuck down my top from behind me. I closed my eyes as he slid his hand inside my bra and teased my nipple.

"Lacey," Andy said, a warning tone to his voice.

"You better watch it, I'm going to take you into one of Andy's bedrooms," I said, ignoring Andy.

His hand gently squeezed my breast as he began kissing my neck. I leaned my head to the side, allowing him better access. I'd never let someone touch me in front of other people. The coke was doing some weird shit to me.

"What the fuck?" Xander yelled. His hand left me quickly, pulling out of my shirt.

Andy jumped out of his chair and leaped to the other side of the room. I turned just in time to see a lamp crash against the floor and shatter.

"What the hell?" I asked, standing up and covering my chest with my arms. My mouth dropped as Xander pinned a guy named John to the floor, raised his fist, and punched him in the face over and over again.

"Xander! What are you doing? Stop! Please, stop!" I ran over and tried to pull Xander off John, but I couldn't. He was too strong.

"Someone help me before he kills him!" I screamed.

Arms wrapped around me, picked me up, and moved me while several other guys pulled Xander off John. I screamed as he lay there unconscious, blood pooling on the floor.

"What did you do? Dammit, what did you do?" I looked at Xander's fist. It was covered in blood. Xander stared at me and then walked into the kitchen.

What had just happened? I sat in the corner as a few of the guys picked John up and took him outside. I wasn't sure where they were taking him, but I hoped it was to the hospital. My God, Xander had almost killed him. Why?

I stood up and leaned against the wall. My legs were still unsteady, but I managed to make it a few steps toward the kitchen. Xander was washing his hands off. Andy gave him a towel.

"What the fuck? Why didn't you stop it, man?" Xander asked.

I stopped before I walked into the kitchen and waited for Andy to reply.

"Are you kidding me? You were in my bathroom getting your dick sucked. Why weren't you out here taking care of your girlfriend?"

Xander turned and slammed Andy against the refrigerator.

"You want me to fucking kill you too?"

My breath hitched, and I stepped back so I couldn't be seen. What was Andy talking about? Xander wasn't the one who'd been touching me?

I backed up, not wanting to hear any more. My stomach churned as I pieced everything together.

*Xander was cheating on me while I was in the same house. And all the guys knew.*

Did they pass the girls around at these parties? Why in the world would John think it was okay to touch me?

I made my way to the front door, grabbed my purse, and walked out. The cold wind slapped me in the face as I pulled on my coat and ran. This was my only chance, and I had to get out while I could. I didn't know what Xander was going to do, and whoever he'd been with, he could just stay with her.

I ran down the driveway and turned left down the street. The rain was coming down harder, and I struggled to see against the darkness. I'd only made it a little way when Xander's truck pulled up and he rolled down the window.

"Get in, Lacey," he demanded.

I stopped and turned toward him. My wet hair clung to my head and rain streamed down my face.

"No," I said.

"Get in the fucking truck and let's go home. I'm not in the mood for your shit."

"My shit? *My* shit? Were you with Brittney? Was she sucking your dick?" I screamed.

The truck lurched to a stop and Xander got out. I stepped backward as he came toward me. His hand connected with my cheek and sent me flying backward. I stumbled and fell flat on my ass. Pain shot through my entire body. He grabbed my hair and jerked me into a standing position.

"Get in the fucking truck and shut the hell up," he hissed.

I whimpered as he led me back to the truck by my hair, put me in the seat, and closed the door.

Silent tears streamed down my cheeks all the way home.

Coming down was a bitch. I still hadn't said another word to Xander. He made coffee while I searched for a towel to make an ice pack for my cheek. I felt like shit. No wonder he was pissed at me. He'd watched another guy feel me up. What the hell had I been thinking?

The morning light filtered through the curtains. I struggled to grasp the idea we'd stayed up all night snorting coke, gambling, and fighting. My life had turned into a secret hell, and I had no way out.

The phone rang and interrupted my thoughts.

"Hello?" Xander asked. "Yeah, is he in the hospital?"

I held my breath and waited.

"Yeah man, thanks for letting me know," Xander said and replaced the phone in the cradle.

"Is John okay?" I asked. "Did anyone tell the cops what happened?"

"He's okay. I broke his nose—that's why there was so much blood."

Xander handed me a small baggie filled with ice. I held it against my cheek as I sat down at the table.

"Now you know why I didn't want you to go. I just got crazy seeing his hands on you, Lacey. You can't be pissed. I was protecting you."

"Who were you with last night? I could smell her perfume," I whispered.

"You're kidding me, right? I went to take a piss, and when I came back, you were acting like a total slut. You just rolled over while John had his hand down your shirt."

I winced at his words. It wasn't the first time I'd been called a slut, though.

"It was the coke, Xander. You know I'd never let anyone else touch me. You know I'm not like that! But apparently you are. How long? How long have you and Brittney been hooking up? The entire time we've been together?" I bit my lip and fought the tears that were pooling in my eyes.

"No! Dammit!" He stood up and kicked the kitchen chair, which clattered to the floor with a bang. I cringed at the noise.

"And it was the coke that made you hit me?" I asked, laying the ice pack down on the table and glared at him.

Xander took one long step toward me, lifted me out of the chair by my shoulders, and slammed me against the kitchen wall. My breath shot out of me as I struggled to regain my footing on the floor.

"Yes, that shit makes me crazy, but so do you. Do you have any fucking idea what it was like seeing him touch you? Seeing you enjoy him kissing your neck and having his hand in your bra? Do you know how much that upset me? You're mine," he whispered as he ran his fingers over my bruised cheek, down my throat, and to the opening of my shirt.

"You're mine," he said again and backed up. He stared at me for a moment as he ran his hand through his hair. Then he turned around and walked into the living room.

I slid down the wall, crumpling to the floor, and swearing I would never use coke again. I never wanted to see his so-called friends again either, especially Brittney, and I never wanted him to go to another party. But I knew better. His nights out were becoming more and more frequent the longer we stayed together.

I picked myself up off the floor and somehow made my way upstairs and into bed. Sleep claimed me Sunday morning.

WHEN I WOKE UP, Xander wasn't in bed next to me.

I showered and made my way downstairs. The house was eerily quiet as I searched for Xander, but he wasn't there. I peeked through the living room curtain and realized his truck wasn't there, either.

*Maybe he left me a note*, I thought.

I wandered back into the kitchen almost relieved he wasn't home, but the longer I searched for a note, the more irritated I became. My shoulders tensed and I warmed up some leftover coffee. Maybe some food would help. But I wasn't really hungry; I just felt like shit.

What had happened the other night? Who had I become? I sipped my coffee as I sat down at the kitchen table and looked at the clock on the stove. It was 11:04 A.M.

I gently rubbed my cheek where he'd smacked me. It was swollen and black and blue. I wasn't sure how I was going to explain it to everyone. *Oh hey, yeah, we were all high and we did some really stupid shit.*

I'd already tried asking him and it didn't work, and that was before I knew there was a lot more going on at those parties. My stomach clenched as I finally considered he was cheating on me.

There was a good possibility I hadn't heard Andy correctly. I was high. Hell, I was so high I couldn't even tell Xander's hand from someone else's. I guess if you really thought about it, I'd cheated on *him* last night, and he'd witnessed it. Plus, I had no proof he was messing around on me at all.

Finishing my coffee, I grabbed the rum, and made a drink. My body felt heavy as I walked into the living room, plopped down on the love seat, and turned on the TV. I missed Emma, but more than that, I missed myself.

Xander and I were so intertwined I didn't know who I was without him. I wanted to call Emma and tell her how crazy everything was, but I knew I wouldn't be able to handle her reaction. And no way in hell could I tell her about last night. She wouldn't understand. I never thought I'd have a life without her in it, but I guess I did now.

"Where the hell do you think you're going?" Xander asked.

"What do you mean? It's Monday, and we have class," I said, frowning at him.

I grabbed my books off the coffee table and stuffed them into my backpack.

"You can't go to class looking like that. Your face is black and blue. I'm not answering a bunch of questions, and neither are you. None of this would've happened if you hadn't gotten high and let some guy feel you up."

"I told you I was sorry. I thought he was you. Please, Xander, I can't stand it when you're mad at me. I can put makeup on the bruise —I'll cover it. Just let me go to class today."

"Nope, sorry," he said. "We can see if it's better by next week."

"Next week? Are you kidding me? I can't miss a week of classes," I said as my voice jumped up an octave.

"Guess you should've thought about that earlier. I'll see if I can get your assignments so you don't get too far behind. Watch some TV until I get home this afternoon, or work on the next chapter in your textbooks. Whatever. I have to go now or I'll be late."

My mouth dropped as I watched Xander walk out the front door and leave me standing there. I couldn't miss an entire week of school. There had to be a solution. I threw my backpack across the room as his truck roared to life and I watched him drive away.

I ran upstairs and grabbed my makeup to try and cover the bruise, but it showed no matter what. Leaning against the sink, I finally allowed the tears to flow. How was I going to make things right with him again? How could I get him to understand I really thought it was him and not John? Nausea rolled in my stomach at the thought of John's hands on me. How was I going to fix this awful mess I'd made?

I stood up and turned the cold water on, splashing my face and patting my skin dry. Then I took a deep breath and gathered the laundry. I could at least clean the house and have a nice dinner ready for him; maybe that would be a good start at repairing the damage I'd done.

By three o'clock, I'd dusted, vacuumed, mopped, cleaned the bathrooms, and finished all the laundry. The house sparkled and smelled amazing. I grabbed my lemon meringue pie recipe and began grating the lemons. It was Xander's favorite.

By five o'clock, I had wrapped the baked potatoes and prepared the steaks. We would be ready to eat by six. I glanced around the kitchen and living room and smiled, wincing slightly as pain shot through my face. Then I made a rum and Pepsi to drink while I waited for him to walk through the front door.

"Hello?"

"Hi," I said, poking my head out of the kitchen and smiled.

"It looks amazing in here. Wow, I should keep you home more often," Xander said and laughed as he closed the door.

"You are so not funny," I said. "I'm making your favorite dinner for you. It'll be done in a few minutes."

Xander entered the kitchen and wrapped his arms around my waist.

"Mmmm, it smells so good," he said as he nuzzled my neck.

I giggled and leaned back into him. It felt like it had been a long time since he'd held me. I turned and peered up at him.

"I guess I know what you did today," he said.

"The house is all clean, the laundry is caught up, and dinner in the oven. I had to do something—I got bored," I said.

"Yeah? I'm pretty sure I can help you after we eat," he said as he leaned down and kissed me.

"Mm, I like the sound of that. I just want things to get better again. I love you."

"I love you too. In fact, I have a little surprise for us tonight."

"You do?" I asked, unable to hide the excitement in my voice. I kissed him as he pulled me in closer.

Heat traveled through my body as our kiss deepened. Maybe he'd had the day to think about everything and he had decided things should get better. Hope filled me. I didn't want to lose him.

I pulled away to take the baked potatoes out of the oven, set the table, and we sat down to eat.

"Were you able to get any of my assignments for me?" I asked.

"No, sorry, babe. I'll see what I can do over the next few days. You know my classes are on the other side of campus. I just didn't have time today."

"Okay." I didn't want to push anything and mess up our evening. So far things had gone well.

We finished eating, and I poured another rum and Pepsi as I cleaned up the kitchen. I joined Xander in the living room after I was finished.

"So, what's this surprise?" I asked, sipping my drink.

"Well, I know the other night was a bit rough, so I was hoping we could have some fun tonight."

I tilted my head and waited for him to continue. He stood up and grabbed his backpack. He opened it and pulled out a small plastic baggie. I realized what it was before he even held it up for me to see.

"What the hell?" I gasped.

"Now wait just a minute. You've gotta try it again. This time it's just us, no one else. Come on. You can at least give me a fun night after the shit you pulled with John."

I gawked at the baggie. Was he insane? I'd barely recovered from Friday evening.

"Don't get all freaked out," he said as he sat back down on the couch. "The sex is fucking amazing. Try it one more time and if you don't like it, fine—I won't ask again."

I stared at him and then looked at the baggie. Was he right? Had we just had a bad night? I wanted to be with him, and I'd do almost anything to move past the episode with John. But not this. I couldn't.

"I've been drinking. I made a rum and Pepsi while cooking tonight. You said I shouldn't mix the two."

"Shit, I didn't even notice. I guess you always have a drink in your hand, huh?"

"What? We drink together," I retorted.

He stared at me for a minute and then opened the baggie, put some on the coffee table, and began cutting it.

"Wait. You're going to use without me?"

He ignored me, leaned over, and snorted a line. "Yup, that's exactly what I'm doing. You don't need to be high for me to fuck you."

"Baby," I whispered. "Please, we were having a good night. Can't we figure things out? I want to be with you, but not while you're high. Xander, making love to you is everything to me, but not like this."

"Making love?" Xander laughed. "You think that's what we do?"

My face clouded with confusion.

"Don't you love me?" I whispered.

He leaned his head back on the couch and smiled. I bit my lip as I waited for him to say something, but he sat in silence.

"Xander?"

"What?"

"Don't you love me?"

"Well, I sure as shit don't when you're fucking nagging me. I just wanted to get past everything, figured we could have a little fun, and now you're whining again. I hate it when you whine. Can you even hear yourself? Your voice changes and you sound like a little girl. You're almost twenty. When the fuck are you going to grow up?"

My mouth dropped as his words cut into me like knives. I'd rather have him hit me again than hear the words he'd just spoken to me.

Xander stood up and grabbed his backpack. He put the baggie inside the hidden zipper.

"Well, since you're being a drag, I'm outta here."

"What? What do you mean? I thought we were going to spend the evening together?"

"Guess not," he said as he pulled his keys out of his pocket and walked out the front door.

3 3

I sat in the dark as I heard the front door open. At least he'd made it home by 4 A.M.—I guess it was progress. I didn't have to ask where he'd gone; I already knew.

His footsteps were heavy as he approached me from behind the love seat.

"What are you still doing up?" he asked as he sat down beside me.

I scanned his face to see if he was still high. A small sigh of relief escaped me. He didn't seem coked out.

"I was waiting for you," I whispered.

He leaned his head back and stared into the darkness.

"Did you win or lose tonight?" I asked.

"I lost my ass," he said as he rubbed his face.

My stomach flipped as I thought I smelled a slight hint of perfume. Maybe I was wrong, though—it was so subtle I wasn't sure. I leaned forward and kissed his cheek, confirming my suspicion. My eyes didn't leave his face as I leaned back into my seat.

"Who is she?" I asked.

"What? You're gonna start that shit again as soon as I walk in the house?"

"Who is she? Is it Brittney?" I asked, my voice barely above a whisper.

Xander put his feet up on the coffee table and stared straight ahead.

"What can I do?" I asked. "Why don't you want me anymore? Is this about John? I've told you I'm sorry over and over again. I don't know how to fix it," I said as tears slipped down my face.

"Are we really going to do this now?"

"Yes. Yes we are. I need to know. The only time you want to be with me is when you're high. Am I that bad? What's so wrong with me you don't even want to screw me?" I hiccupped.

"It's not you. There's just a lot of complicated shit going on."

"So you're telling me it's not my fault you're fucking Brittney?"

Xander leaned forward and put his head in his hands.

"Is this it?" I continued. "Are we over? Have you made your choice, and you're going back to her?" I wiped away the tears now flowing freely down my cheeks.

"Don't cry. It's . . . I'm all fucked up. There's just . . ." He paused for a moment. "No, we're not over. It only happened tonight, and it just got out of control. I'll stay away from her. I'll tell Andy I don't want to be there if she's there. I screwed everything up tonight, and I'm so so sorry," he said as regret filled his face.

"You're breaking my heart. God, I don't think I can do this anymore," I said, covering my face.

"What? No! Don't say that," he pleaded as he turned toward me. His brown eyes were rimmed with red. Was he crying?

"I'm not sure we can fix this," I said and shook my head.

He wiped his eyes and tried to clear the tears.

"Babe, don't leave me. I can't take it if you do. I love you. You're everything to me. It's over with her, I promise."

"How can I believe you?"

"I'll stop everything. If you promise you won't leave me, I'll stop the coke, and I won't see her again. Please."

I put my head in my hands and cried quietly. How could I forgive him? He'd just admitted to cheating on me with Brittney. What the hell was it with girls named Brittney?

"I'm going to bed. You can do whatever the hell you want," I said, standing up and leaving him sitting alone on the love seat. My head throbbed while I walked up the stairs, slipped into the guest room, and locked the door behind me. I crawled underneath the covers and cried myself to sleep.

THE AFTERNOON SUNLIGHT streamed through the curtains, and I rubbed my eyes. There was no good reason for me to wake up. I didn't want to get out of bed and face my screwed-up life. My heart ached as I lay there and stared at the ceiling. Our conversation replayed through my head.

Tossing off my covers, I rubbed my bare feet on the rug. I wanted to feel something other than pain and focus on the soft fabric against my skin; anything that might feel good.

My stomach growled, and I unlocked the door and made my way downstairs and into the kitchen.

"Hey," Xander said.

I jumped at the sound of his voice. "What the hell are you doing here? Shouldn't you be at school? You scared the crap out of me."

"Sorry," he said as he ran his hand through his hair. "I didn't want to go. You weren't in our bed, and after last night, I couldn't leave you. I can't lose you. So, I thought if I stayed home, maybe we could talk about everything and move forward."

I shook my head as I grabbed a coffee mug and filled it. "And how are we going to move forward? How do you think I'm going to be able to do that?" I asked, leaning against the kitchen counter. The idea of sitting with him at the table wasn't appealing. I needed some space.

"I meant what I said this morning. I won't even be around her. It was a stupid mistake. We were coked up, and it happened, but it was the first time."

I winced at his words.

"Stop it. I don't want to hear another word about her." My jaw clenched at the thought of them together.

"Okay, I understand. I got crazy over John, so I can't imagine how you're feeling right now. Just please tell me we can fix this," he pleaded.

I paced across the kitchen as I tried to find the right words. My stomach churned as I thought about my life without him, but I couldn't allow him to cheat on me, either.

"*If*, and I mean if, I decide to give you one more chance, no more coke, no more women except me, and no more late nights at Andy's or anywhere else. If you want me, then you have to act like it. I'm tired of being treated like your whore. You either love me or you don't. And you have to tell me now."

"I love you. I do. No more late nights, no more Brittney, and no more drugs. I swear, just please tell me you'll give me another chance."

I sighed and stared at him. If I were honest with myself, I wanted things to get better, I loved him. He'd become my entire world, and I couldn't stand the thought of him not being it in. What if he really did stop using? Would it fix everything?

"Okay. *One* more chance," I said, placing my coffee cup on the table.

Xander stood up so fast his chair almost toppled over. He grabbed me and picked me up. I wrapped my legs and arms around him while he hugged me. His fingers dug into my back as we clung to each other.

I blinked my tears away as he sat me down.

"I'm taking you out tonight."

"I can't go anywhere until my cheek gets better."

He gently ran his fingers across my bruise.

"I'm so sorry," he whispered.

I grabbed his hand and squeezed it. "It's over, right? It won't happen again, so let's not dwell on it. I just want us to move past this and let things get better."

Xander leaned down and kissed me. "I have an idea. I'll be back in a little while."

My eyebrows knitted together in confusion. Was he leaving again? Would he be back? Was he already going back on his word?

"Hey, it's okay. I'm running to school, and I'll be right back. I have an idea, and if it works, we'll be going out tonight."

He kissed me goodbye and walked out the door once again.

3 4

The door opened again forty-five minutes later.

"Xander?" I asked, confused. He never went out for only a short time unless it was to the liquor store.

"Hey, babe. I'm back."

I stared at him as he came into the living room and sat down with me on the love seat.

"Listen. I have good and bad news. Which do you want first?"

I bit my lip and searched his face.

"The bad," I whispered.

"I ran into your mom on campus."

My eyes widened as his words registered.

"What? Oh my God! Why won't she give up and leave me alone?"

The thought of running into her again sent chills through me. I rubbed my arms in an attempt to warm up.

"It's okay, babe. I talked to her."

"What?" I asked and leaned toward him. He had my full attention.

"When I saw her, I walked right up to her."

"Did she remember you from that day?"

"Oh yeah. I don't think she likes me much," Xander said and chuckled.

I scooted over and closed the gap between us.

"She doesn't like guys much in general, so I wouldn't take it personally."

"Trust me, I'm not gonna live my life based on your mother's opinion of me."

"Was Patsy with her?"

"Yeah, they were close to PLC Hall, where I have my English class. When I spotted them, I walked right up to her and asked what the hell she wanted."

"Oh my God! You did? You actually said that to her?" Xander had just become my hero. No one ever talked to Mama like he had.

"Yup."

"And?" I asked as I lightly patted his arm to continue.

"She said she wanted to see you, and she wasn't going to stop until she could sit down and talk to you."

I rolled my eyes. Mama wanting to talk meant her telling you what was wrong with you and how to fix it. It was always a one-sided conversation.

"What did you say?"

Xander ran his hand through his hair and smiled.

"I told her if she showed up again, I would not only call campus security, but I'd call the police. And I told her you no longer lived on campus and if you were interested in contacting her, you would. But until then, she needed to stay away from you or she would have bigger problems to deal with."

"Ohhh! I wish I could've seen her face!" I squealed. "Thank you. But if that was the bad news, then what's the good?" I was unable to hide the excitement in my voice.

Xander reached into his pocket and pulled out a small makeup compact. I frowned as he handed it to me.

"It's concealer from the drama department," he said. "It's way better at covering than the stuff you have. A few dabs and your bruise won't show, which also means you can go back to class."

"Really?" I asked, opening it. "I'm gonna go try it," I said. I kissed him on the cheek and ran up the stairs to the bathroom.

A few minutes later, I walked back into the living room and smiled.

"What do you think?"

Xander stood up and tilted my chin toward him. He turned my face to the left and then to the right. "That's some good shit."

"I know, right?" I said and beamed up at him.

"Go get changed. We should go out."

I jumped up and down and then wrapped my arms around his neck.

"I love you. Thank you for taking care of Mama and getting the makeup for me."

"Love you too," he said as he kissed the tip of my nose.

I ran upstairs, all smiles. This was the Xander I'd fallen in love with. I'd missed him so much. Hopefully things would be good for a while now. I'd do everything in my power to make him happy.

I smiled as I approached George, who was waiting for me on the steps outside of our health class.

"Girl, I'm pissed at you," George said as he hugged me. "Where the hell have you been? Have you been sick? I couldn't even find Xander to see why you weren't in class."

"Yeah, but I'm all better now," I said, smiling. The pain had lessened, but I was still aware of my bruise. Thank goodness it had faded a little bit—with the makeup, no one could see it.

"You'll never believe who I talked to," George said. His smile lit up his entire face.

"Who?"

"Andy!"

My face fell as I remembered the conversation I'd had with Andy. I'd told him to call George. Crap, what had I done? Andy used coke as much as Xander, and I didn't want that for George. He deserved better.

"Lacey?"

"Yeah?"

"I know that look on your face. What's going on? Why aren't you happy for me?"

"Oh, I'm so sorry. I can't tell you how I know this, but Andy isn't the right guy for you."

"What are you talking about? He said you were the one who told him to call me."

"I did, but it was before I knew him very well."

"What do you mean? You know him well now?" he asked, as his brow furrowed.

"I know more than I'd like to. Listen. I can't explain it, but he's not a good guy, and I don't want you to get involved with him."

George frowned as he took a step backward. "You're serious, aren't you? And why can't you tell me?"

"Because it's not my place. It also involves a lot of other people. Just please trust me and don't go out with him."

He shook his head as he stared at me.

"I don't get it. You used to tell me everything, but I don't even know who you are anymore. Xander is almost always with you, you don't go anywhere except school and home, you skip classes, and you're secretive."

He paused as he kicked at the ground. "Well, I guess if you decide I'm worthy of your friendship and you can trust me, come find me," he said as he turned and walked into the building.

My mouth hung open as I watched him walk away. What had just happened? What was he even talking about? I hadn't changed. The situation was intense, and I couldn't tell him about Andy without implicating myself and Xander for having illegal drugs. I bit my lip and made it up the stairs and into class.

I slipped into my normal seat next to George, but he refused to look at me.

"What's with you two?" Adalyn asked as she entered the class and sat in her seat.

"Nothing, it was just a misunderstanding," I muttered.

"Mmm, I don't think you can misunderstand that expression on his face. He looks pissed."

My shoulders slumped and I leaned back in my seat.

"He said I've changed," I said, glancing at her.

"You have—you're totally different since you started dating Xander. Hell, we never see you anymore except in class. You pretty much disappeared."

"I didn't mean to."

"Look who decided to join us today," Megan said as she slipped into her seat across the aisle from me.

"Hey," I said and attempted a smile.

Megan leaned forward and peered at George, who continued to stare straight ahead.

"You two fighting?"

I loved how they both just spoke their mind.

"I guess so," I said, glancing at him. He was really upset with me. I couldn't do this.

"Okay, let's go," I said as I stood up, grabbed George's hand, and dragged him out of class and into the closest women's bathroom.

"What the hell?" George screeched.

"Hush," I said, checking for feet under the stalls and confirmed we were alone.

If Xander found out about this I'd tell him what happened, but I needed to fix things with George. I didn't have a lot of friends, and I couldn't lose him.

"Oh, your bathroom is way better than the men's. Much cleaner," he said, suddenly distracted as he took everything in.

"Come on, seriously. We have to discuss this. You're my best friend out here, and I can't deal with us not talking."

He glared at me as he leaned against a sink.

"I'll tell you how I know about Andy, but you have to promise me you won't tell anyone. Remember our deal—you can't tell the girls, or your brother, or his cat," I said as I attempted a smile.

"I'm waiting," he replied as he crossed his arms in front of his chest and tilted his head.

"Well, things got all messed up. It's better now, but barely, and I'm scared if I tell you about it you're gonna open your mouth and get me into trouble."

"Fine, we don't even have to have this conversation," he said as he turned and walked toward the door.

"No, please stay. I'll tell you."

He stopped and returned to lean on the sink.

"Xander and I were at a party. We were actually at Andy's house." I paused, contemplating if I was doing the right thing. One glance at George and I decided it was.

"There were a lot of people there, including Brittney."

"Go on," he said, motioning for me to hurry up.

"The guys were playing poker, and I was at the card table with Xander. Anyway, Andy had some cocaine, so we all started doing lines."

"I'm so sorry, like, back the fuck up because I could've sworn you just said you guys were doing cocaine."

I closed my eyes for a minute. Maybe I shouldn't have said anything. Well, it was too late now.

"That's what I said. I was high when I told Andy to call you. I'm so sorry, George. I just got really chatty, and I wasn't thinking straight. Then, after everything was over, I realized I'd screwed up. I would never want you to date someone who was using drugs," I gushed.

"But are you? I mean, cocaine? Really? Like, what the hell is happening to you?"

"I know. It was one night and it was so stupid. I can't even tell you how stupid. The whole night was . . ." I couldn't tell him any more.

"What about Xander? You thought he was using a while ago, so is he?" he asked as his eyebrows knitted together.

"Not anymore," I whispered.

"Hey! Look at me," George demanded as he stomped his foot. "This is important, dammit."

I glanced at him and then down at the floor. I couldn't stand to see his disappointment.

"What's he doing to you?"

"No, it's not like that. I promise," I said, shaking my head.

"It sure as hell looks like it from here."

"Things got bad for a little while, but it's fine now. We're doing a lot better."

"How bad? And no sugarcoating it. Tell me the truth," he demanded, putting his hands on his hips.

I walked over to the paper towels, pulled one down, wet it, and gently removed a small part of the makeup revealing my bruise. Tears began to stream down my face I turned toward him.

"Shit," he whispered as his eyes scanned my cheek. "Please tell me he didn't do this to you."

"I can't tell," I hiccupped through my tears. "This is why I wasn't at school. That night at the party got completely out of control. I thought Xander had . . . had slipped his hand down my shirt, but it wasn't him. It was this guy named John, and when Xander saw him he beat the shit out of him. I thought he was going to kill him. It was horrible. There was blood everywhere, and a few other guys had to pull him off John. I was high and panicked. I took off running, out of Andy's house and down the street in the pouring rain. It was pitch black, and I couldn't see very well. The next thing I knew, Xander pulled up in his truck and told me to get in. I was so terrified after what he did to John that I said no. Then . . . this," I said as I pointed at my cheek.

I wiped my tears away and began reapplying the drama makeup to my bruise.

"That's not okay," he whispered. "Are you in danger? I know someone who can help if we need to get you out."

A sad smile spread across my face, and I shook my head.

"I'm okay, and it won't happen anymore. He promised me, no more parties or coke. The coke makes him a different person. He gets mean when he's using, but we've worked things out, and we're okay now. It's been good again. I feel like I'm back with the guy I fell in love with," I said.

"You can't stay. Please tell me you want to leave him."

"It's not like that, and this is why I didn't want to tell you. It wasn't Xander who hit me, it was the stupid coke, and as long as he isn't using, he's fine. Please, I'm okay. It won't ever happen again."

"Did Walker ever hit you?"

"What? Walker? Where did this come from?"

"Because you don't stay with someone who abuses you. Normal people *don't stay*."

"What? Now I'm not normal? Oh my God, don't blow this out of proportion. I told you it's over. He's not getting high anymore."

"Answer me, though. Did Walker ever hit you?"

I rubbed my forehead. "No," I said as I glanced at George. "Walker, at least until the end, treated me better than anyone ever has."

"Did your mom ever hit you?"

"Yeah, I guess, is that what you wanna hear? She's hit me before?"

"Lacey, I'm not trying to be an ass. I'm trying to get you to see this is important, and you need help. You wouldn't stay with someone like him if you weren't already used to it."

"I have no idea what you're talking about, but this conversation is over. The only reason I even told you was because of Andy. And after seeing your reaction, you can understand why I was being secretive."

I closed the compact and tossed it back into my bag. "I miss you and I want to tell you things, but this—I pointed to my cheek—was a one-time incident. You need to trust me."

He closed the gap between us and hugged me. I wrapped my arms around him and hugged him back. My heart ached as I realized how much I missed him. He'd been my first friend in Oregon, and I'd lost so much already. I wasn't willing to let him go, too.

"Promise me—not another word about it, and you won't tell anyone, ever," I said.

"I promise, but only on one condition."

"What?"

"If it happens again, if he hurts you in any way, you'll tell me and let me help you."

"And how are you gonna do that? Where am I gonna go? Mama's still searching for me. Xander ran into her the other day. I'm not safe here."

"You're not safe with him, either," he said.

"Enough!"

"Okay, I'm sorry, but promise me you'll tell me if anything happens again. If you do, then I won't tell anyone about this conversation."

I held his gaze as I mulled over my options.

"Promise," I said.

"Me too," he said.

"Okay, so are we good again?"

"Yes, we'd better get you out the front door before Xander comes to meet you."

I nodded in agreement and checked my bruise coverage one last time before we left the bathroom.

George grabbed his books from the now-empty classroom as I waited by the door.

"You two all better now?" Megan asked as she entered the hallway.

"Yeah," I said and smiled. "Like I said, it was all a misunderstanding."

"Yup, it's all good," George said as he joined us.

I didn't miss the expression he shot me as we all walked outside.

The May sunshine peeked through the trees and warmed my back. I couldn't believe we only had six weeks of school left and then we'd be out for the summer.

Xander had stayed true to his word, and for the last month, everything between us had been better. There hadn't seen any signs of him using, and he'd stopped staying out all night. He was still moody, but nothing compared to before. I made sure I didn't piss him off, too, which helped.

I'd taken to digging in the dirt for something to do. Xander had given me a designated area in the front yard where I could plant flowers. He had such a beautiful home, but it needed a splash of color.

Slipping on my garden gloves, I carried my rose bushes to the place I'd dug for them. The roses reminded me of home, and I'd chosen a pink-and-white variety to plant. I hummed as I moved the dirt and prepared to plant the bushes. Xander had just left to run errands, and I was enjoying my time alone.

A car pulled into the driveway, and I peered over my shoulder. I shaded my eyes with my hand and squinted, but I couldn't make out who it was until it was too late.

"Where's Xander?" Agnus asked as he stepped out of the Mustang.

I took a step backward and my foot slipped into one of the shallow holes I'd dug for the rose bushes. My ankle twisted, and I fell against the house, wincing. I leaned against the wall as they approached, and realized I had nowhere to go.

"Ah, look, Mike. Goldilocks hurt her ankle," Agnus said, laughing.

"Good, it means she can't run," the taller man said.

"Yeah, Mike here is getting impatient with your boyfriend, so I think you need to help us out so we can stop bothering you," Agnus said as he rubbed his chin.

"What do you want?" I asked unable to control the shaking in my voice.

"Well, I don't know if you know this or not, but your boyfriend is causing a lot of trouble, and he's pissing people off."

"Yeah? He pisses me off too," I muttered.

Agnus took a few steps toward me. Chills traveled down my spine as he stared at me. I didn't know how, but I had to get to the front door. I glanced at Mike as he stood still, his hand on his gun.

"I can't tell you what you want if I don't know who you are."

"Little girl, you don't want to know who we are," he replied.

Agnus closed the gap between us and ran his fingers down my cheek.

"He'll kill you if you touch me again," I said as my body betrayed me and trembled.

"He can't touch me, and he knows it," Mike said. "In this world, Xander Koffman ain't shit," he chuckled as his finger slowly moved down my neck and to the top of my shirt. "But, you . . . how in the world did he get so lucky?"

"Don't you think she's beautiful, Mike? Maybe we don't need to wait for Xander. Hell, maybe we can take her instead. It might be a fair trade."

"I'm not property you can just take!" I yelled.

Agnus's hand covered my mouth, and he leaned into me. I shuddered as his body trapped me against the house.

"The only talking you get to do is telling me where Xander is. And the only thing that's going to save you is I have a boss to answer to, and he wants his money. So, I'm going to remove my hand, and you're going to be a good girl and tell me where your sorry excuse for a boyfriend is." He stared at me as he slowly removed his hand.

"I don't know," I said. "He left about thirty minutes ago. I have no idea when he'll be back or where he went. He said he had errands to run."

Agnus laughed and stepped backward.

"What do you think? You think she's telling us the truth? I say we take a look inside the house and see if he's acting like a scared bitch and hiding somewhere. Don't let her move. I'll be right back."

I watched in horror as Agnus walked up the porch steps and right into our home. Would he take anything? Were they going to rob us? What did they want Xander for? What money? My head pounded with every question.

I stared at Mike. He hadn't moved, but I had no doubt he could outrun me in a split second—especially since I'd be running on a twisted ankle.

"She's telling the truth," Agnus said as he closed the door behind him. "Let's go, Mike. I think I know where he might be."

I stayed glued to the side of the house until their car disappeared from sight. I slid onto the ground, rolled down my sock, and grabbed my ankle. It had already begun to swell. My eyes squeezed shut, and I bit my lip, refusing to cry.

I leveraged the wall of the house and stood up. Somehow, I put the rose bushes in their holes, but didn't bother covering them up. I hobbled up the porch steps and into the house and turned the deadbolt behind me. Hobbling into the kitchen, I pulled the ice tray from the freezer. With a quick twist, the cubes loosened, and I dumped thems into a kitchen towel. Then I grabbed the rum bottle as I hobbled to a chair and sat down.

I slipped off my shoe and situated the towel on my ankle. It hadn't swollen anymore, and I hoped it would be okay by tomorrow. I twisted the cap off the rum bottle, took a drink from it, and winced as it burned its way down my throat. My shoulders shuddered as I took another swig and placed the bottle on the table.

What in the hell was I going to do about Mike and Agnus? I didn't want to tell Xander again. He would lose his temper, and things had gone so well lately. How much money did Xander owe them? My ankle throbbed as I contemplated what to do. If they showed up again, hopefully I wouldn't be outside.

I laughed out loud. I knew damn well they'd be back, and it scared the shit out of me.

Xander walked through the front door, and I took another drink.

"Hey, babe, I'm home," he yelled.

"I'm in the kitchen," I replied.

"Well, what have we here?" Xander asked as he put some bags on the table and kissed me on the forehead.

"Ugh," I said, rubbing my forehead. "I wasn't paying any attention and stepped into the hole I'd dug for the bushes. How stupid was that?" I asked and laughed. "I don't think it's too bad, but I wanted to put it up and get some ice on it."

Xander picked up the towel and turned my foot from one side to the next.

"I don't think it's bad, but you should stay off it. Which means I'm really glad I picked up dinner for us while I was out."

"I was about to ask you what smelled so good."

"Chinese," he replied as he pulled several small containers out of the bag.

"Thank you!" I said, grabbing some chopsticks and opened the containers. I dipped my chopsticks into the chow mein and took a bite.

"Are you hungry?" Xander asked.

"I'm starving! Guess I worked up an appetite digging in the dirt," I said and grinned.

I wanted to tell Xander about Mike and Agnus, but I was terrified it would ruin his good mood. Maybe I could test the waters.

I waited until Xander had filled his plate with food and taken a few bites.

"Did you go anywhere exciting other than to get our dinner?" I asked.

"Not really, everything was pretty busy. I stopped by the bank, grabbed a few groceries, and picked up dinner. Maybe I should've taken you with me and protected you from the war of the rose bushes."

"You're so not funny," I said, glancing at my food and moving it around on my plate. At some point I'd gotten really good at acting. I was scared to death right now, and he thought everything was fine.

"Can I ask you something without you getting mad?"

Xander's chopsticks stopped midair as he stared at me. "What?"

I didn't miss the "tread lightly" tone in his voice, and I took a deep breath.

"A while ago, I told you about two men who showed up and asked for you. Who are they?"

Xander put his food down and ran his hand through his hair. I held my breath and waited for him to respond.

"Nothing you need to be concerned about."

"Please, you can trust me."

"Enough. I'm not mad you asked, but you need to drop it. Don't ever bring it up again, do you understand?" he asked as his jaw tensed.

"Okay," I whispered. He might not be angry now, but if I pushed, it would only be a matter of time.

"I picked up a movie, too," he said, changing the conversation.

"Which one?"

"*Indiana Jones and the Last Crusade.*"

"Oh, it looks really good," I said, following his lead. If he wasn't going to open up about Agnus and Mike, I sure as hell wasn't going to tell him they'd stopped by again. Dealing with his anger would be worse than dealing with theirs. I would just have to take my chances.

"Hang on a minute," Xander said as he stood up and grabbed our plates. He walked to the living room and returned empty-handed. Then he bent over and picked me up out of my chair. I grabbed the bottle of rum as he carried me to the love seat and set me back down.

"Thank you," I said. I placed the alcohol on the coffee table and grabbed my food again. Xander put the movie into the VCR and pushed play as he settled in beside me.

As hard as I tried to focus on the movie, I couldn't. My mind kept wandering back to Agnus and Mike. What if they found Xander? What if they came back? Maybe I should buy some pepper spray, but how would I get any since Xander went everywhere with me? I'd have to ask George. I couldn't tell him about the men, so I'd have to make something up.

I hated the thought of not being honest with George, but he would think I needed it for Xander, and I wasn't interested in his dramatics. Maybe I wouldn't talk to him after all. Adalyn and Megan would be a safer bet. They probably wouldn't even ask why I wanted it. Walking around on campus was a good-enough reason.

We hadn't talked during the movie, but somehow we'd managed to finish the bottle of rum between us.

"Hey, are you asleep?" Xander asked.

"No, not yet," I said and yawned. I hadn't even realized the movie had ended.

"That was a great movie."

I nodded.

Xander stood up and lifted the towel from my ankle.

"It's looking pretty good. I think you'll be fine in a few days, maybe even by tomorrow."

"Good, I don't want you having to carry me across campus."

"I'd just throw you over my shoulder, like this," he said as he grabbed me and tossed me over his shoulder like I was a sack of potatoes.

"Hey!" I squealed. "Put me down," I said as I giggled.

He smacked me on my ass, turned off the TV, and carried me up the stairs and into the bedroom. I laughed as he plopped me on the bed. He stared at me as he removed his shirt and jeans. A smile pulled at the corners of his mouth as he unbuttoned my jeans and slid them down over my hips and legs. I sat up, slipped my shirt over my head, and removed my bra. I tossed them both on the floor.

Xander laid next to me on the bed and teased me through the thin fabric of my red-lace panties.

I dug my fingers into his biceps as he rubbed my clit. No one took me over the edge like he did. I took him in my hand and stroked him.

"I've missed you," he whispered as he lowered his head to my breast. His tongue flicked across my nipple, and I moaned as I arched into him. He trailed soft kisses down my stomach and slid my panties off. I opened my legs and welcomed his warm mouth. My fingers played with his hair as his tongue danced across my clit. He lifted my hips off the bed and quickened his pace. I dug my fingers into the blankets as the familiar feeling began to swirl inside me.

"Oh, Xander . . . baby, I need you inside me," I gasped.

Xander slid his finger inside me as I bucked against him. I couldn't wait any longer, and I lost control. I tried to pull away, but he pinned my hips in place and continued. He held me firmly and continued sucking me, finally stopping a second before I came again. He stood up in front of me and brought me to the edge of the bed. I gasped as he entered me.

"Shit, babe," he said as he moved in and out of me. He closed his eyes, and at that moment my brain betrayed me and I thought about him with Brittney. Was he thinking about her when he was with me? I bit my lip and tried not to think about it, but I couldn't shake the image.

His pace quickened, and I pushed Brittney out of my mind. I focused on how good he felt and reminded myself he was with me right now, not anyone else. *I* was with Xander Koffman, in his bed. Heat flooded through me as his excitement built, and I rocked with him.

"Harder, babe," I whispered.

"Yeah, that's it. Come for me."

I gasped as he leaned over me. I dug my fingers into his back as we moaned and released together. Xander relaxed and settled on top of me. He smoothed my hair away from my face and smiled.

I gazed into his brown eyes and reminded myself he had chosen me.

We got situated on the bed, and I laid my head on his chest as we drifted off to sleep.

My eyes shot open as a fist slammed into my arm.

"What?" I said as I grabbed my arm. "What the hell, Xander?" Tears filled my eyes as my arm throbbed. I glanced at the clock; it was 1:20 A.M. Xander stood up and paced the room.

"What's the matter?" I asked, sitting up in bed, still rubbing my arm.

He turned toward me and glared. I didn't understand why he was pissed. What had I done?

"Are you fucking around on me?"

"What?" I gasped. "No! When would I even have the opportunity? I'm with you all the time, and if I'm not, I'm here waiting for you to come back home. I don't understand how you could even think something like that."

Xander grabbed the flower vase from his dresser and threw it at the wall. I screamed as the glass shattered.

"What's wrong? I don't understand," I said as tears streamed down my face.

He crossed the room and grabbed my shoulders. I flinched as his fingers dug into me.

"You're hurting me. Please let go," I whimpered.

"Who the hell is Walker?" he asked without loosening his grip.

"What?" I gasped. "No one," I said as my heart pounded. How did he know about Walker? I'd always been careful to never mention his name. Had George slipped up and said something?

"Are you screwing him?"

"Please, just let me go and I'll answer any questions you want me to," I pleaded.

Xander released me and took a few steps back. I tried to catch my breath, but my chest ached, and I struggled to calm my breathing.

"Who is he?" he asked again. The calmness in his voice made the hair on the back of my neck stand up. "Is he someone at school?"

I shook my head.

"Answer me! Don't sit there and shake your head. Look me in the eye and tell me you're not fucking him."

"I'm not sleeping with anyone else. Only you." My voice was barely above a whisper as the tears spilled down my cheeks.

"You called for him in your sleep," he said as his jaw tensed.

*Oh my God. Oh my God. What have I done?*

I racked my brain, but I couldn't remember even dreaming about anything. Why would I call out for Walker?

"He lives in Arkansas. We were friends in college. I must have been dreaming about home."

"Arkansas?"

"Yes, he was a friend from back home. Emma knows him—we all hung out together." I hoped I hadn't said anything else other than his name. I'm not sure I could explain if I had. "Come back to bed. We have classes in the morning," I said and patted his side of the bed.

"I can't fucking sleep now," he said as he stormed out of the bedroom.

After I slipped my house shoes on, I grabbed the broom and dustpan from the hall closet. I turned on the bedroom light and swept up the pieces of the vase. My arm smarted as I swept.

Why had I called out for Walker? My stomach flipped at the thought of him. I'd pushed him into the depths of my heart when I'd left Arkansas. When I'd met Xander, Walker had all but slipped away from my thoughts.

As I dumped the dustpan into the trash can, a rush of fear shot through me, but I pushed it aside and returned the broom to the closet. I wasn't expecting Xander to come back to bed tonight.

Exhaustion filled me as I slipped under the covers and then my eyes closed. There was nothing I could do to smooth things over for tonight; I'd have to deal with it tomorrow. I took a deep breath before drifting back to sleep.

THUMP, thump, thump. My eyes fluttered open as I sat up. What in the hell was that noise?

I got up and opened the bedroom door. It was bass: there was music coming from downstairs. It grew louder as I went down the stairs and toward the kitchen.

"Xander! Xander! What are you doing?" I yelled over the music. "It's one-forty in the morning! What are you doing?"

Xander dipped a piece of chicken in flour and placed it in the frying pan.

"You're cooking chicken?" I rubbed my forehead, completely confused.

"I'm too pissed to sleep, and a guy's gotta eat," he retorted.

"Can we turn the music down?" I didn't wait for an answer, but walked into the living room and turned the stereo off. "Now I can hear you. What are you doing?"

"Like I said, I can't sleep, so I'm cooking."

My eyebrows knitted in confusion. I couldn't believe what I was seeing.

"Fine, cook your chicken, but can you keep the music off? We have class tomorrow."

"This is *my* house, Lacey. Or have you forgotten? Why don't you go back to bed and dream about Walker some more?"

"It's not like that. What else do I have to say for you to believe me? The guy is two thousand miles away, and you're upset?"

Xander turned toward me, his icy stare burning holes through me. I rubbed my arms as he stood there without speaking.

The grease began to pop, and he turned the chicken over.

"If I find out there is anything going on . . . I'll kill both of you. What I did to John was nothing compared to what'll be in store for you and *Walker*."

A gasp escaped me as I realized what he'd just said.

"Get out of my sight," he said and waved me away with the spatula.

I wasn't stupid enough to stick around and try to talk to him. I ran upstairs and locked myself in the guest room. If he was really going to hurt me, at least I'd hear him coming.

I crawled into bed and stared into the darkness. Why had I called out for Walker? I rubbed my arm where Xander had punched me. It was the rudest awakening I'd ever had. He apparently didn't trust me, and I had no idea what to do about it.

Seconds after I closed my eyes, loud music and the thump of the bass filled the house again. I grabbed the pillow and covered my head. There wasn't a single thing I loved about Xander Koffman at that moment. In fact, I might have hated him a little.

## 3 8

"How was your weekend?" Megan asked.

"Good, except for this," I said, pointing to my foot. "I twisted my ankle."

"What?" George asked as he entered the classroom and sat in his seat next to me.

"I twisted my ankle while planting rose bushes, and I accidentally stepped into the hole I dug," I said and rolled my eyes. "I've never been the most graceful person in the world, but it's doing a lot better. It's still pretty sore, though."

"Hey," Adalyn said as she joined us.

"Lacey had a boring weekend except she twisted her ankle," Megan said to Adalyn.

"That was stupid," Adalyn said as she smacked me on the shoulder.

I yelped and grabbed my arm.

"Geez, you'd think a country girl would be a little tougher," Adalyn said, laughing.

"You would think, huh?" I said and stared down at my desk. No way would I even dare a look at George. He would take one look at me and know something was wrong.

I rubbed my arm and opened my textbook. The girls chatted with

191

George until the professor walked in. I peeked out of the corner of my eye at George, but he was focused on the instructor. Maybe he hadn't pieced anything together.

Xander was waiting for me after class. I waved goodbye to everyone, and he took my hand as we walked toward the truck. Maybe he was seeing reason, but I couldn't tell with him. He hadn't spoken to me since he'd decided to fry chicken in the middle of the night.

Half an hour later, we pulled into the driveway and entered the house. I put my books on the coffee table and went to the kitchen to grab a Pepsi.

"I'm still pissed," he said as he followed me.

I sighed and grabbed the rum from the cabinet. I poured us both one and handed it to him.

"Would it help you feel better if I told you he was married? And I was friends with his family back home until his mom died? Would that make things better?"

"He's married? How old is he?"

"Twenty-one, I think."

"Shit, why in the hell did he do that?"

"No clue. He married his high-school sweetheart right before his mom died. I assumed it was because he wanted his mom there, but I don't really know. It's been over a year since I've talked to him."

"Then why'd you call out for him last night?"

"Hell if I know," I said as I took a swig of my drink. "Sometimes I get homesick. I had a wonderful group of friends—Emma, Joss, Walker, Tammy . . ." I smiled as my mind drifted back to the times I'd had with them. My heart ached. I missed them so much. I loved Oregon, but here, I only had George—sort of—and Xander.

"I've never given you a reason not to trust me," I continued.

Xander laughed. "Yeah? And I should trust you after John? You seemed like you enjoyed it."

"I thought that was over, and I didn't screw him. And have you already forgotten what *you* did?" I said as I glared at him. "Only one of us had sex with someone else, and here you are punching me in the arm because I said some other guy's name, even though he lives two thousand miles away. What the hell is wrong with that picture?"

"Stop being a bitch," Xander muttered.

My breathing hitched. I was about to cross the line with him, and I couldn't afford any more bruises. My hands raised up in surrender. "I didn't mean to make you mad—I'm just asking for a break. There's nothing going on with anyone else. I'm all yours and only yours."

"Don't forget it, either," he said as he walked out of the kitchen.

I refilled my glass, went into the living room, settled into my spot on the love seat, and grabbed my books. I had a ton of studying to do, and I was grateful for the distraction.

"I'm going out tonight," Xander said as he grabbed his keys from the coffee table.

"What?" I said and closed my book. "You said you weren't going out anymore." Dread filled me at the thought of him at Andy's again.

"I won't be out all night. Don't start your whining. I need to get out of the house for a while. You're suffocating me."

"Are you going to Andy's?"

"I'll be back later," Xander said, ignoring my question.

"Don't go, please. I'm begging you."

Xander didn't respond as he walked out the door. I rubbed my forehead. I had no choice but to wait and see what mood he was in when he came home. He hadn't been to Andy's for a while, at least that I knew of, so maybe he was just going to stop by for a couple of hours.

I turned on the TV and tried to distract myself, but it wasn't working. There was nothing on. I turned it off and watched the darkness settle in across the sky.

My mind returned to Emma and Joss. I needed to call Emma and make things right, but that would mean having to lie to her and tell her how wonderful everything was, and I just didn't have the strength to do it. Joss was more understanding about things, but she wouldn't be okay with Xander either. Her tolerance was seriously low after having to deal with her mother's boyfriends.

A knock at the door startled me from my thoughts. I froze. Xander couldn't possibly be home this soon, and he always used his key to let himself in. The house was dark; I hadn't bothered turning on the lamp yet.

My bare feet didn't make any noise while I crept from the living room into the kitchen. I stayed out of the line of the windows, made my way to the door, and moved the curtain just enough to peek outside. I jumped as someone pounded on the door again.

Mike and Agnus were standing on the porch. A shudder ripped through me. No way in hell was I going to open the door for them, and if I stayed still, they couldn't see me on this side of the window. I watched them as they looked at each other. Agnus hopped off the porch and walked around the side of the house. I pressed myself against the wall as his shadow passed by the windows. Mike pounded on the door again.

Several minutes later, I heard their footsteps heading down the sidewalk and watched as they returned to their car. I stood still, watching them drive away.

I made my way back to the love seat, curled up on it, and left the lights out. I didn't trust they wouldn't be back. Which meant I would just have to wait for Xander.

## 39

I sat up as the front door opened. Xander's footsteps broke the silence as he walked into the kitchen. He turned the light on, and I winced at the sudden brightness.

Startled, he stepped backward as he realized I was sitting on the love seat.

"What the hell are you doing? Why are you sitting in the dark?"

"Waiting for you," I said, staring straight ahead.

"Well, I'm home and it's only midnight. I told you I wouldn't stay out all night," he said as he sat on the couch across from me.

"Yeah," I muttered.

"What the fuck is your problem? You all pissed I went out?"

"Depends on what you did."

He threw his head back and laughed. It was at that moment I knew he was high. I also recognized the perfume.

I shook my head as I stared at him.

"So, this is how it is? I say some guy's name in my sleep, and you go snort coke and screw Brittney?"

"Fuck you, Lacey. You're not gonna do anything about it anyway. I tried it your way for over a month. As long as I give in to whatever you want, then everything is great, but the minute I wanna go hang out with my friends you're a total whiny bitch."

His words pierced my heart, but this time, something inside me snapped.

I jumped up and crossed the room to where he sat. My hands balled into fists as anger overwhelmed me.

"Cheating on me and using coke isn't 'hanging out with your friends,' and I don't deserve to be treated this way."

"You're so naive," he spat.

"Think about this for a minute," he said as he leaned forward. "Nobody wants you around. Oh, wait, except your crazy mother, and God only knows what she'll do to you. And even then, she doesn't want you for who you are. You drive me crazy with your rules, and you think you're better than everyone else. I guess you're good for the occasional fuck, but that's about it. Hell, even then I go elsewhere or take care of myself."

My mouth dropped as I stared at him. Was he serious or was it the coke talking?

"You bastard," I whispered.

Xander shot out of his seat, and I flinched as I covered my head with my arms. He grabbed my shirt and tossed me across the living room. Everything was a blur until I made contact with the coffee table.

Pain exploded inside me and traveled through my shoulder and back. I reached for my head, winced, and then stared blankly at my hand. It was covered in bright-red blood.

Xander crossed the room and straddled me, pinning me to the floor. His lips curled into a snarl as his eyes darkened with hatred. He lowered his face until it was a mere inch from mine.

"Get used to it—this is your life now. And no matter what you tell yourself, I had no remorse about killing my brother, and I won't even think twice about hunting you down if you walk out the door. *You are mine*. Do you understand me?" He grabbed my shoulders and shook me violently.

"You don't mean that," I whispered once he'd let go of me.

"You tell yourself whatever you need to," he said and stood up. I scrambled backward and away from him as fast as I could.

Xander turned and walked away. His footsteps echoed through the hallway as he went up the stairs and slammed the bedroom door. I wiped my bloody hand on my jeans and huddled in the corner the rest of the night, afraid he would come back downstairs and hurt me again.

MORNING FINALLY ARRIVED, and I locked the bathroom door as I showered. My head throbbed, and it took me several extra minutes to wash the dried blood out of my hair. I put my makeup on and used a bit of the heavy concealer for my bruise and under my eyes. I hadn't slept at all, and my eyes were puffy, with dark circles underneath them.

*Thank God for good makeup*, I thought.

I went downstairs and cooked us breakfast. I'd planned on acting as normal as possible; then maybe everything that happened wouldn't come up again. But now, I knew the cycle, and I knew he would be back to normal this morning, or at least I hoped. It'd never gotten as bad as it had last night.

My chest ached as his words about Brittney and how this was my life ran through my head. He might seriously hurt me if I did try to leave. In all the craziness, I'd forgotten to tell him about Mike and Agnus stopping by, but there was no way in hell I was going to tell him now.

"Morning," Xander muttered as he entered the kitchen and filled his coffee cup.

"Hey," I said, placing a few pancakes on his plate. "I figured you might want some breakfast this morning."

"Thank you," he said as he sat down.

I sat across from him and took a few bites of my pancakes. But I didn't feel like eating, and I pushed my food around more than I ate.

We finished our breakfast in silence, and I cleaned up the kitchen as Xander went back upstairs. I was ready to leave for class by the time he came back down.

## 40

Unfortunately, I didn't see George or the girls on campus. We only had class together three days a week, so I wouldn't see them again until tomorrow.

I couldn't stop George's words as they played through my head on a loop. He was right: I had changed, and all for Xander. I thought he loved me and wanted to protect me from Mama, but now I wasn't sure which one of them was worse.

What would happen if I did leave him? I had nowhere to go. I couldn't call Emma and simply ask to come home, and it would break her parents' heart if they knew what kind of trouble I'd gotten into. George and the girls couldn't help me without putting themselves in danger, and I couldn't do that to them. Mama would keep me safe from Xander, but who would keep me safe from her? There was nowhere to hide anymore.

I'd manage to re-create my own personal hell.

There were only four more weeks of school left, and I had to figure something out before then. At least I saw George during the school year, but that wouldn't be the case in the summer. I would be cut off from everyone I knew. I had no job, no car, and no place to live.

My laugh split the silence. Who the hell was I kidding thinking I could ever make it out of his front door?

Xander met me after class and walked me back to the truck. We only spoke when necessary, and the silence hung in the air between us as we drove home. He pulled into the driveway and he shifted the truck into park.

"Get out," he said without looking at me.

"You're not coming in?" I asked, reaching for the truck's door handle.

"Don't bother waiting up, I won't be home tonight."

Tears pooled in my eyes and I quickly turned away before he could see. I hopped out of the truck and went into the house, locking it behind me as I heard his truck drive away. Suddenly relief flooded through me at the thought of him not being home. I wasn't sure what to expect tomorrow, but tonight I would curl up on the couch and sleep.

My backpack slipped off my shoulder and I tossed it on the floor. Then I went to the kitchen, grabbed the rum, and took a deep swallow straight from the bottle. I walked to the hall closet and grabbed a spare pillow and blanket. Even though he said he wouldn't be back until tomorrow, I didn't trust him. I'd be safer on the couch. At least he couldn't sneak up on me if he did come home.

I made my bed and took another drink. It was only 7 P.M., but every part of me ached, including my heart. Life had mentally and physically drained me. I stretched out on the couch and fell asleep within minutes.

THE MORNING LIGHT streamed through the living-room curtains and woke me. I rubbed my eyes as I sat up. Xander hadn't come home, just like he'd said. Although, I was still tired, but I felt a little better. The clock read 8:16 A.M. I stretched, realizing I still had plenty of time to shower and eat before classes. Xander would be back to pick me up soon, and I needed to talk to George. I'd made a promise to him and I needed to keep it, no matter how he reacted.

After a hot shower fresh clothes, I felt better. I made some eggs and coffee and waited for Xander. I grew restless as the time passed and he still hadn't shown up. We were going to be late for class. Had he gone without me? *Shit.*

A few hours later, I realized I wasn't going anywhere, and I wouldn't see George until after the weekend. I was screwed.

EVERY EMOTION possible coursed through me over the next thirty-six hours. Not only had Xander not bothered to call, I didn't hear from him once. I knew he was angry about Walker, but I was at a complete loss as to how I could earn his trust back. And what did *I* want?

I had run every scenario through in my head, including leaving or staying and what either of those choices might look like. But no matter what, I could no longer dismiss the nagging in the pit of my stomach. As much as I tried to stop it, my mind wandered back to Walker. Were he and Brittany still married? Had he asked about me again? But those were dangerous thoughts, and I quickly pushed them aside. No matter what, things would never be the same.

I slept on the couch all weekend in case Xander came home or Mike and Agnus showed up again, but the house was quiet and peaceful, which gave me time to think.

Loneliness crept over me with every hour that passed. I glanced at the phone every time I was in the kitchen, wishing I could reach George and the girls. *Maybe I should patch things up with Emma,* I thought, but I couldn't. What would they all think if I told them the truth, anyway?

The door finally opened on Sunday around 11 A.M. Xander's keys jangled as he placed them on the kitchen table. The fall of his footsteps let me know he'd gone upstairs. He didn't even bother to come back down when he must've noticed I wasn't in the bedroom.

## 41

"Hi," Xander said as he wrapped his arms around me.

"Hi?" My eyebrows knitted together. I poured my coffee, grabbed a cup for him too, filled it, and handed it to him.

He released me and accepted it. I stared at him as he pulled a kitchen chair out and sat down.

"Did you have a nice weekend?" I asked softly.

"Yeah, I just needed a break. I had to think some things through, and I couldn't do that here. I knew you were okay—I'd just done the grocery shopping. So I took the opportunity and left."

My eyes narrowed, and I sipped my coffee. I had no idea what to expect from him anymore. He'd most likely stayed at Andy's, and with Brittney.

"I think I needed the break too. I'm tired of fighting," I said, placing my cup on the table.

"I didn't see her."

"What?" I asked and tilted my head as I waited for his response.

"I didn't see her this weekend."

"Oh? Was she out of town?" I retorted. I bit my lip and reminded myself where talking back had gotten me the last several times. "I'm sorry," I said. "I shouldn't have said that."

"I don't know where she was, but I wasn't with her or anyone else. Like I said, I needed time to think."

"And?"

"I think it's what I needed, and I'm back."

"What does that mean, exactly?" I asked, more confused than ever.

"I'm home. I want to be here, I want to be with you and work things out."

My stomach tightened at his words. What if I didn't want the same thing anymore?

I stood up slowly and walked toward him. He reached out, took my hand, and pulled me into his lap.

"I love you," he whispered.

"I love you too," I replied, laying my head on his shoulder.

We sat together for several minutes and then grabbed our books and headed out the door to go to school.

❧❦❧

XANDER WASN'T in any hurry to walk me to my building; he held my hand as we strolled across campus. I wanted to talk to George in health class, but I was going to be late at this point, and now I would be lucky if I could even find an open seat. I sighed softly as irritation rose inside me.

We finally got to my building, and he pulled me in for a deep kiss. I smiled as he let me go. At least for this morning, I had my Xander back.

I waved goodbye, walked into the building, and slipped into my class. I scanned the back of everyone's head and searched for George. Finally spotting him, I noticed the empty seat next to him. The moment the professor to turned his back, I hurried down the aisle and slipped into the seat next to George. I spotted Megan and Adalyn across the room and gave them a quick wave.

George's eyes lit up when he saw me, and he reached for my hand. I squeezed it before letting it go and pulling my notebook out of my backpack. Then, I scribbled something on a piece of paper and quietly tore it out of my notebook, sliding it over to George.

My attention remained focused straight ahead as I heard the paper being unfolded. George gasped and then whispered, "Let's go. We need to talk, right now."

"I KNOW WHO CAN HELP," George murmured as we quietly closed the door to the classroom.

My shoulders tensed as I glanced around at the other people milling around in the hallway. I wasn't sure if Xander followed me or if he had other people do it, but I was terrified someone would hear us talking.

"I don't know how," I whispered. "I can't get anyone else involved."

"No, I actually know someone who can help. We just have to figure out how to get you to her."

"Who's we? I don't think you understand how risky this is."

"I do, and the girls are gonna help too, so we need to tell them."

"How am I going to do that? He's everywhere."

"Looks like we need another meeting in the bathroom."

I laughed as I remembered the expression on George's face when I pulled him into the women's restroom for our last meeting.

"Okay, but you're going to have to get them together. If we're gonna do this, you all will have to do most of it. He knows when I skip class, and where I am at all times. I'm not sure how we're gonna pull it off."

"You're going to have to trust me."

"I do. I trust you," I said. Even though I trusted him, I was terrified we would get caught.

"Go to the bathroom and wait for us." He pointed to the same bathroom we'd used the last time. "I'll go get the girls—it'll just take a minute—and we'll meet you there."

I nodded and walked down the hallway and into the bathroom as casually as I could.

"He can't do this to me," the girl cried.

"It'll be okay. He was a loser anyway," her friend said, patting her on the back.

I groaned inwardly as I watched the crying girl stand at the bathroom sink and dab her tears away. *Shit. George is going to walk in any minute, and someone else is in here.* Judging by the conversation these girls were having, they had no intention of leaving anytime soon.

My gaze remained on them, hoping they were telepathic and would leave. I scanned the stalls for anyone else, but they were the only ones left. I glanced at my watch; I still had forty-five minutes before class got out and Xander would be waiting for me out front.

I leaned against the wall and crossed my arms in front of me. They were completely unaware I was there.

The bathroom door opened, and Adalyn strolled in. She glanced at me and approached the girls.

"Okay, party's over. Get out," Adalyn said.

"What?" the crying girl asked, frowning.

"Out. I'm sick, and I'm gonna have the massive shits, and you don't want to be anywhere around."

"Eww, oh my God," she said as they both bolted out the door.

"Oh my God, I can't believe you just said that!" I said and giggled.

"Well, George said it was an emergency, so it means we don't have time to deal with her," she said as she crossed the bathroom, opened the door, and ushered in Megan and George.

I checked the stalls one last time, and then we gathered in the middle of the room.

"Okay, we have to talk fast, and I can't take any chances of anyone hearing anything," I said in a hushed whisper. Megan frowned and rolled her eyes.

"Isn't this a bit James Bond, or whatever? I mean, it's a tad dramatic."

"Lacey is in trouble," George said.

"What do you mean, in trouble?" Megan asked.

"We need to help her leave Xander. He's hurting her."

"Xander Koffman? Star quarterback, sexy as hell? Hurting her? I kinda doubt it," she said as she rolled her eyes again.

"Seriously?" Adalyn asked. "Don't be stupid. Just because he's gorgeous doesn't mean he isn't capable of being a douche."

They both went quiet and looked at me, wide-eyed, silently asking me to confirm what George had just told them.

I winced as I slipped my shirt over my head and revealed the black-and-blue bruise on my shoulder and the other one on my back. Then I parted my hair and uncovered the gash on my head. George gasped and turned away. Finally, I removed a little bit of the makeup from my cheek.

"Shit," Megan said as I put my shirt back on. "Why didn't you tell us before now?"

"I was scared," I whispered. "He knows if I'm in class or if I'm skipping to spend time with George, and . . . I'm afraid for all of you now that you know. He's crazy, and he swore he'd hunt me down if I left."

"Son of a bitch," George muttered. "I should've paid closer attention when you started disappearing.

"Don't say that," I whispered. "I wouldn't have told you anything. Not only was I not ready to leave—I have nowhere to go."

"You can come to Portland with me," Megan said. "If Xander

showed up at my house, my stepdad would invite him in and then shoot him and call it self-defense. He doesn't put up with men hitting women. He's kind of cool like that."

"I can't do that to your family, Megan. I can't bring this into someone else's home."

"What about going back to Arkansas?" Adalyn asked.

My eyes fell on George for reassurance. Could I really trust the girls? He took my hand and nodded.

"I can't. I ran away from home to come here, and . . . my mother is sick."

"Like cancer?" Megan asked.

I shook my head and sighed. George squeezed my hand.

"There's too much to explain right now, but the short version is she didn't like a guy I was dating back home, so she drugged me and held me hostage for over a week. She believes I'm demon-possessed."

Their mouths gaped open.

"Her mom is mentally unstable you guys, so close your damn mouths," George said. "The other part of it is that her mom moved here to Eugene and almost kidnapped her at the start of the school year. She's been trying to find her ever since."

"That's what you were running from that day?" Megan asked. "When Xander grabbed you, and you didn't even say goodbye?"

"I'm sorry. I was trying to keep everyone safe from my mom. I thought Xander was protecting me, but he's a monster," I said and bit my lip. Tears spilled down my cheeks.

"Oh honey, don't cry," Megan said as she hugged me. "We can help. You're going to be okay, and we're here with you."

I hugged Megan and took a deep breath as I glanced at the clock on the wall. Twenty minutes until class got out.

"Okay, here's the deal," Adalyn said. "Megan, you get in touch with your friend and let her know we're bringing someone to her. Lacey, we'll let you know as soon as it's safe and ready. I'd plan on the next few days. Everytime you come to class, stick a few pieces of clothing into your backpack, but not enough to tip off Xander. You'll give it to me, Megan, or George—we'll figure out times to meet on days we don't have class together."

"Ummm, no panties if you have to hand clothes to me," George said.

"George, man up," Adalyn said. "Besides, I need to you go to the drama department and borrow a wig and some glasses—something we can use for Lacey. This way, Xander won't know if she skips class or leaves. Find a wig that looks like Lacey's hair for Megan. When we know what day Lacey will need to slip away, Megan will wear the wig and attend Lacey's classes. We'll figure out the rest when we know what day this will happen."

Adalyn stared at all of us. I was in a bit of awe how she'd just stepped up and orchestrated a plan. How did she know how to do all this?

"Who will I meet with?" I asked.

"I can't tell you yet," Megan said. "I promise you we'll all be with you, though, and you can trust her. But for now, the less you know, the better."

I peered at George.

"It's going to be okay," he said.

"Thank you," I whispered.

"Don't thank us yet—we have to get you out first," he said.

I took a deep breath and hoped it would work.

"Time is running out and Xander will be waiting for me."

We all nodded at each other. Megan and George filed out the door, and I tugged on Adalyn's sleeve, holding her back.

"I need to talk to you," I whispered and closed the door.

"What is it?" She asked, worry lines creasing her forehead.

"Please, don't tell anyone..."

"You have my word," she promised.

And while the seconds ticked by, I confided in her and asked for help one more time.

The next few days passed by without incident. Xander stayed home in the evenings, and I made sure I didn't piss him off. I kept busy studying, cleaning, and taking care of the laundry. I was able to slip a few pieces of clothing into my backpack each day without him noticing.

I'd at least have a few days' worth of clothes if I were able to get out this week, and I hadn't heard anything yet, so I just stuck with that plan. I was too scared to do anything else.

"You should take a study break," Xander said as he entered the living room and took my book away from me.

"Yeah? And why is that?" I asked and attempted a smile.

"Because all you've done is study today. I thought maybe we'd go out and get a bite to eat."

"Oh, that sounds nice. I would like to get out of the house for a little bit," I said. "Where are we going?"

"How about a good steak?" he asked and reached for my hand.

"Are you sure? I know it's expensive," I said as I stood up.

Xander pulled me into him and wrapped his arms around me. I laid my head on his chest and listened to the steady drumming of his heartbeat. My stomach flipped as I remembered the last time he'd taken me out for dinner and what he'd told me about his brother that night.

Had he found out I was trying to leave? Had he followed Megan or Adalyn? Had someone overheard us making plans? I squeezed my eyes shut and tried to remain calm. I was close to getting out, just a few more days . . . I hoped.

I tried to enjoy dinner, but my mind kept drifting to my escape plan as he talked.

"Hey, are you okay? You seem distracted," Xander said between bites of his steak.

"I'm sorry, I'm just so exhausted. I guess all the studying and preparing for finals has drained me a little bit," I replied and frowned I wasn't hiding my feelings better.

"Yeah. The end of the year gets pretty intense—this is my fourth time," he said and chuckled.

"It's hard to believe I met you for the first time on the airplane," I said, setting my fork down. "I would've never thought nine months later I'd be sitting across the table eating a steak dinner with you," I said. "Life's crazy, isn't it?"

He reached across the table and took my hand.

"I know it's been a bit up and down, but I love you."

My heart fluttered as I realized I was sitting across the table from my Xander. I knew a part of him loved me; it was all the other parts I couldn't live with any longer.

"I love you too," I whispered, holding his gaze.

We finished our dinner, Xander paid the check, and we chatted about classes and plans for the summer as we drove home.

"We should go camping," Xander said as he unlocked the front door of the house for us.

Nausea swept over me at the thought of being in the woods alone with him.

"What's wrong?" he asked. "Have you never gone camping?"

"No, and the thought of snakes and bears is a little scary."

Xander laughed as he put his arm around me and led me into the kitchen.

"We'll put the tent in the back of the truck. Will it make you feel better?"

"Much!" I said and laughed.

Xander grabbed the rum from the cabinet and made us drinks. We settled into the living room and turned on the TV. I snuggled into him and laid my head on his shoulder. If I did anything differently, he would know something was wrong. I had to rely on my acting ability. It had become a matter of life and death.

My belly was full, and the alcohol relaxed me. I hadn't realized I'd drifted off to sleep until the phone rang. My eyebrows knitted together. The phone rarely rang. I pulled away and began to stand when he tugged on my arm.

"Let the answering machine get it," Xander said.

I sat back down on the love seat as the beep on the machine went off. Xander muted the TV so we could hear who was on the line.

"Lacey, it's me, Emma. I know you don't want to talk to me right now, but it's really important. Please, if you're home, pick up, or call me as soon as you get this. I don't care how late it is."

Xander frowned at me and hopped off the couch. I wasn't sure if he was going to answer the phone or not.

"It's about Walker—" Emma started before a loud crash in the kitchen shot me up off the couch.

"What happened?" I asked as I ran into the room.

"What the fuck was that?" Xander asked. I glanced around and identified pieces of the answering machine scattered across the floor.

"What? What happened?"

"*Walker?*" he asked as his hand clenched into a fist.

"No, I told you, we were all friends. I haven't talked to Emma since Christmas, and I have no idea what she's talking about!" My eyes widened. Emma's timing couldn't have been worse. I stared at the floor.

"You're lying!"

"No I'm not," I said as I put my hands in front of me and backed away from him into the living room. "He's married. And I haven't seen him in a year and a half. I don't know where he lives, or anything else about him," I stammered as he followed me.

Xander's fist flew up and smacked my cheek. A sharp pain traveled through my face as I reeled backward and into the back of the couch. I flipped over it and landed on the floor with a thud.

"Please, don't, you've got it all wrong," I whimpered, covering my head. He jerked me off the floor, and I found myself standing on my feet. His breathing came fast and hard as he stared at me.

"I love you," I whispered. "Only you."

He released me and shoved me backward. I stumbled but caught myself. My legs wobbled as I reached out to regain my balance on the couch. Xander turned around and went upstairs. I sank down and sobbed as quietly as I could.

4 4

After I showered I applied my bruise concealer before Xander woke up. For some stupid reason I didn't want him to see the bruises. But now, I had to cover both cheeks. At least the older bruise was almost gone. My head throbbed, and my body ached. I had no idea what kind of mood he'd be in, but I had to get to school. I'd even chanced it and rolled up a pair of jeans to give to Megan today. My backpack looked bulkier than normal, but if I turned it toward me, he wouldn't notice.

Silence hung in the air between us as we rode to school. He walked me to class as usual; I wasn't sure if he wanted to or he was just trying to keep up appearances.

I entered the building and noted Megan waiting by the women's restroom. She nodded, and I glanced around to see if anyone was following me. I bit my lip as I followed her in.

"You're meeting with her in a few minutes," Megan said as she pulled a dark wig and glasses from her backpack. "Let's put these on, but first, we need to switch shirts."

I nodded as we traded. Thank God we were similar in size.

"Hey, are you okay? You're super quiet."

I held her gaze, remembering our fight last night. "I can't wait much longer." My voice shook. "He hurt me again last night."

"Son of a bitch," she spat. "Look at me. We've got this. Stay focused, okay? I know you're scared shitless right now, and no one should ever have to go through what you've been through. Unfortunately, you've had a double share of it between your mom and Xander, but we're so close. Hang on, okay?"

Tears slid down my cheeks, and I nodded. I tugged the dark-haired wig on, and Megan tucked my hair underneath it. She pulled a pair of eyeglasses from the bag and slipped them on my face.

"This will work. George did good," she said and smiled. I adjusted my glasses in the mirror and gawked at how different I looked. It wasn't just the wig and glasses, but how flat and lifeless my eyes were.

"Let's do this," she said. "I would go with you, but I need to make sure everyone thinks you're here and not sneaking off. Adalyn is waiting for you at Grayson Hall. If you go out the back door of this building, you shouldn't be seen. George will also join you there. I'll fill in for you in class, and I've already told my friend about what you've been going through so we can get this done as quickly as possible. Any questions?" she asked as she adjusted her wig.

I shook my head as Megan leaned in and hugged me.

"We got this," she said one more time and then walked out of the bathroom.

With a deep breath, I opened the door, and turned the opposite direction from the front doors I normally entered. I glanced behind me, but the hallway was empty. Pushing through the exit doors, I walked across the car filled parking lot. I spotted Adalyn standing outside the main doors of Grayson Hall. She nodded as I approached, and then she walked into the building.

Thirty seconds later, I slipped in the door behind her. I followed her down the hallway and then took a right. She paused for a moment so I could see her enter an office. My heart pounded as I looked around again. I took a deep breath and slipped inside the door.

"No one would ever know it was you," she said as she hugged me.

"Yeah, George did well. Speaking of, where is he?"

"Here," George said as he slipped into the office.

"Hi!" I said and hugged him.

I scanned the walls and the chairs. It almost resembled a doctor's exam room, with two different doors and a desk. The walls were blank, but overall it seemed quiet and safe, and it's all I needed.

I was in the middle of removing my wig and glasses as the second door clicked open and a voice said, "Hi, everybody."

I looked up to see Mrs. Walters walk in. My mouth hung open for a second.

"Hello, Lacey," Mrs. Walters said. Her smile lit up her face as she made herself comfortable at the desk.

"Hi," I said softly.

"I hear you're in trouble, and I understand we only have about twenty-five minutes to talk before you need to head back. Megan's already told me the basics of what's going on to save us some time—I hope it's okay."

I nodded. "Of course."

"First of all, Lacey, I need you to understand this isn't your fault. There isn't anything you could've said or done that warranted you being hit. Ever. I don't care if you let some other guy touch you, used drugs, or argued with him. No human being deserves to be hit. Did you screw up? Sure, but haven't we all. I sure as hell have. In fact, I was in your shoes fifteen years ago."

"You were?" I asked, unable to hide my surprise.

"Yes, and I had three kids to take care of. We ran from my abusive husband, and after we were safe and had had some time to heal, I dedicated my time to helping other women escape abusive men. We aren't affiliated with the police or any other organization, so we have the ability to do things differently. We're similar to an underground railroad, so to speak. We're quiet and effective. We're an all-volunteer group, and we have a seventy-five percent success rate with the women we've relocated."

"Only seventy-five percent?" I squeaked.

"One thing I've learned over the years is you can only help someone as much as they want to be helped. Twenty-five percent of women go back. My responsibility is to sneak you out of here and get you to safety. There are people along the way to help you move and take care of you, but it's ultimately your choice.

"Are you ready to leave and start your life over? You won't be able to reach out to your friends, you won't know anyone except maybe one family, and you'll be in a new state. Our program sets you up with a new identity, and you will start completely over. You will no longer be Lacey Beaumont."

My eyes widened as her words registered with me. I couldn't talk to George, the girls, or Emma, at least for a while. No one would know where I was, but that also included Xander and Mama. I was so tired of trying to start over and it not working. There was nowhere else to turn.

"Yes," I whispered. "Yes, I'm ready."

"Okay, I'll put everything into motion then. Since it's Friday, and from what I understand you are well guarded, we have two choices. I can show up at Xander's house tonight with the police and arrest you on some trumped-up charge, or we can be ready for you when you return to classes on Monday."

"No, no police," I said adamantly, shaking my head. "I think Xander has friends there. I'm scared they would tell him the truth and he would come after me even harder."

"Okay then, Monday it is. You stay as safe as you can over the weekend."

A surge of panic set in as I realized I had to get through three more nights with Xander.

"He's been nicer the last several days," I said, "but I never know when it's all about to change. I typically don't have any warning."

"I've been there, hon—you're talking to someone who lived through the same thing. You're about to take action. You'll no longer be a victim," she said as she smiled comfortingly.

*Can I have that too? Can I be safe and find peace?*

I nodded, attempting to process everything that was about to happen.

"We need to go," Adalyn said. "Thank you for meeting us, Mrs. Walters."

"You all did the right thing by bringing Lacey to me. Let's get her safe."

I adjusted my wig again and slid my glasses on as we slipped out the door one by one, a couple of minutes apart.

I was hurrying down the hallway toward the front doors when I heard a loud whisper. "Pssst! Lacey!"

"Shit, Adalyn, you scared me!" She was standing just inside an empty classroom's doorway.

"I almost forgot to give you this," she whispered as she slipped a small bag into my hand.

"Thank you." I shoved it into my backpack and hugged her. I left her standing in the classroom doorway as I practically ran down the hallway, across the parking lot, and into the back of my building.

I went straight into the bathroom, shoved the wig and glasses into a bag, and left it under the sink for Megan to pick up later. Fear rolled through me as I realized I'd forgotten to change shirts with Megan.

*Shit! Shit!* I had no other choice than to walk out of the bathroom as though I owned the T-shirt I was wearing.

## 4 5

———————

I smiled, descended the steps of the building, walked over to Xander, and kissed him.

"You're in a good mood," he said as he wrapped his arm around my waist.

"It's Friday, and we're almost done with the school year. I can't believe it. And you're graduating, Xander. Does it feel weird after four years of college? I mean, you're almost done."

He chuckled as I babbled on about the year, how fast it had flown by, and how different everything was from the first day I'd arrived. Xander hadn't mentioned the phone call from Emma, and I sure as hell wasn't going to. If he was going to be sweet for five minutes, I knew better than to rock the boat.

Besides, Emma and Walker no longer mattered. The only thing I needed to focus on was getting through the next few days.

On the way home, I talked about how nice it was to not need the air conditioning at the end of May, and how back home your makeup was melting off the moment you stepped outside.

We arrived home and agreed to watch a movie and order pizza. I made drinks and wandered onto the front porch. The gentle breeze

219

rustled the leaves as I checked on Laverne and Shirley, my rose bushes. I smiled as I realized I'd managed not to kill them. They were taking to their new home well. I reached out and touched the soft petals as their sweet fragrance filled my nose.

"They're doing well," Xander said from behind me.

"I'm excited. These are the first flowers I've ever planted. It's so beautiful here with all the trees. I remember it was one of the first things that stood out when I came to Oregon—how green everything was, even in the summer," I said and took a drink.

"You sure are taking a trip down memory lane today," he said.

"Yeah," I said and stared at my shoes. "I do that sometimes. A lot has changed in the last year."

"It has," he said as he took my hand. "I want to have a good summer too. I think we should take a few different camping trips. I'd love to show you Crater Lake. It'll take your breath away. We can go up to Washington as well. How does it sound?"

"It sounds great," I said, reaching up and kissing him. "I need to go pee and get a refill. I'll get you one, too," I said and took his glass.

I opened the front door and went to the kitchen. Xander hadn't followed me back into the house. I put our glasses on the kitchen counter, ran up the stairs as quietly as I could, grabbed my backpack from his bedroom, and hurried into the bathroom. I checked I'd locked the door three times before I opened my backpack.

My stomach flipped as I pulled out the small bag Adalyn had given me. I slid the package out, turned it over, and read the back of the box. My hands shook as I unwrapped it. I followed the instructions and then sat on the side of the tub and waited.

I mulled over the conversation with Mrs. Walters from earlier in the day, trying to imagine what my life would look like in a few days. How was this all going to work if I didn't even know where I was going to live? My chest ached with the thought, but I brushed the fear aside. I needed to grab one or two more items of clothing. Xander hadn't said anything about my shirt; I owned a few black shirts already, so maybe it wasn't obvious.

With a few minutes left, I rubbed my forehead and refused to go to a dark place mentally. Megan's voice filled my thoughts saying, *We got this*. I don't know where her confidence came from, but the last time I thought I was safe, Mama drugged me and locked me up. I wouldn't make the same mistake again and think things were okay before I'd crossed the finish line.

Standing slowly, I peered at the results. I gasped and doubled over. *Oh my God. Oh my God.*

"Hey, you okay in there?" Xander asked as he knocked on the door.

"Yeah, I'll be out in a minute," I replied, grabbing the pregnancy test, shoving it back into the box, wrapping it up in the brown paper bag, and tossing it into the trash.

I hopped down the stairs and joined Xander in the kitchen.

"Pizza's here," he said as he handed me a paper plate.

"It smells really good," I said and grabbed two slices.

He refilled my rum and Pepsi and handed it to me. I took a long drink and set it down on the table. I was starving.

UNABLE TO SLEEP, I lay still in bed and stared at the ceiling. The moonlight trickled in through the curtains and Xander breathed softly next to me. My mind raced with the plan of me leaving in a few days. I would no longer live in the state I'd worked so hard to get to. I wouldn't be able to have any contact with Emma, George, Adalyn, or Megan. Honestly, I didn't care anymore about Mama. This was the only way I'd ever break free from her. A tear slid down my cheek as I thought about everything I was going to say goodbye to.

I watched Xander as he slept. Anger and fear rolled through me at the same time. Why had everything turned out this way? Why couldn't he leave the drugs and women alone? He'd been so good to me in the beginning; he'd been my rock. He'd protected me from Mama as she tried to drag me off, and then everything had turned to shit.

I'd focused too much on the good side of him, which had also been my downfall. I continued to hold on to that part of him and hope it would resurface, but it had cost me everything, including my soul. Now, I was a hollowed-out shell of a person. I'd tried hard drugs and allowed myself to be hit, lied to, and cheated on. And now everything was about to change again, but this time, I didn't have Emma or her parents to help me. I would have to trust total strangers.

46

I yawned.

"You look exhausted," Xander said over breakfast the next morning.

"I couldn't sleep last night," I replied. "I hate it when that happens." I took a bite of my eggs. "Maybe I'll lie back down for a little while if you don't care?"

"Are you not feeling well? You've never been sick before."

"I know, and I don't get sick often. Maybe it's the stress of getting ready for finals and finishing the school year."

"Yeah, I'm gonna mow the lawn since it's not raining, so lie down for a while. Maybe you'll feel better this afternoon."

I nodded as I rinsed my plate and loaded it into the dishwasher.

"Thanks," I said as I kissed him and went back upstairs. After I crawled back into bed, I fell asleep within minutes.

It was almost 7 P.M. when I went back downstairs. I didn't feel any better, but maybe it was my heart hurting more than anything else. I was torn between leaving everything or staying. An uneasy feeling filled me as I walked into the living room. Neither outcome sounded good, but I had to make a choice—and fast.

"Hey, how are you feeling?"

I shook my head and joined Xander on the love seat. "Can't seem to shake it," I muttered, rubbing my eyes and glancing at him.

"Do you think you have the flu? Because if you do, stay away from me."

"Thanks," I said and leaned my head back.

"Do you want a drink? I can make you one."

"No, I don't think it's a good idea. I feel kind of sick to my stomach."

"Don't puke on my rugs."

My eyes squeezed closed, and I reminded myself not to piss him off. "I won't."

I only had to get through tonight and tomorrow before I left. Surely, I could keep my mouth shut for that long.

"I think I'm gonna go back to bed." I stood up and walked out of the living room.

I stayed in bed until the next morning; I wasn't even sure when Xander was home and when he wasn't. The timing of getting sick sucked, but maybe it was also a blessing in disguise. If I could manage to stay out of his way I was safer, but I knew it wasn't going to happen.

Kicking off the blankets, I stood up slowly. I grabbed some clean clothes and got into the shower. My stomach growled, which was a good sign, and I wondered if Xander had left me any pizza. I'm not sure why I was so exhausted, but I needed to get my shit together before tomorrow.

I dressed and made it to the kitchen. The pizza was gone, so I grabbed some chips and a Pepsi and made my way into the living room.

"Hey," I said as I sat down.

"You feeling better?"

"Yeah, a little bit. I'm hungry, so it's a good sign."

Xander closed his textbook and stared at me.

"What's going on?"

"What do you mean?" I asked as my heart slammed into my chest.

"Something's wrong, and you need to tell me."

I chewed my chip and took a sip of soda. I wasn't sure what to do, and it had literally made me sick all weekend.

Turning toward him, I set my food and drink down on the coffee table.

"I'm pregnant," I whispered.

"No," he said, his eyes widening.

"Yes. I took a test yesterday, and it came back positive."

"You sure it's mine?"

"Are you in shock, or are you just being a total asshole?" I asked. I hadn't really expected him to say anything different if I'd been honest with myself.

Xander stood up and stared at me. His brown eyes scanned my body as though he could see inside me and make sure I really was pregnant with his baby.

I picked up my chips again and nibbled on one. The salt settled my stomach, and the stupid things tasted so good. I wondered if that was what I had to look forward to over the next nine months.

"I'm outta here," Xander said as he grabbed his keys from the kitchen table. The door slammed behind him.

I sighed as I took another chip. I'm not sure I'd planned everything out very well, but he always seemed to know when I lied, and I figured I would only have tonight to fight with him before I left. I probably would've told him anyway, just in a note or something. I wanted to leave with a clear conscience, and he had a right to know he was going to be a father.

Mentally, I reviewed the exit plan for tomorrow. Megan had retrieved the wigs, and we'd put them back on so I could sneak back to Grayson Hall, where Adalyn and George would be waiting in the same little office. A tear slid down my cheek as I realized I wouldn't see or talk to them again.

I had no idea where Xander had gone, and I hoped it wasn't to Andy or Brittney. But I was too tired to try and figure it out right now. My eyes fluttered closed as I got situated on the couch and closed my eyes. Just before I drifted off to sleep, I had a fleeting thought that maybe, just maybe, this would inspire Xander to get his shit together, and we could make it after all. I guess part of me still hoped for the best with him, as naive as it might've been.

THE NEXT MORNING, I peered through the living-room curtains and waited for Xander. I was going to miss class, not to mention my meeting with Mrs. Walker. My timing officially sucked. I should've told him on Friday, but I was scared of his reaction, and I had to stay safe.

There was no way of contacting George or the girls, and I couldn't find the phone book to call Mrs. Walters on campus.

I paced back and forth and continued to glance at the clock every five minutes. A sigh escaped me as I plunked down on the couch. It was over. I'd missed the rendezvous with Megan, and they were all probably wondering where I was by now.

To make matters worse, I had no idea what kind of mood Xander would be in when he got home. I made breakfast while I waited, and the uneasy gnawing in my stomach got worse with every minute I waited for him to come home.

"Wake up."

My eyes popped open and I realized I hadn't heard Xander come home.

"What time is it?" I asked as I sat up.

"It's five."

"Thanks for not showing up to take me to class this morning," I muttered.

"I needed some space."

"I know I surprised you, and I'm sorry."

"You need to make a doctor's appointment and take care of it," he said as he joined me on the love seat.

"I know. I'll need to start on prenatal vitamins and get checked out."

"No, I mean you're not keeping it."

My mouth dropped as I realized what he'd said.

"No, I'm keeping the baby. This isn't open for discussion. If you don't want us, fine. I'll leave, and you'll never hear from me again," I said, standing up.

"Sit the fuck back down!"

I jumped at the volume and anger in his voice. My stomach shook as I stared at him and did what he told me to.

"You're not keeping the baby, and it's final. I don't want a kid. I've never wanted a kid. I thought I told you to get on the Pill. How could you do this to me?"

"Do this to *you*?" I asked as my eyebrows rose. "I didn't just sit around thinking I had nothing better to do with my time than try to get knocked up. And I am on the Pill."

"Then how did this happen?"

"I don't know!" I cried. "Maybe I missed a pill or two on accident. With classes and everything going on with us, I . . . I don't know," I said as my voice trailed off.

"We're too young, Lacey. We can't have this baby. I'll pay for the abortion since you don't have shit to your name."

"It's not that easy. I can't abort a baby. It's *our* baby. "

"Yeah, I fucking got it!" he yelled as he ran his hand through his hair. "Shit!"

"Do you love me?"

Xander leaned back in his chair and closed his eyes. If he was wishing we weren't sitting here having this conversation, I couldn't agree more, but he was so unpredictable I had no idea. Several minutes passed before he replied.

"Yes, I've told you I love you," he said.

"Well, I'm scared. We're not in the best place right now, but I want this baby. The question is, are you going to be with me, or am I going to have to raise it on my own?"

"You're that serious?" he asked as he opened his eyes and turned toward me.

"Yes, and I realize I've had a day or two extra to process it. But it happened, I'm pregnant, and . . . and I'm going to have this baby."

"Okay."

"Okay? What does that mean, exactly?"

"Okay, we'll have this baby. It's not like I can force you to go to the clinic and make you have an abortion anyway."

"Really? You mean it? You want to have our baby together?" I asked as tears filled my eyes. Hope and joy flooded over me. Maybe he would do the right thing now. Maybe this could fix what was broken between us.

"Yeah. I'll even get my shit together before it gets here."

"I love you," I said, leaning over and kissing him.

"I love you too, babe," he whispered. "I love you too."

Was I mistaken or was there a hint of defeat in Xander's voice? I hoped he meant what he said. I hoped we could figure this out and take care of a baby together. And I would tell George and the girls I wasn't leaving. At least, no matter what, I had them.

A small smile tugged at the corner of my mouth as relief flooded through me. I wasn't going to leave, change my name, or not be able to see my friends again.

"Are you gonna get all round on me?" he asked.

"Really? You just asked me that? Yes, I'm gonna get 'all round' on you, and I'll probably even waddle," I giggled as the image ran through my mind.

"Why don't I go to the store and grab us something to eat? You're feeling better, so I bet you're pretty hungry."

I nodded as he smoothed my hair from my face.

"You're going to be a daddy," I said.

The doorbell rang and interrupted our conversation.

"I got it," Xander said as he stood up and made his way to the front door. I peered after him. He peeked through the curtain before he opened the door. I wondered if he was watching out for Mike and Agnus. My heart fluttered with the thought of them showing up again.

"Hey, man, what's going on?" Xander said as he opened the door.

"I'm looking for Lacey."

"Lacey, George is here," Xander said as he stepped away from the door. He removed his keys from his pocket. "I'm going to run a few errands and grab something to make for dinner," he said. "Be back in a little while."

"Okay, babe. Thanks," I called out as he walked out the front door and gave a small wave goodbye to George, who smiled and waved back.

The truck rumbled to life, and he pulled away.

Worry flashed across George's face as he stepped inside and I shut the door behind him.

"Where were you today?" George asked.

"I'm sick," I replied.

"Really? You're really sick?"

"Yeah, I know how it looks, but things have changed, so . . ."

"What do you mean, things have changed? Did he find out? Did he hurt you again?"

"No, no, he's been fine actually, and I don't think the drugs and stuff are going to be a problem any longer," I said.

George's eyebrow rose as he waited for me to explain.

"I'm staying. I can't go now. We agreed to try and make things work between us. I want to stay with you and the girls, and this is my home now."

George's mouth dropped as I spoke. "You're not serious, are you?"

"Yeah, I am," I said, crossing my arms in front of me.

"What happened to change your mind? I don't understand. You were ready to go."

"I don't know what to tell you, but things are gonna be okay. Promise," I said.

A pang of fear ran through me as I heard my own words. I didn't fully believe them, but here I stood, in front of one of my best friends, trying to convince us both to swallow the lie.

"Okay," he said as he raised his hands in surrender. "I was worried about you, and I wanted to stop by. Will you be back at school?"

"Yeah, I'll see you on Wednesday like always," I said and attempted a smile.

George took a deep breath and hugged me. "You're sure?"

"Yes."

He pulled away, and I stood in the doorway as I watched him leave. I stepped out onto the porch and sat on the steps. The early evening sun peeked through the trees as the wind rustled the leaves. It was beautiful.

I leaned back and took a deep breath. The urge for a drink

surfaced, but I reminded myself I couldn't have one, at least for a while. Tears slid down my cheeks as my new reality crashed down on me. I was staying, and I was pregnant. I was going to have a baby.

How in the hell was all of this going to work out? My hand hovered over my stomach. I'd figure out something. For now, I had a roof over my head and food to eat. I had nine months to work on my degree, get a job, and buy a car. I could do this, right? I hiccupped as the tears came faster. What in the hell was I doing?

Maybe Xander was right; maybe we really couldn't do this. Maybe I shouldn't have this baby. I wiped at my tears and chided myself for even considering something like that. It was just the fear.

I went back inside the house and locked the door behind me. Then I grabbed a Pepsi and wandered upstairs. I opened the guest-room door and tried to imagine it as a nursery. What would Xander think? If we kept the spare room between the bedrooms empty, he could still sleep when I was up with the baby. Maybe I'd talk to him about it when he got back.

"I'm back," Xander hollered.

My stomach growled as I went downstairs to see what he'd bought for us to eat.

"I thought you could make your hamburger stroganoff. I bought garlic bread, too."

"Yeah, sounds really good," I said, relieving him of the groceries and grabbing a pan.

"What did George want?" Xander asked.

"Oh, he was just wondering why I wasn't in class today. Just said I was sick and would be back tomorrow."

I browned the hamburger, and within forty-five minutes we were eating together at the table.

"You cook a mean stroganoff," Xander said between bites.

"Thanks," I said and smiled. Had he had time to process our news? Was he doing okay with everything? He seemed so calm.

He cleared the dishes, and we settled in on the love seat in the living room.

"So, I was upstairs when you were running errands," I said. "I wondered which room you thought would work for the baby?"

Xander held my gaze, and a smile spread across his face. At that moment I flashed back to the first time I met him, on the plane. I remembered how his brown eyes danced, and how his beautiful smile made my heart stutter. Would the baby look like him or me? I hoped for a combination of both: my eyes, and his smile.

"I guess I hadn't gotten that far yet," he said and chuckled. "You're a little bit ahead of me."

"Sorry, I'll try and give you some time to process everything," I said, snuggling up to him.

"I'll catch up," he said and patted my knee.

"Hey, can I ask you something?"

"Sure. What is it?"

"It's about Mike and Agnus."

"Who?" I felt his body and jaw stiffen.

". . . They stopped by again."

"Today? They stopped by today, and you didn't tell me?"

I sat up so I could face him.

"If you'll recall, you asked me not to ever bring them up again. And, no, not today. I didn't tell you when it happened because you came home and . . . we didn't have a good night. I'm not trying to be a bitch, but if they come back, I need to know what to do. They scare me, they aren't good people, and now we have the baby on the way."

"Goddammit! Shut the hell up about the fucking baby!"

I stepped away from him as he stood up and paced the floor.

"Please, tell me who they are and why they keep coming back here. What do they want with you?"

"You just had to push it," he said as he walked into the kitchen. I followed him and watched as he refilled his glass with rum.

"I'm sorry, but what should I do?"

"Nothing, just don't open the door. I'll take care of it."

"Take care of it? You told me that months ago when they first showed up. You've never answered my questions or even made sure I was safe. It's not just me I have to take care of now."

I winced, realizing I'd brought up the baby again. What was wrong with me? Why couldn't I stop talking about the pregnancy?

"Are you saying I don't take care of you?"

"No, of course you do, but who are they? Can't you tell me? Don't you trust me?"

Xander laughed as he guzzled his drink and refilled his glass.

"This is great. Are you gonna replace your coke habit with alcohol? That'll make you a fantastic daddy," I spat.

My breath whooshed out of me as I made contact with the living room floor. Anger ripped through Xander's handsome features, contorting them into something evil. I'd pushed him too far. I wasn't sure why in the hell I'd said anything to him at all.

I wrapped my arms around my stomach as he stood over me.

"You can't hit me anymore," I whispered.

"I can do whatever the fuck I want. You're such a stupid little bitch," he sneered.

My eyes widened. His words hurt deeper than any bruise he'd left on me.

I scrambled backward, but he grabbed me by my hair and jerked me to my feet.

"I'm sorry," I whimpered. "Please stop, don't hurt me."

"Let's go upstairs and talk for a little bit."

Xander never let go of my hair as he dragged me through the kitchen and stopped to get something out of a drawer. I tripped up the stairs behind him and tried to get my footing, but my socks only slipped on the wood floors.

"Xander, please," I begged as he tossed me into his bedroom. I tried to stop myself from hurtling forward, but I landed facedown on the hardwood floor, rolling over onto my back as he approached me. I doubled over as his foot connected with my stomach and sent a sharp pain through me.

"Stop! You'll hurt the baby!" I tried to protect myself from his foot, but his legs were strong from years of playing football. His shoe connected with my stomach again and again. I sobbed as my screams ripped through the air and the pain tore me in two.

"Shut up. My God, you've been driving me fucking crazy," he said as he tore off a piece of duct tape and slapped it across my mouth. My eyes widened, and I screamed against the sticky material, but only a muffled sound escaped. Tears rolled down my eyes as he grabbed my wrists and taped them together behind me. I kicked my feet and smacked him in the face, but he still grabbed my ankles and bound them together.

He sat on the bed and stared at me while I squirmed on the floor.

"Okay, I'll tell you, but no interrupting," he said and laughed. "Mike and Agnus. Yeah, those two guys," Xander said and then paused. There was no remorse in his voice or his expression as he stared at me lying there bound and gagged on his bedroom floor.

"So, Lacey, I—I just didn't deal well with our relationship after a while. I don't do commitment, and you started getting under my skin with your whining and nagging all the time. It was tough, and I struggled because part of me didn't want to leave you, but I couldn't stand to be around you, either. There was this crazy tug-of-war inside me, and when I couldn't take it any longer, I'd go to Andy's and take a break. We'd all hang out, snort a few lines, and play some cards. It was all harmless fun for a while, ya know? Just a bunch of guys blowing off steam.

"But, then, one night after a game, I walked outside and these two guys were hanging out at my truck. They offered to let me in on the big poker games and said they'd front me the money to get in. I agreed since I was tired of playing with the losers at Andy's anyway. So, I started going somewhere else. You'd never believe who was at these tables, Lacey. My God, I walked in the first night and almost pissed myself when I recognized all the city and state politicians and cops." He paused.

"I did really well at first, and I was pretty happy about it. I'd take you out to celebrate, or we'd have great sex those nights. But then it started to change. I lost a game here and there and lost some money. I figured I could get it back, though. But by then, I'd gotten sloppy and was doing coke during the games. I couldn't stop the gambling or the drugs, and before I knew it, I'd lost everything."

I shook my head as tears streamed down my cheeks.

"*Everything.* And they want me to pay up." He peered down at me as a smile snaked across his face. "Everything means everything, don't you get it? You cost me every fucking thing I owned. Oh wait, I can see by the expression on your face you still have questions."

Xander walked over and crouched down next to me.

"I lost the house, my truck, every penny my grandma left me. Everything I owned now belongs to them. Why, you ask? Why? It's all your fucking fault. If you hadn't driven me out of my own home, we wouldn't be in this predicament, now would we? And to shake things up just a bit more, you're pregnant, or you were, anyway," he said and nodded toward my blood-soaked jeans.

Fear splintered my heart as I saw the red stain. I glanced at him and pleaded with my eyes, but I wasn't sure if there was any decent part left inside him.

"I told you, but you didn't wanna listen. That's the thing, Lacey. People will tell you exactly who they are, but most of the time we aren't interested in the truth. And then they wonder how the hell their life got all fucked up. They want to make excuses or see the *good* in people. I was up-front with you about who I was, that night in my bed when I told you about Steven. But you talked yourself out of believing me. And you stayed. I figured, what the hell? I had a piece of ass at home, and I was banging Brittney the whole time. Yes, that's right, and don't look so surprised. You knew all of it, deep down. You knew it all, and you talked yourself out of it," he said and shook his head.

49

Xander grabbed his suitcase from the closet and opened the dresser drawers. He pulled his clothes out and tossed them into his bag.

"It was sorta funny when you told me about Mike and Agnus the first time. You do realize Agnus isn't his name, right? I mean, what parent in their right mind would name their son Agnus? Know what his real name is? Donald. Yup, plain old Donald. Agnus is code for 'we're coming after you and you owe us a lot of money.'

"So, Lacey, I can't stay. I've gotta go, and you're not going with me. Don't look so disappointed, babe. I must tell you, this all came together just a few hours ago. You were yammering on about this stupid kid and the nursery when it dawned on me. It just clicked. The perfect plan that would take care of everything. I'm going to burn down this beautiful home, collect the insurance money, relocate, and start my life over without you. And I'm sure as hell not gonna be a daddy," he said as he packed.

I strained and yelled against the tape on my mouth, but I could barely make a sound.

"I think back on it, and you were *so* easy. You were a scared little girl running from mommy. At first, I figured I'd play the good guy and at least get a good piece of ass, but then, something totally unexpected happened. I fell for you, and it started making me crazy. I couldn't stand the thought of you with anyone else. And the night with John. What the fuck? I thought I was gonna kill that stupid fool."

Xander put the last few items into his suitcase and went into the bathroom. He came out a minute later and tossed his toiletries in with his clothes.

He sighed and ran his hand through his hair. He glared at me and shook his head.

"It could've all been different. *We* could have been different. But now, I have to leave, and you're not coming with me," he said as he shrugged his shoulders.

I whimpered against the tape.

"You hold that thought. I'll be right back," he said and walked out of the room.

My head swam as I tried to grab on to any coherent thought of how I could get him to let me go. Then an acrid smell drifted toward me. I attempted another scream as he walked into the bedroom with a can of gasoline.

"If I can't have you, if I can't have my house, then no one will."

I watched as he placed the gas can next to the closet. He ran his hand through his hair again and glanced around.

"Ya know, come to think of it, I'm gonna hang out with you for a few more minutes if that's okay," he said as he unzipped his suitcase and pulled out a baggie with white powder in it.

"I figure this'll be for old time's sake. We *have* spent the last seven months together in an intense relationship. And I'm rather excited I can leave now and I don't have to waste my time hunting you down, which is what I'd do if you left me. I think this'll all work out better. I'll let the insurance company know I wasn't home when the house caught fire and play the grieving and distraught boyfriend. After the money comes in, I'll pay my gambling debt, and boom. I'm gone. I think I might try the East Coast."

I watched as Xander took his time and cut the coke. He grabbed his wallet out of his pocket, pulled out a dollar bill, rolled it up, and snorted a line. He laid back on the bed and sighed. My head throbbed with every second that passed by.

"You know what, now that I'm feeling a bit better, I'm gonna see if you have anything to say. But if you scream when I take off the tape, it goes right back on. Don't forget, we're out here in the country surrounded by five wooded acres. No one would hear you anyway. Be a good girl, and just say your last words."

Xander crouched down and ripped the tape from my mouth. I cringed as it pulled away from my skin, but the pain was nothing compared to the cramps in my stomach.

"Please, Xander, I know you love me. You don't want to do this. I can forgive everything—the drugs, Brittney, the gambling. Take me with you, and we can start over. I promise I won't nag or even care if you're out all night. Please. Don't do this. Do you really want to leave me here? Do you really want to have my death on your conscience?"

Xander frowned at me. Was I getting through to him? Would he consider taking me with him?

"I just can't," he replied. "I think the baby was the last straw, and if you're still pregnant and I take you with me, we have the same problem. I can't trust you, not only with Mike and Agnus, but to not get yourself knocked up. I don't like kids, and I never wanted them. And, if you'll recall, I *murdered my own brother*. Why in the world would you think I wouldn't do it again?" he asked.

He paused as he lowered himself until he was a mere inch away from my face. "What makes you think I haven't murdered other people, Lacey?"

"What? No, it's the coke talking," I whispered. "And if you're really going to do this, then I want one last thing from you."

"What?" he asked, surprised.

"Kiss me goodbye."

His eyes searched my face for a long moment, and then he closed the small gap between us. His lips lingered for a second longer than I'd expected and I took my chance. I tilted my chin up and bit the end of his nose as hard as I could. He doubled up and grabbed his face. As he leaned forward, I pulled my head back and smacked his forehead with as much force as possible. I gasped from the pain in my head as I laid back on the floor.

"You bitch!" he yelled as he fell backward and blood dripped down his face. I watched and prayed he would pass out; then maybe I could somehow make it to the phone and dial 911.

His body went limp and he laid still on the floor. I began rolling my way toward his nightstand. My head throbbed so bad black dots danced before my eyes. I'd almost knocked myself out, too.

I reached the bed, positioned my hands on the bed frame, and pulled my feet underneath me. I took a deep breath and used my legs to push myself up and onto his bed. I stared at the phone and then glanced back at his motionless body. I leaned forward and knocked the phone from its cradle. Thank God for push-button phones. I leaned into the phone and pushed the nine with my nose. I heard it beep and aimed for the one. A beep followed it as well. I only had one more number to push. A tear slid down my cheek as the last tone sounded. I gasped as I heard the operator answer.

"Help me, he's going to kill me," I whispered, praying he wouldn't regain consciousness.

"I'm sorry, ma'am, I can barely hear you. Please say it again," the operator encouraged.

"He's going to kill me, please hurry. 842 Hickory—" I screamed as Xander ripped the phone from the wall and jerked my hair so hard I fell off the bed and landed with a thud on the floor.

"My God! I can't believe you just did that."

"Xander, stop, you can't hurt the baby and me anymore. Please," I cried.

"Yeah, you might still be pregnant, but it doesn't matter anymore. You just signed your death certificate."

"No! You can't do this!"

"Oh yes, I can, and I have to do it now," he said as he slapped the piece of tape back over my mouth.

He turned toward the closet and began splashing the room with gasoline. The stench burned my nostrils as I watched him continue to pour it into the hallway. I heard footsteps descending the stairs and imagined him pouring gasoline through the kitchen and his beautiful living room. Fear gripped me as I realized how quickly the curtains and rugs would catch fire, then the walls, then the wood floors and the staircase. It wouldn't take long before it traveled through the entire house.

A small glimmer of hope rose inside me as I heard footsteps coming my way. Had he realized what he was doing and changed his mind? Had he come back for me?

"It's all done. One single match will have this place up in flames," he said. He stared at me as I laid on the floor and silently pleaded with him. "Goodbye, Lacey."

My heart sank as Xander turned and walked out of the bedroom. His footsteps echoed through the hallway and down the stairs. I don't know why I tried to scream again; maybe it was just instinct. With one final attempt, I tried to pull my wrists and ankles apart, but the tape was too tight.

I'm not sure how long I laid there. The smoke crept up the hallway and through the door. The shadows of the flames danced off the walls not far behind it. I had no way to escape. Even if I could make it to the window across the room, I couldn't open it, nor would I have any way to land safely after a two-story fall.

I laid my head down and closed my eyes. If I'd only gone with George, if I hadn't told Xander I was pregnant, I'd be out of this house and somewhere safe.

Tears continued to slip down my cheeks as I grasped at any possible way of getting out of the house before it burned down. I gave one more tug at my bound hands, but it was no use.

My mind turned to Emma. Our last conversation had been an argument. I'd been bullheaded, and I hadn't called her back when I should have. Memories of my last day in Arkansas with her family ran through my head. I'd never have a chance to make it right. I hoped she knew I loved her; she was more than my best friend. She was my family.

My eyes closed even tighter as I thought about George showing up on the porch. He didn't have to say a word to me; his expression had said it all. The sadness that filled his eyes when I told him I'd decided to stay tugged at my heart. I wished George and the girls really knew how much they'd saved me. They were my first friends in Oregon, and I loved them.

I had so many regrets in my life, and I wasn't even twenty. I couldn't imagine if I'd continued down this path. Maybe Xander had done us both a favor. What kind of mother would I have been? I had nothing to offer. I was empty and broken.

I'd heard most people died of smoke inhalation before the flames ever reached them. Maybe I'd go that way. I peered around the room one last time, took a deep breath, and closed my eyes. The intense heat was traveling up the stairs, and I took another deep breath through my nose. The only favor I could do for myself now was to die before the flames reached me.

My head jerked off the floor as I heard something. I strained to listen as footsteps echoed in the hallway, but I couldn't tell if they were coming this way or going down. Straining against the tape on my wrists one more time, the room began to spin, and my eyes fluttered closed.

5 0

"**L**acey! Honey!"

I gasped as the tape was ripped from my mouth.

"Mama? Is that you?" Dark spots danced across my vision, and I squeezed my eyes shut. Forcing them open again, Mama's image shimmered into Emma's.

"Emma?" The smoke had entered the bedroom now, making it hard to breathe. My vision blurred again as a firefighter walked in.

"Do you have her?" he yelled, his voice muffled by his breathing apparatus.

"Yeah, I'll get her out," a loud voice right above me yelled back.

I glanced around the room and tried to make sense of what was happening.

"I'm here, don't you worry," Mama said as her image reappeared.

"Please help me."

"It's going to be okay. I've got you now."

The house filled with voices as the flames continued to crackle all around us.

"How did you know? How did you know where I was?" I asked Mama.

"I'll explain everything later—let's just get out of here right now," she said as she cut through the thick tape on my ankles and then my hands. Although I tried to move, I couldn't. My arms and legs were completely numb. The flames grew closer, and I whimpered.

"I want you to know I love you, and I've always loved you. I'm so proud of you. You came out to Oregon and started all over and pursued your passion. You followed your heart, and I never did. I never had the courage you do. It's something I wanted to tell you, but I couldn't. I struggled to find the words, and the last few years were so difficult. We just kept growing apart. I know we haven't agreed on a lot of things, but I wanted you to be happy. I didn't want you to make the same mistakes I made. I'm so sorry. You're my baby, and I'm going to make it up to you now."

My tears fell freely as Mama scooped me off the floor and into her arms. I wasn't sure if we would make it out of the fire or not, but I'd longed to hear those words from her mouth for almost my entire life. No matter what happened, if we got out of the house or died together, my heart had just healed a little bit.

I leaned my head into her shoulder and buried my face into her neck. The familiar smell of her perfume lingered on her skin. My mind flipped through memories like a Rolodex as she carried me out of Xander's bedroom.

I smiled, remembering how Mama had read me a book and rocked me every day at naptime when I was little. She did that until I was in the first grade, and then everything began to change. I wanted that again with her. I wanted her to love me again.

Voices drifted through the house as Mama carried me down the stairs. The heat radiated as she moved toward the front door. The orange-and-red flames licked up the staircase we'd just come down. I watched through squinted, tear-filled eyes as the upstairs hallway burned. I smiled as I thought about the first time George and I had stayed the night in this house. How had everything gone so wrong?

My head swirled as I struggled to stay awake. I was so tired. Tired of running, tired of fighting, tired of crying. My heart had been broken more times than I could take. I couldn't hold on anymore. I couldn't live like this.

"I love you, Mama," I mumbled as I took a breath and slipped away into the darkness.

Mama used to tell me stories she'd read about people dying and experiencing a bright-white light, and then coming back to tell everyone what heaven was like. She said they reported feeling so much love and peace they didn't want to come back. If she were in a bad mood, she'd also tell me how she couldn't wait to die so she'd really be loved. Apparently, Patsy, Krissy, and I were never enough, but I knew that already.

Since I'd grown up in a religious home, I honestly hadn't considered the possibility I'd even make it to heaven. I'd messed up the short life I'd lived so badly. I'd gotten pregnant out of wedlock, not to mention all the times Mama told me I was possessed. I guess it all just stuck.

If I was doomed to an eternity in hell, I figured I'd at least live my life the way I wanted. But it didn't turn out that way at all. I'd hurt people, myself, and my unborn baby. And now, it was over. I allowed myself to surrender and sink into oblivion.

I squinted as a white light pierced through the darkness. As I raised my hand to shield my eyes, a sharp pinch traveled through the back of it. I blinked my tired eyes and tried to adjust to the light, but it was too strong, and I was forced to turn my head away. The pinch in the back of my hand returned, and I frowned. Wasn't heaven supposed to be pain-free? It definitely wasn't: my head throbbed, my lungs hurt, and my lower abdomen cramped. If I wasn't in heaven, was I in hell? I panicked as I tried to understand.

I glanced around as my vision cleared enough for me to realize I hadn't made it to heaven at all. Not even close. Fear ripped through me as I realized something was on my face. Frantically, I grabbed the mask and tore it off. Blinking, I tried to focus through the grit, and my mind kicked into overdrive. The memories ran full speed ahead: the baby, the fight, Xander kicking me in the stomach, the fire. My heart pounded as all the pieces spilled into place.

*Oh my God, Xander set the house on fire with me in it. He tried to murder me.*

What in the hell kept stinging? I glanced at the back of my hand, located the culprit, tugged out the IV, and tossed it away. My mind began to clear, and I sat up. I was in the hospital? How? Who brought me here? What happened? Where was Xander? Oh my God. I had to go. If he were anywhere near me, he'd finish what he started.

Panic clutched my heart, and I grabbed at my chest. I had to be strong. if I'd just made it out of a burning house alive, I could find my clothes and sneak out of the hospital.

But before I could make it out of bed, strong hands grabbed my shoulders and pinned me down. I screamed as I fought against them, but my throat was raw and scratchy. My voice only came out as a hoarse shout.

"No! Don't touch me! Get away from me!" I swung my arms and tried to free myself from his grip, but he was too strong. I could only hope a doctor or nurse had heard me. If anyone had and they came in, I'd tell them he'd tried to kill me. I'd have them call George to come get me. He and the girls could sneak me to safety. I wouldn't screw up this time. This was my second chance.

"Shhh, it's okay. You're at the hospital."

I froze at the sound of his voice. My body trembled as I swallowed the bile that had risen from my stomach.

"Lace, it's okay. I'm here," he whispered.

My mouth dropped as I stared into the most beautiful blue eyes I'd ever seen in my life.

"Walker?" I gasped.

THANK you so much for reading CAPTURED! This story ends with Lacey being rescued, but who really saved her? Follow Lacey into FREED as she continues her journey in the final book of the series.

SIGN UP FOR J.A. OWENBY'S NEWSLETTER and receive bonus scenes, updates, and participate in giveaways.

Enjoy giveaways, the inside scoop about J.A. Owenby, and never miss a new release again! Sign up today at https://www.author-jaowenby.com/newsletter

Let's Get in Touch! Connect with me here:

Author J.A. Owenby Website

Join my Newsletter

Follow me on Facebook

Join my Facebook Group

Follow me on Amazon

Join me on Goodreads

Follow me on BookBub

Follow me on Twitter

Follow me on Instagram

Join me on Pinterest

# ALSO BY J.A. OWENBY

*OTHER BOOKS BY INTERNATIONAL BESTSELLING J.A. OWENBY*

**New Adult Romance**

**The Love & Ruin Series**

Love & Ruin

Love & Deception

Love & Redemption

Love & Consequences, a standalone novel

Love & Corruption, a standalone novel

Love & Revelations, a novella

Love & Seduction, a standalone novel

Love & Vengeance

Love & Retaliation, coming June 2021

**Romantic Mystery**

**The Wicked Intentions Series**

Dark Intentions

Fractured Intentions

**Coming of Age**

**The Torn Series, inspired by True Events**

*Fading into Her, a prequel novella*

*Torn*

*Captured*

Freed

*Standalone Novels*

*Where I'll Find You*

Published by Kindle Direct Publishing

www.jaowenby.com



Edited by Molly McCowan

Cover Art by iheartdesigns

Second Edition

ISBN-13: 978-1-7321510-9-3

ISBN-10: 1-7321510-9-1

Click here to gain access to previews of J.A. Owenby's novels before they're released and to take part in exclusive giveaways.

*This book is dedicated to Jeremy Hand, who was an amazing friend and author. The world lost you too soon.*

ACKNOWLEDGMENTS

The outpouring of support for the first book in The Torn Series, *Torn*, has been amazing. I'm so grateful to all the readers who reached out to me personally, and to everyone who took the time to give the book such thoughtful reviews.

Brett, I couldn't do this without you. I love you so very much.

My friends are amazing, and I get misty-eyed when I think about all the love and support they give me. Thank you to Sheri Kaye Hoff, Jeannie Kemper, Kara Long, Sarah Jones, Nancy Schnauefer, Cristel Olive, Pat Harvey, Rochelle Miller, Savannah Earnst, Shannon Barnard, Bonnie Gortler, Vivienne Smith, Aubrey Minear, Angela Fowler, Brittney Valencia, Gabriel Jones, Dawn Plummer, and the fantastic people from Lake Hamilton High School who shared posts, left reviews, and recommended my novel to others.

# ABOUT THE AUTHOR

International bestselling author J.A. Owenby grew up in a small back-woods town in Arkansas where she learned how to swear like a sailor and spot water moccasins skimming across the lake.

She finally ditched the south and headed to Oregon. The first winter there, she was literally blown away a few times by ninety mile an hour winds and storms that rolled in off the ocean.

Eventually, she longed for quiet and headed up to snowier pastures. She now resides in Washington state with her hot nerdy husband and cat, Chloe (who frequently encourages her to drink). She spends her days coming up with ways to torture characters in a way that either makes you want to throw your book down a flight of stairs or sob hysterically into a pillow.

J.A. Owenby writes new adult and romantic thriller novels. Her books ooze with emotion, angst, and twists that will leave you breathless. Having battled her own demons, she's not afraid to tackle the secrets women are forced to hide. After all, the road to love is paved in the dark.

Her friends describe her as delightfully twisted. She loves fan mail and wine. Please send her all the wine.

*You can follow the progress of her upcoming novel on Facebook at Author J.A. Owenby and on Twitter @jaowenby.*

*Sign up for J.A. Owenby's Newsletter:*
  *BookHip.com/CTZMWZ*

*Like J.A. Owenby's Facebook:*
  *https://www.facebook.com/JAOwenby*

*J.A. Owenby's One Page At A Time reader group:*
  *https://www.facebook.com/groups/JAOwenby*

www.ingramcontent.com/pod-product-compliance
Lightning Source LLC
Chambersburg PA
CBHW032100050726
47590CB00001B/352